THE JIBE

Robyn Cotton

The Jibe

Cover design by Betty McCready.

ISBN: 978-0-473-70886-3 (Paperback)
ISBN: 978-0-473-70887-0 (e-PUB)
ISBN: 978-0-473-70888-7 (Kindle)

For permission requests, write to the author:
Hatherop Books, 133 Alec Craig Way, Gulf Harbour 0930, New Zealand

First printed in New Zealand. This book is available in print at selected bookstores and online retailers. For more information, please visit:

www.hatheropbooks.wordpress.com

I dedicate this story to my husband Geoff who first kindled my love for sailing and who has encouraged me, making it possible for me to write this book.

Acknowledgements

This book could not have been completed without the support and help from a number of friends and family. It began as a cognitive challenge, brought on by a fear of losing some ability through my Parkinson's and the drugs I take to manage the symptoms. Thanks to the encouragement of those around me, it has turned into a story that I hope others will read and enjoy.

There are a few people that I want to single out.

Margaret, Robert, Lesley and Matt read my early drafts and provided invaluable critique for which I am extremely grateful. Their comments have helped me hone the story into a better yarn.

Thanks also to Murray for his insights into the work of the Maritime Police Unit.

A special thanks to Glenys for her careful editing of the manuscript, as well as for helping me navigate the changing conventions around the use of commas—a source of frustration and at times despair as I agonised over their use.

A huge thank you to our talented niece Betty, who designed the cover and turned this book into a visual work of art.

Above all, I acknowledge Geoff for his patient support, encouragement and wise counsel. I cannot imagine a life without you at my side.

1

The boat lurched as a wave rolled under the bow. She barely noticed the rise and fall of the deck underneath her. There had been no time to tidy the sails away and they billowed and flapped at the mercy of the wind. The vibrations of the motor reverberated through her feet and up her entire body, amplifying the fear which threatened to overwhelm her. The moving seascape surrounded her, making her feel small and vulnerable. Neither man nor boat were in sight; even the islands were invisible behind the misty horizon. The swells ebbed and flowed, a continuous pattern yet random in its rhythm, broken only by the occasional seabird floating on the surface.

The search was pointless and deep down she knew it, but she had to keep looking, to be sure. It was unlikely he was conscious when he hit the water. Now she was certain he was gone, his body lost beyond the waves. Time seemed to stop as she maintained her vigil. A sentinel on the ocean. Scanning back and forth. Searching. Searching.

A loose lock of long blond hair whipped her eye. She tucked it behind her ear. Dean always said her hair was one of the things that'd attracted him to her. Dean. Tears blurred her vision and she absentmindedly wiped them away with the back of her hand. The colour had drained from her world and her soul had emptied, losing all clarity. It should have been different. She shivered in the seasonably warm wind, her eyes probing the sea, wishing she could put things right. How could they have come to this?

The sea had always been a place of solace for her. But today that peace was replaced with anxiety and apprehension for what might lie ahead. She scanned the swells again, looking for something that didn't fit with the seascape. Nothing. As the gravity of her situation sank in, nausea hit the pit of her stomach and she shook uncontrollably. Tears flowed down her face unchecked. A wail came from deep within her. The sound was loud and long and gut-wrenching; directed at the waves, at herself and at all of the last six months. It exploded with the power of her pent-up stress. Using the wheel to steady herself, she cried until she was spent.

Everything she'd done had been for Dean. She and Dean had begun their relationship on *Aurora*. And that had been followed by countless sailing holidays. The first time they'd made love was on board, before they'd even left the marina. And in those early days it was heaven. She scanned the empty ocean again, her heart racing and the adrenaline pumping.

At times it felt like you were a world away from anyone else, like you were the only people left on earth. How she loved the freedom of following the wind, never quite knowing where it would take you. The Gulf offered so many options for islands to visit and bays in which to shelter from all winds. Many of these islands were sanctuaries for New Zealand's unique native species. How she longed for the safety of her own sanctuary.

Sailing had introduced her to a whole new world and one that she'd come to love more than anything else. *Aurora* had become her second home. But now... what would the future hold? The nice comfortable life they'd enjoyed thanks to the business he'd built was gone, replaced now by a frightening dark void.

The sound of the thrashing sails became insufferable, so she reigned in her rising panic and tried to restore her inner calm. Now was the time to be strong. The autopilot controlled the rudder while she hauled on the genoa furler and wound in the foresail. With a deep sigh, she moved to pull the mainsail sheet in tight before lowering the mainsail into the lazy jacks that guided it down onto the boom. Then up on the cabin top where she tied the mainsail to the boom with Velcro straps, her steps anticipating the movement of the sea that comes from years of experience.

Only the sound of the sea and the gentle hum of the motor remained as she climbed down the companionway and into the cabin.

She picked up the radio handpiece and pressed the button. "Mayday, mayday, mayday. This is *Aurora, Aurora, Aurora.* Oscar Romeo Bravo nine four two zero. Over."

*

It had been a quiet morning for Coastguard volunteer Jack Currie. Summer holidays were over and the inclement weather meant that there were fewer boats out and about on the Hauraki Gulf. With things so quiet he made a third cup of coffee for the morning and stirred a second heaped spoonful of sugar into the strong brew. It brought a smile to his weathered face knowing he couldn't get away with two at home. His wife of forty-five years would point to the substantial gut that clung to his tall and otherwise lean frame and nag him to diet. But here at HQ he was free to do as he pleased. And strong sweet coffee was what he liked.

The radio burst into life with some static and as a veteran of twenty-five years serving the Coastguard service, he was quick to respond.

"Mayday, mayday, mayday. This is *Aurora, Aurora, Aurora.* Oscar Romeo Bravo nine four two zero. Over." The woman's voice had a Kiwi accent.

Jack's vast experience kicked in and he responded with calm professionalism. "Mayday *Aurora*, this is Coastguard radio. What is your position and the nature of your distress? Over."

Intently focused on the radio, he took a sip of hot coffee while he waited for her response.

"My husband fell over-board and I can't find him. I'm roughly five miles west of Tryphena Harbour. Over." The signal was strong, the words rapid and the voice slightly shaky.

Sensing her panic, he slowed his voice in an attempt to keep her calm. "Mayday *Aurora*, can you give me your coordinates? Over."

A short pause followed. He readied his pen over the pad on his desk.

"The chart plotter tells me I'm 36.4156 degrees south and 175.3023 degrees east. Over." Her ability to read her location told him she was coherent and had some experience.

He read the numbers back to her to check he had them correct.

"I've been searching, but I can't find him. He wasn't wearing a life jacket and was hit on the head before he went overboard. I don't know what to do." Her voice quavered.

"Mayday *Aurora*, please stay close to the radio and maintain your location. I will mobilise a search and rescue party. Stand-by."

"Okay, will do. Over."

Coffee was now forgotten as Jack put the 'all stations' call out to any boats in the area to assist in the search. The next call was to the Police Maritime Unit who would coordinate the search as was their function in Marine Search and Rescue. They were already out on the water attending another callout in West Harbour, however their priority was where life was in immediate danger. The skipper advised they would immediately re-route to the search area. Next he mobilised the Coastguard rescue launch based in Great Barrier and the rescue helicopter from the Auckland base. Then he placed the Navy on alert and advised them a search was underway. Time was of the essence as every second wasted could mean a life lost. The odds were poor for a person surviving for long in the water without a life jacket, and infinitely more so if they sustained a head injury.

Once satisfied the launch and helicopter were on their way, he turned his attention back to the woman aboard *Aurora*.

"Mayday *Aurora*, this is Coastguard radio. Do you copy? Over."

"Coastguard radio, this is *Aurora*. Over."

"Mayday *Aurora*, the Coastguard launch and rescue helicopter have been dispatched. Please advise state of the person in the water, the colour of clothing and what time he actually went in. Over."

"It's-it's a man, my husband. He's wearing khaki shorts and a green sweater. Forest green." She sniffed. "I'm afraid I've lost him. It happened at around 11 o'clock. He hit his head before falling overboard." This time a sob.

"Mayday *Aurora*, please stand by."

Jack quickly and succinctly relayed the information to the search and rescue teams as well as the Maritime Police Unit.

"Mayday *Aurora*, please confirm the number of souls on board your vessel and are you in any danger? Over."

"*Aurora* to Coastguard. There's only me on board and I don't know what to do." Her voice was quieter this time.

"Mayday *Aurora*, please continue to hold your position until the rescue teams get there. The police *Eagle* helicopter search team should be overhead in 15 minutes and Coastguard's rescue boat will be alongside in 35 minutes. They will take over the physical search which will be coordinated by Marine Search and Rescue. Are you able to get your vessel home single handedly? Over."

"Is there someone who could help me bring *Aurora* back to the marina? Over."

"Mayday *Aurora*, copy that. The Coastguard rescue team will provide any assistance required. In the meantime, please continue to stand by. Coastguard out."

Jack relayed the information to the search crew and sat back to reflect. He could only imagine the anxiety that the poor woman must be feeling. To lose your husband in an accident is a tragedy at any time, but for it to happen at sea always seems worse. And to be left on your own, to have searched in vain, it was little wonder she sounded so panicked.

With nothing to do until the rescue teams reached the search area, he left his station and crossed the room to reheat his coffee in the microwave, all the while listening for a transmission.

Back at his desk, he checked the E.T.A. of the rescue crews. The helicopter was three minutes out from the target area and would soon be commencing its search in a grid pattern. He took a sip of the hot brew and updated *Aurora*. Although not necessary, this gave him the means to check in on the woman sailor. She seemed to be holding it together, sounding like a person operating on autopilot.

The chance of success in locating the man was not great. It would be a tall order to identify a person wearing khaki and green colours, especially under a deeply overcast sky. The swells and foam from the waves would make the task even more difficult. Added to that, the tidal movement would be close to peak flow and could drag a person out towards the treacherous Colville Channel, the stretch of water that lay between Coromandel and Great Barrier Island. If the person was a strong swimmer, they might stand a chance, especially as the water temperature was less of a problem at this time of year. If they were injured, or worse, concussed or unconscious, recovering a body in these conditions would be nigh on impossible. And then there were the sharks, not a thought he wanted to contemplate. He took a long swig of his coffee.

*

Pete Drury watched his skipper, Alan Paine, anticipate the swells with an experienced hand on the wheel and expertly adjust the throttle to maximise their speed. The conditions were difficult as the wind whipped the swells up into peaks. The *Awhina*, a former America's Cup chase boat, cut through the water with ease. She was the jewel in the Coastguard's fleet making him doubly proud to be part of her voluntary crew. He checked his watch as Alan nudged the throttle a nick further and felt *Awhina* respond immediately.

Tom Avery was the other crew member on board. Like Pete, he had many years of experience, both as a yachtie with his own recreational boat and as a Coastguard volunteer of more than ten years. They both scanned the waves, looking for the man-overboard.

Alan turned to him. "Pete, Coastguard has advised that the woman on board *Aurora* needs help to get back to the marina. I want you to board and assist her with taking *Aurora* home. As soon as you're aboard, Tom and I will join the search."

"Can do Skipper."

"It's going to be a big ask finding someone out here today with no life jacket and without any bright colours," Tom yelled over the sound of the motor.

"In this current they're likely to be well south of here by now, past Channel Island," Pete shouted back.

"Likely he's already shark bait."

"Poor sod." Pete's eyes roved back and forth as he searched the greyish water on either side. If he was lucky, he might catch a glimpse of the man before he disappeared over the next swell, but that would require a lot of luck. Time and again they were called out to search for someone in the water who didn't have the appropriate safety gear or in the very least, bright coloured clothing. Pete shook his head in disgust.

The sleek outline of a sloop-rig yacht with a dark blue hull grew larger as they hammered the waves. A few kororā, the little blue penguins, floated by and a small flock of storm petrels flitted past dancing from one swell to the next, but he saw no sign of a person in the water. A helicopter whirred overhead. He looked up to see the police helicopter *Eagle* make a pass over them.

"Pete, prepare to board her," Alan called over his shoulder. "I'll ease us up to the stern."

"Aye aye Skipper."

Awhina had an inflatable tube around her fibreglass hull enabling her to safely come alongside a vessel without risk of damage. After checking his life jacket fastenings were secure, Pete picked up his gear bag and moved carefully onto the forward deck to crouch in preparation.

"Ready Skipper," he yelled.

As they came alongside *Aurora*, a tall slender woman emerged from the cabin and waved. Despite the grim situation, he couldn't help but notice that she was attractive in tight fitting jeans and a bright red hoodie with a blonde ponytail poking through the back of a black cap.

"I'm coming aboard!" Pete yelled over the noise of the engine and across the narrowing gap between the two boats.

"What do you want me to do?" Her voice sounded slightly panicked.

"Catch my gear bag." It came out as a command, but now wasn't the time for niceties.

"Sure."

Moving with the grace of someone who was familiar with the movement of the ocean, she caught his bag with ease.

"All set Pete?" Alan asked.

"Ready."

Alan brought *Awhina* up behind and eased her forward so that her bow was touching the stern of *Aurora*. The swells made this manoeuvre tricky and there was little time to waste. Judging just the right moment when the swells held the boats steady, Pete leapt across the gap, taking extra care under the bulk of his wet weather gear.

"I'm Pete Drury," he said, putting out his hand.

She shook his hand and said, "Ella Hampton. I'm so relieved you're here." Her eyes looked red and tired.

"I'll help you bring *Aurora* into shore and *Awhina* will join the search."

"I'd be grateful for the help as I've not done it on my own before. But shouldn't we join the search?" Her voice had a slightly desperate edge to it.

"No, we'll leave that to the experts. Just give me a moment and I'll despatch *Awhina*." He turned back to the stern and shouted to Alan, "All good here, I'll take her in."

With a wave from Alan, *Awhina* raced away and Pete slipped in behind *Aurora*'s wheel.

"Tell me exactly what happened," Pete said.

"We left Whangaparapara Harbour this morning, heading for home." Her voice quavered.

"Where's home?"

"We keep her in Westhaven Marina." She fidgeted with the hem of her sweater. "We were sailing with full sail and Dean was standing on the seat when the boat lurched with a swell, and the boom came across hard and fast. It hit Dean and he... he disappeared overboard. It all happened so quickly and before I knew it, he was gone. I couldn't see him in the swells. It seems like I was searching for ages."

"How badly was he hit? Can you be sure if he was conscious when he hit the water?"

"It gave him a real smack. I didn't see him in the water. By the time I got to the starboard side he was out of sight already behind a swell. I had my hands full starting the motor and turning *Aurora* around—I never saw him again." Tears welled up in her eyes and she dabbed them with her sleeve leaving small dark smudges.

"What time did it happen?"

"I think it was around eleven, although I can't be sure of the exact time."

Pete checked his watch. The man had been in the water for nearly an hour and a half already, so he didn't like his chances. "We were told he's not wearing a life jacket, is that right?"

"We never wear one unless it's really rough."

Pete tried not to show his annoyance over boaties who think they are invincible when out on the water despite the hostile environment where things can go wrong so fast.

"How about you go and put one on now, while I head us for home?"

Without a word, Ella climbed down into the saloon.

Once the autopilot was set to the correct GPS coordinates, Pete checked that the gear was well stowed topside. *Aurora* appeared to be set up for offshore sailing with lifeline netting around the sides, four solar panels and a marine wind turbine for energy generation. A dinghy was strapped securely on the forward deck. The ropes had all been neatly coiled. Three fishing rods and a net stood in a row like soldiers on a watchtower, secure in their holders on the aft rail. She was ready for the trip back to the marina.

The swells were increasing with the wind and beginning to peak sharply as they turned into them to head for Westhaven. Heading into the wind meant the wind was coming over the bow and if sailing, the boom would be pulled in tight. If sailing downwind, the boom would be set out wide to capture the wind in the sail, enabling a jibe if the wind came around to the back of the sail, sending the boom, at times violently, across the boat. When the accident happened, *Aurora* must have been travelling downwind, and not heading to Westhaven.

Awhina was already some distance from them and was turning, obviously working a grid pattern across the search area that had been devised based on the tidal flow and windage. The search helicopter buzzed low overhead.

"Mind if I check below deck and use your radio?"

"Sure."

The saloon was spacious with a large table dominating its centre. Around the table were seats upholstered in smart blue fabric with brightly coloured cushions strewn over them. The galley was offset to the starboard side with everything neat and secure. A chart table and radio were on the port side. He poked his head through the closed door to the forward cabin and noted the bed was unmade with rumpled sheets and a few clothes lying about but nothing that needed to be stowed away. The doors either side of the cabin doorway opened to well organised storage lockers. Tools and consumables were well secured on shelves in one and the other stowed the wet weather gear and life jackets. To the rear of the saloon was a small head. He smiled at the sign above the toilet that read *Don't put anything down the toilet unless you eat it first.* Nothing was loose that could fly about in the head. The aft cabins were also ship-shape—one had a bed made up and the other appeared to be used for storage. *Aurora*'s woodwork gleamed with new varnish, giving the appearance that she was well loved. He sat down at the chart table and lifted the radio handpiece to check in with Coastguard radio, relaying the information Ella had given him.

Once back on deck, he resumed his position behind the wheel. Ella was stretched out on the cockpit seat, her eyes staring vacantly across the water. The wind had come around and was now close to head-on, making motoring the best option in the circumstances. An air of misery hung over them as they settled in for the trip back to Westhaven. Normally he loved to be behind the wheel of a boat, but there'd be no pleasure in today's excursion amidst such a tragedy. If only the circumstances were different.

In an attempt to put Ella at ease, Pete asked, "Have you been on holiday for long?"

"Dean and I have been holidaying out at Great Barrier over the past week. Last night we were at anchor in Whangaparapara Harbour. It was a bit of a rough night because the wind changed causing waves to start coming down the harbour. Between that and the noise of the wind I didn't get much sleep. I lost count of how many times I got up to check we were okay." Her deeply tanned face looked strained.

"Yeah, that can be tough going. Were you planning to go home today? I'm surprised you were sailing downwind."

Ella's eyes widened. "Um... Dean wanted to go down to Coromandel, however I was tired and wanted to go home. We have work on Monday, but Dean won so we changed our minds and headed southeast."

She turned her back and stared out over the frothy water of the wake, giving the subtle message that the conversation was over. He respected her need for quiet reflection. She sat like that for a long time. There was an elegance about her that bespoke money and her body was shapely, like a woman who got the most out of a gym membership. Probably the type that had it all, until now. He couldn't imagine how hard it must be to lose a loved one overboard, nor how he'd react in the circumstances, especially when you have little hope of them being found alive. It was safe to assume she was already grieving so he'd need to be sensitive to that.

The recognisable aluminium hull of the police boat *Deodar III* came towards them at speed. A beamy 18.5metre jet powered twin engine catamaran, it carved through the water effortlessly as it made its way to the search area. Pete exchanged waves with the skipper and crew as it passed them on their port side.

Aurora sliced through the swells heading for the marina. The sea is an environment that despite man's great advances can't be harnessed or tamed. It is moody and mysterious, like a living organism that requires respect. It nurtures life and can take it away. Today it was a dull grey-green with white caps topping the swells, looking bleak and unwelcoming. Tomorrow it could be aqua blue and calm or hostile and ominous. A body of water forever moving, forever changing. A place of calm and quiet contemplation or a place of adventure and challenge. And like so many other sailors, this was what drew Pete to it. It captivated him and he could watch it for hours without ever being bored. Nothing could stir his emotions quite like the sea.

After a half hour or so of silence, Pete asked, "Can I make you a hot drink?"

She turned and gave him a forced smile. "Thanks, a coffee would be great."

Though a small gesture, he welcomed the chance to do something more for this sad lady and gladly went down the companionway steps to boil the kettle and make the drinks.

The coffee seemed to unlock something in her and she began to talk as though a cork had come out of a bottle. She spilled her life story. Dean, her husband, had been passionate about sailing. *Aurora* had been his long before they'd met and had been a big part of his previous family's life. Sailing was new to her in those early days when he'd taught her the craft, kindling in her a passion that grew to where she loved every minute spent out on the water. While they'd had no kids themselves, he had a daughter from his first marriage who was close to her dad and whom Ella struggled to get on with. Her two previous marriages had failed and throughout it all her love of sport and the outdoors had helped her survive. In Dean she'd found her soulmate. Pete let her talk, figuring it helped her to come to terms with her loss.

Suddenly she stopped and turned to him, as if just noticing him standing at the helm. "Do you think they'll find him?"

Pete carefully considered his answer. He didn't want to give false hope. "I don't know. But the search crews are very experienced and good at what they do."

"How long before you sink if you are unable to swim?"

"I wouldn't expect it to be very long, unless he had some sort of buoyancy aid." While vague, he didn't want to upset her further.

They lapsed into another long silence.

"Do you have a partner?" she asked.

The question sounded strange coming from someone who's loved one had just been torn away from them. "No, my wife and I have recently split."

She looked at him with appreciation, almost as if they had shared circumstances. "Why didn't it work out?"

He hesitated, wondering how much he should share, but decided to oblige her as it was more for her good than his own.

"We grew apart, what with work and interests and then she met someone else. It was all over before I realised what was happening." This was the truth and it still hurt to talk about it.

"Any kids?"

Something alluring about the way she looked at him made him think she was a woman who could get a man into trouble, making him uncomfortable about being drilled by this stranger. "Nope, we didn't get around to it."

Her face took on a whimsical expression. "Dean wanted more kids, but I didn't want any. I've never been the nurturing type."

"I guess some people just aren't... I think I'll go get an update from Coastguard." Pete escaped down the companionway and into the main cabin.

Coastguard advised there was as yet no sign of a person in the water and they would continue their search until dark.

Back in the cockpit, he asked, "Do you have someone to call? Perhaps someone who could meet you? You probably shouldn't go home alone."

Ella looked pensive. "I guess I could call my mum. And I should give Dean's sister a call—they're close. She'll let the family know."

The calls were made and Dawn, her mum, agreed to meet them at the marina. *Aurora* made good progress up the Waitemata Harbour which provided shelter from the swells and Pete brought her safely into the marina berth without any drama.

2

Amy Fagin held onto the mobile phone and stood staring out the window. Although her accountancy office overlooked a small park, she saw nothing, felt nothing. Dean was missing—it just couldn't be. Dean, her precious brother, had been sailing since they were kids. Out on the water was where Dean was happiest, his experience built up over a lifetime of sailing. It was devastating news, unbelievable. If only it were a mistake, but it couldn't be. Ella had been there, there could be no mistake. Nevertheless, Dean had always been a survivor. The Coastguard would find him, of course they would.

The hand holding her mobile phone shook, something she was beginning to get used to. She'd recently been diagnosed with young-onset Parkinson's disease, a neurological degenerative condition usually afflicting old people. At only 47 years old it had come as a shock. Even after all the research over numerous decades there was still no cure. And if they didn't come up with something soon it would eventually consume her to the point where she'd be fully dependent on carers—not something she was ready to accept. For her the diagnosis was embarrassing, making her reluctant to share her news, especially at work, as she didn't want to be treated as though she were disabled.

Right now, she wanted a calming influence so she dialled her husband's number and put the phone on speaker. She sat with elbows resting on the desk, holding one trembling hand in the other, watching them shake as if they didn't belong to her. Terry's kindly eyes watched her from the wooden picture frame on her desk.

16

"Hi, what's up?" Terry asked.

"It's Dean, he's lost." She picked up the phone, turned off the speaker and put it to her ear.

"What do you mean lost?"

"Missing off his boat." The phone rattled against her earring as the tremor increased and she stifled a sob.

"Where? What happened?"

"I don't know the details. Ella called, poor thing. The Coastguard is searching for him." She drew a deep breath. "I just can't believe it."

"Don't worry, I'm sure they'll find him. Do you want me to pick you up?"

"No, it's okay." Knowing she needed to be strong and support Ella through this, she clicked into big sister mode. "I need to let the family know and I'm going to leave early and go round to Ella's. She'll be needing some support—I'll offer to cook her a meal. She must be devastated."

The call ended with Terry promising to come home early. The next call was harder. Her Mum, Diane, broke down when she shared the news with her. She had recently moved into an elder care facility as she had been showing the early signs of dementia. Amy promised to keep her up to date the moment she heard anything. Lastly, she rang Maddie and Tracy, her two teenage daughters, to give them the bad news. Like her, they adored their uncle and he'd always made a big fuss of them. It broke her heart to hear them crying at the other end of the phone, causing her to be torn between going to comfort them or supporting Ella. However Terry would soon be home to look after them and it was only right that she should go to Ella.

Alistair, her workmate and good friend, poked his head through her doorway. "You did well in the meeting with Clarkson

Engineering today. I'd say you nailed it. They'll be bringing their books over to us pronto. It's a good win—they're a big outfit." He paused before saying, "What's up? You look like you've seen a ghost."

"Um, I've had some family news. My brother was on his yacht and fell overboard today. As far as I know they're still searching for him."

"That's terrible news!" Al stood awkwardly, his angular face contorted in a deep frown, as if desperately trying to think of the right words. "Look, I'm sure they'll find him soon. Why don't you go home now, I can cover for you."

"Thanks Al, I owe you. Don Striker is coming in at four p.m. with some query on his account. Do you think you could meet him and find out what he wants? Give my apologies and just tell him I was called away."

"Of course, anything at all. Let me know if you need anything else. Now go!" His expression conveyed genuine concern.

She collected her things, closed the door to her office and walked the short distance to the carpark building. Ella and Dean lived in a central suburb and in no time at all she was pulling into their driveway. The rain was heavy as she made the dash across to the front door. The doorbell chimed loudly before soft footsteps approached and the door swung open.

"Amy, it's good of you to come around." Ella looked remarkably composed apart from the telltale smudges of mascara under her eyes.

Amy moved towards her and wrapped her in a hug. "Ella, I can hardly believe it. Dean is so sure footed on the boat, it's such a shock."

"I know. Come in out of the rain."

"Have you heard anything more from Coastguard?" Amy asked, closing the door behind her.

"No, I expect to hear soon. I've not been home long myself."

"What exactly happened?" Amy followed Ella into the kitchen where Ella's mum was getting mugs out. "Hello Dawn."

"Amy, I'm glad you came by." Dawn's voice had a cultured ring to it. A striking woman in her sixties, she was always beautifully turned out with perfect make-up and manicured nails. "Can I make you a hot drink while Ella fills you in on the details? Tea or coffee?"

"How about something stronger, like a gin and tonic?" Ella chipped in.

"I'll settle for a coffee, but I'll pour you a gin." Amy found a glass and retrieved a bottle of tonic from the fridge while Ella brought the half-full bottle of gin from the sideboard. Amy poured, with little focus on the job at hand. Gin spilled down the side of the glass and onto the bench. She silently cursed her tremor as she wiped it up. Worry increased the shaking making it more difficult for her to conceal it.

"You alright?" Ella asked, staring at Amy's hand.

"It's nothing. Tell me what happened." Other than Terry, she hadn't shared her Parkinson's news with anyone, swearing him to secrecy until she was ready to talk about it.

"It was awful. It happened so fast," Ella climbed onto a barstool. "We spent an uncomfortable night anchored in Whangaparapara Harbour last night, with the wind coming round to the west. We were both tired and decided to head for home. It happened about five miles west of Whangaparapara. We were under full sail when *Aurora* unexpectedly jibed—the boom came across and knocked Dean on the head. He went overboard. He didn't even scream. I lost sight of him behind the swells." She sniffed into a tissue. "By the time I managed to release the sails and turn around, I couldn't see him. He was gone." Ella sobbed loudly with her face hidden behind tissues.

Not knowing what else to do, Amy moved around the bench to hug her. This time Ella seemed to stiffen in her arms, so Amy quickly released her and went back to slicing a lemon for the G and T.

"I don't suppose he was wearing his life jacket?" Amy had told Dean many times that he should wear one when he was on a passage.

"No, you know how we don't tend to wear them unless it cuts up rough."

"Wasn't it rough out there today?" Amy passed the gin to Ella.

"Not too bad. It started out at about 25 knots nor'westerly and one-metre swells." Ella took a sip of her drink.

"Dean's a strong swimmer. If anyone can, I'd put my money on him making it to shore." Amy tried to hold back her tears. "How badly was he hit?"

Dawn passed her a steaming mug of coffee and they both sat down next to Ella.

"I don't know, I heard the thwack..." Ella twisted some loose strands of her hair that had escaped her ponytail.

Amy's gut squeezed tight. She was struggling to hold it together, but Ella seemed so strong and calm in the circumstances. She hadn't seen this side of Ella before and realised she had some real steel. This revelation made her feel guilty that she'd underestimated her in the past, when she'd unfairly judged her to be lacking in substance.

Just then Ella's mobile buzzed and she pounced on it. "Hello."

Amy held her breath and listened, willing it to be good news.

"Oh." It was almost a sigh, a release of air. "Will you continue searching?"

A pause.

"I understand." She sounded beaten. "Please keep me informed. Goodbye."

Amy sensed the news wasn't good and reached for the tissue box on the worktop. "News?" she prompted.

Ella faced her, eyes brimming with tears. "They say they've not found any trace." She dabbed her eyes with the tissues.

Amy could no longer hold back her own deluge of tears and they flowed down her cheeks. If they hadn't found him by now, the chances of his survival were diminishing rapidly. She wished she could do something instead of sitting here, but she knew Dean would want her to be here with Ella even though they'd never been particularly close.

Ella took a long sip of the gin and tonic. "They're sending a cop around to talk to me about what happened."

Amy was surprised they hadn't done so already, however she held her tongue, not wanting to upset Ella further.

"Look, why don't you take your drink and have a soak in the bath. I can help Dawn fix you something for dinner. We'll give you a call if anyone comes."

"Good idea. You'll feel better for a bit of pampering." Dawn ran her fingers through her stylishly short white hair. "How about I go and prepare the bath for you."

"No, I can do it. You should go, you've got your cards group tonight. I'll be fine, honest. And Amy is here." Ella turned to Amy. "There's not much food in as I left everything on the boat. Take a look in the freezer, you might find something there."

"Don't worry, I'll sort it, or else I can order in. You go and have a soak and wash away the salt."

Dawn made her exit and Ella topped up the gin in her glass before taking it down the hallway towards her bedroom.

Amy took her time finishing the coffee, desperate for a strand of hope to cling to. Her mind was numbed by the overwhelming fear that was growing deep inside, filling her with an all-consuming sense of dread. Tears flowed and dripped onto the benchtop. She'd experienced loss before, but Dean? Memories came to her; Dean and her playing in a mud bath as children, dress-up parties, family holidays, sailing, tennis, his weddings, various family events. He was such a big part of her life. Sobs escaped and she allowed herself to let it out. Eventually she calmed herself and wiped her eyes. She went through to the living room and checked her eyes in the mirror, touching up the mascara smudges with a damp tissue.

The living room was a mess, so unlike Dean and Ella. A pile of washing lay on the couch where it'd been dumped, presumably before the holiday, so she folded it into neat piles. Then she plumped the cushions and arranged them along the backs of the lounge suite. Papers and magazines were strewn over the table which she automatically sorted into tidy stacks of reading material, advertising brochures and correspondence. One was a printout from a crypto dealer. Odd, she hadn't remembered Dean having an interest in crypto currencies. The room was dark and stuffy, so she drew across the shade curtains and opened a window. The rush of fresh air felt good as she filled her lungs.

The light settled on the small array of photographs in silver frames on a cabinet, several of which portrayed Dean smiling, as if at her. One in particular caught her eye. Dean was grinning at the camera from behind the wheel aboard *Aurora*. He looked so happy. A cloud settled over her as she realised how little she'd seen of Dean in recent times, even though they lived in the same city.

To busy her mind, she went on the hunt for some dinner. The fridge was as bare as expected, with only a few condiments, a bottle of wine, the bottle of tonic and a droopy looking carrot. The freezer fared a little better with frozen bread, various bags of vegetables, meats and a quiche which she decided to thaw.

The doorbell rang and she hurried to open it, longing to see Terry. Instead she was greeted by a tall and heavily built stranger with a grim expression. Although he wore blue overalls he didn't look like a tradesman. Something about him, perhaps it was the notebook he carried or his upright posture, distinguished him as a cop.

"Mrs Hampton?" He ran his hand over his thinning hair that had streaks of salt and pepper.

"No, I'm Amy, her sister-in-law. You are?"

"Frank Smythe. I'm with the Maritime Police Unit."

"Oh yes, we were expecting you. Come in and I'll go and fetch Ella." She led him to the living room.

Ella was fixing her thick blond hair into a braid, looking fit and healthy in a black top and leggings. Even without make-up she looked stunning, especially with her darkly tanned skin.

"The policeman is here," Amy announced.

"I heard...tell him I'll be there in a moment."

Amy dutifully went back to the policeman and passed on the message, offering to make him a hot drink, which he declined.

Ella entered, offering him her hand in a graceful gesture. "Ella Hampton."

"Frank Smythe, Maritime Police Unit. I've been coordinating the search and rescue efforts today. I'm so sorry you are having to go through this." Wrinkles turned up the corner of his eyes and he smiled good-naturedly. "I knew your husband—he was a top man and a good sailor. We used to crew together on a classic yacht in the regattas, years ago."

"I think that must have been before we got together. I do remember him saying something about sailing classic yachts—in fact he's pointed the odd one out to me more than once. Please, sit down. Do you bring news?" She fiddled with her wedding band.

His expression fell as he accepted a seat, sitting erectly on the edge of the sofa. "I'm sorry, but there's no update. I was on the line to Coastguard just before I arrived here and still nothing. They confirmed they'll keep the search going until dark."

Ella sank into an armchair and put her face in her hands. Her shoulders heaved. Amy grabbed the box of tissues and passed them to her. Ella blew her nose noisily before pulling another out to wipe her eyes. "They're not going to find him alive, are they? Not now?"

"It will take a miracle, but I've known them to happen." He smiled weakly. "Look, I'm sorry Mrs Hampton, I know this is a difficult time for you. I'm afraid I need to ask you a few questions. Just routine stuff."

"Okay, I understand. And please call me Ella."

"Let's start with some background." He opened his notebook and took out a pen.

Ella shifted uncomfortably.

Poised and ready, he asked, "Tell me about yourself and Dean—how long have you been together?"

"We started going out soon after his divorce. After dating for a while I agreed to move in with him—that was seven years ago. I guess you could say we hit it off from day one. I'd been working as the receptionist in his dental practice, so we already knew each other. We are very close and work well together." Her face lit up with a radiant smile. "We see each other virtually all day every day."

"Not many people can do that—it's pretty special," Frank said.

She sat back in her chair, looking a little more relaxed.

"Do you have an up-to-date photograph of Dean that you could give me?" His eyes drifted to the selection of pewter framed photos displayed on a cabinet. "If you don't have a printed one, you can email one through."

She drew her lithe body out of the chair like a cat stretching and went over to the cabinet. Choosing one, she paused and looked at it for a long moment before handing it to Frank.

"Thanks." He took the photo and looked at the picture. "I have to say, he's hardly aged in the time since we last met."

"He's always kept himself fit."

"Is this your most recent photo of Dean?"

"I have some on my phone from our holiday." She picked up her phone and tapped the screen. "This is a good shot taken just two days ago. I can send it to you."

Frank looked at the screen. "Can I have both? I promise I'll return the framed one."

Ella opened a drawer and rummaged through its contents before pulling out an unframed copy of the print. "Here, take this one instead."

He carefully placed the photo on the arm of the chair. "Now I know this isn't going to be easy for you, but would you mind going over the incident again in detail, starting with when you began your holiday?"

Ella sighed deeply. "We had been out at Great Barrier Island on holiday after sailing across on the westerly last Saturday. We spent the first few days in Port Fitzroy, enjoying the usual things:

fishing, bush walking and of course swimming. A couple of days ago we sailed down the coast to Whangaparapara Harbour. We were expecting a southerly last night, but it had a bit more westerly in it and we spent an uncomfortable night listening to the wind and the noises of the boat as it rocked with the small swells coming up the harbour. I didn't get much sleep and spent a bit of time on anchor watch." Her eyes brimmed with tears which she dried before blowing her nose.

"And what happened today?" His voice was gentle and encouraging, his eyes dark and intense.

"Today," she repeated. "Over breakfast we agreed to head for home. The forecast wasn't looking great for the next few days, and I was tired and frankly, a bit irritable."

"I hate to ask this, but did you fight?" He watched her with interest.

"No, I wouldn't call it a fight, more a minor disagreement. Dean and I have a very loving relationship. He also loves his boat and can't spend enough time on her. I love her too, although not so much when it cuts up rough." She was speaking quietly. "We left the harbour under motor and put the sails up once we were in the open. We were about five miles out when it happened. A swell forced a jibe." She put her head in her hands and gave in to quiet sobs.

"Take your time," he said, poised with pen in hand.

She looked up. "Dean was standing on the starboard cockpit seat at the time and the boom came around and struck him on the back of the head. I was sitting on the port side. It all happened so fast!" The last came out more as a wail and this time she sobbed loud and long, her face cradled in her hands.

Amy moved across to sit on the arm of the chair and put her hand on Ella's shoulder. She could barely contain her own tears, but she drew on every ounce of strength that was in her to provide comfort, while desperate to be comforted herself. They waited for Ella to regain her composure.

Ella wiped her face and took a long breath in through her nose and let it out slowly through her mouth. "I searched for him, I really did, for ages and ages. I just couldn't find him." Her voice had taken on a desperate note as if needing to convince them, possibly feeling the guilt now of not being able to find him.

"Did he have a life jacket on?"

"No, I've explained this to Coastguard. We tend to only wear life jackets when it's rough."

"Did you throw him a lifeline or a floatation device like a horseshoe?"

"No, there wasn't time—and I don't think he was conscious. I never heard him call out. He was out of sight behind the swells by the time I let the sails fly and got the motor started to turn *Aurora* around. He disappeared so fast." She sniffed.

Listening to Ella's account brought a rising tide of tears into Amy's eyes and she silently wept while still perched on the arm of the chair.

Frank checked his notes and cleared his throat. "You say you were heading for home... that would be in a west to sou'west direction. How did you come to be under full sail and heading downwind?"

"Ah sorry, I can explain that." She paused to pick up her glass and tossed the remaining contents down her throat. "We were heading for home and then changed our minds—it was simply too soon to finish our holiday. We decided to head down the west side of Coromandel and spend our last few days down there. We have—um—had a few more days before we are due back at work. We like to think we're free spirits when we're on the boat and we go as the mood and weather takes us. We're a bit nomadic when we're out there."

"Right, thanks. I think I've got it all." He pulled a business card out of his pocket before crossing the room to hand it to Ella. "Here's my number, call me if you need anything or think of anything else. Like I said, Dean's a great guy and I'll be praying for a miracle. And please send the photo to my email."

They said their goodbyes and Amy saw him out. At the door she said, "I'm so glad you knew my brother. He's very special to me. I think he'd be pleased to know you're assigned to finding him."

"We'll do our best, but with the light failing they'll soon be calling off the search for the day. I'm sorry." He turned and walked back down the path.

*

Later that night when Amy and Terry were home and preparing for bed, Amy said, "I can't believe Dean is missing. It feels like a bad dream."

Terry stopped shaving and looked at her in the mirror. "It's a shock alright. How are you coping?"

"I admit it's been a struggle. My tremor has been noticeably worse. I think Ella saw it when I spilt some gin, although she's probably forgotten it now—what with Dean to think about."

"Maybe you should tell her."

"No, I'm still not ready for that." Amy rubbed the night moisturiser into her face. "She said something odd tonight to the policeman. She said they were heading for home, but when quizzed by the cop she said they'd changed their minds and decided to head to western Coromandel for a few days."

"That makes sense, doesn't it?" Terry asked, climbing into his side of the bed.

"Why didn't she tell me that?"

"Maybe she wasn't thinking straight. It wouldn't be that surprising given the stress she must be under. I wouldn't read too much into it."

She stripped off her dressing gown and draped it over a chair before climbing into bed next to him. "And why didn't she throw him a horseshoe? They're right there on the transom."

"Everything must've happened so fast, and he probably disappeared behind the swells before she got the chance. No matter how much you drill it, when it happens for real it must be a lot more difficult. Situations can develop rapidly. Be careful not to overthink it. I know you love your brother, but you've gotta see it from her angle. I always thought they were a solid couple. She must be devastated to lose him like that. I guess there's little hope now."

"You can't say that!" She removed her glasses and placed them on the bedside table. "He could be lying on a beach somewhere, alive and waiting to be rescued."

He turned out the light before taking her in his arms, running his hand over her curly hair and tucking it behind her ears. "Honey, the chances that he would have survived that in all honesty are next to none. You know what it means to be hit by the boom under the full force of the wind. I think you have to prepare yourself for the worst."

"I can't give up hope, and I won't. Not yet. He's a strong swimmer."

"From Ella's account, it's unlikely he would have been able to swim after that head blow. I know it's hard, but I don't want you to have false hope."

Her body shuddered beneath his arms as she gave into the full force of her emotions, allowing the tears to run yet again. He continued to stroke her gently while she silently cried, not only for Dean but also for the loss of her own healthy body.

She lay quietly taking refuge in the dark, before whispering, "I don't know what I would do without Dean. I regret not having made more effort to see him since he married Ella, but I will once he's found. We were always so close growing up."

"One day at a time. You need your sleep to face tomorrow and to be strong for Ella and the family. You should take the next couple of days off work." His voice was heavy with sleep.

"I'll call work in the morning. Al will cover for me." She snuggled into him. "I'm glad I've got you to help me through this, my Parkinson's, and everything."

"I've been meaning to talk to you about that. Isn't it time you told the girls? They see your tremor and they're old enough to deal with the news."

"I will, soon. I promise. I just can't cope with it at the moment with everything that's going on. Let's focus on Dean first." She yawned. "I need to support Ella."

3

The next morning Frank Smythe was in the office early to wade through his paperwork, giving him time to check in on Dean's wife before taking out the police launch. He had a number of current cases contributing to a mountain of paper. It was an on-going battle in this job, with no-one to delegate the admin to. They were his cases and as such he needed to close them out himself.

Having made the rank of detective he had come close to burnout in the city's Central Police Station. He simply lacked the ambition needed to manage the high turnover of young staff and dealing with criminal elements all day every day had given him a warped view of humanity. It came as a natural fit to transfer across to the Maritime Unit. With his love of the sea and his sailing experience, this was the perfect job for him. Most of his shifts were out on the police launch doing a lot of the things a land-based policeman does but on the water, which suited him perfectly. He no longer had to deal with the gangs and that was a plus. The change had come with a demotion of rank to the equivalent of sergeant, matched with a corresponding cut in pay, but he was much happier skippering the police boat *Deodar III*. He'd started as crew until he got his Master's papers promoting him to Coastal Master. After gaining practical experience he was signed off as a Police Coastal Master. His wife, Margie, had been supportive of the move, especially now the kids had left home. She was fully aware of his anxiety and the impact it had been having on the family.

Today he was preoccupied with the Hampton case. This was his only case that was personal, having known Dean. His sympathies lay with the poor widow—he was certain that Dean had drowned, especially given the alleged head trauma. The jibe is the most dangerous manoeuvre for a yacht; it happens when the boat turns with the wind going across the stern causing the boom holding the mainsail to slam across the cockpit, often with tremendous force.

Searches like this were coordinated out of his unit and he was grateful to be on deck today. Because Dean Hampton had been a friend, he'd personally made contact with Dean's wife rather than hand it over to Central as normally would be the case. He intended to stay close to it for Dean's sake.

The search would now be to recover a body—that would be like looking for a needle in a haystack, although the day was forecast to brighten up and the wind was due to ease. The search would be difficult, with a large area of water to cover where strong currents ran through the channel and swells steepened dangerously when the wind was against the tide.

He'd never been good at breaking bad news to families, but he felt he owed it to Dean to keep his widow informed—for old times' sake. He pushed the pile of papers aside and put his notebook and pen in the pocket of his regulation blue overalls, standard issue in the Maritime Unit. Then he left the office and went in search of a coffee-to-go to take with him on the drive over to the Hamptons' home.

The traffic was heavy for this hour and he'd finished his coffee by the time he pulled into her driveway. The same cars as last evening were parked outside, so he assumed the sister was there. He strolled up the path that had on one side a barked garden of randomly placed rocks intermingled with native grasses and small shrubs, and neatly trimmed grass on the other. He rang the doorbell and heard footsteps approaching.

Ella opened the door, looking fresh in a buttoned-through floral dress that highlighted her curves and shapely calves. It was obvious what had attracted Dean. Her tanned face had flawless skin, her eyes were wide and clear, made up with expertly applied make-up. "Hi Frank, come on in."

"Good morning." As he followed her inside, he wondered what was good about it and silently chastised himself for being so insensitive.

She led him into the kitchen where Amy was making coffee. Amy's yellow top and denim shorts were strangely incongruent to her drawn face and red eyes behind black rimmed glasses. Her face had a startled look and her mop of unruly dark hair showed no family resemblance to the Dean he remembered.

"Coffee?" Amy asked in a flat tone once they'd greeted each other.

Being polite, he said, "Yes, thanks. I've been trying to cut back, but that smell is irresistible."

"Is there any news?" Ella asked.

"Ella, I'm sorry—there's been no news overnight. We have teams out searching the bays where Dean may have managed to make landfall." It sounded clumsy, so he added, "I have to say it's not looking good for Dean. I'm so sorry."

She drew in a deep breath. "I know you're doing all you can and I, we the family, appreciate that. How long will the search go on?"

"It's likely to be scaled back if we don't find him over the next eight hours. I promise to keep you posted with any developments." It sounded so empty and he regretted he couldn't be more positive.

Amy passed steaming mugs of coffee to Ella and Frank and offered the obligatory biscuits.

"I was thinking I could go down to *Aurora* and pack up the food and clothes and bring it all back here." Amy gave Ella a somewhat forced smile before looking at Frank and adding, "Would that be okay?"

"That's a kind offer," Ella answered. "I left the fridge going, but we could do with the food here. I'm afraid everything was left in a bit of a mess."

"I think that's a great idea," Frank said. "I would appreciate some more of your time Ella, to go over the details again to make sure I got them right. I'll be needing to make my report. It would also be useful to familiarise myself with *Aurora*. Perhaps I could go down to the marina on my way back to the office—if you're down there already Amy, I won't need to get a set of keys."

"Can I pack up the food while I wait?" Amy sipped her coffee.

"That would be okay. Just don't touch anything else until I've seen her. Any tidying or cleaning will need to wait." He looked apologetically at Ella. "It's just standard procedure."

They agreed this was a good plan. While they drank their coffees, Ella quizzed Frank on his experiences crewing in the classic yacht regattas with Dean. She seemed to be holding it together well, showing exceptional fortitude, although he assumed she was putting on a brave front and inside she was probably anything but calm.

Amy tidied up the cups and collected her bag before leaving for the marina. Frank pulled out his notebook and went through the events of the previous day with Ella, taking care to get the details correct. Happy there was nothing new to add, he left for the marina promising to keep her informed as soon as he heard anything.

*

Amy put her empty bags into a marina trolley and dragged it through the security gate and down onto the jetty. Launches and yachts flanked her on both sides. At another time she might have sized them up and chosen her favourite, something she had done since she was a child. But today she didn't have the energy or presence of mind to take notice of the boats. Dean consumed her thoughts.

Her footsteps were heavy, her movements stiff making her body seem older than her age. This was Parkinson's. Everything seemed to be that much more difficult, her actions that much slower.

Alongside *Aurora*, she kicked off her shoes and carefully climbed aboard. Standing in the cockpit, she stared at the starboard rail and imagined the moment that Dean went over. Tears welled up in her eyes and she made no attempt to stop them. The flotation buoys sat on the stern where they had always been. If only someone else had been on board to leap in after him or throw him a lifeline. It could have made all the difference.

The deck was white fibreglass and sleek. Windows wrapped over the cabin top from port to starboard, letting the light into the saloon below. Ropes were all neatly stowed in spirals, something Dean had always liked to do. The heavy aluminium boom was hinged perpendicular to the mast—it must have swung across at such speed that poor Dean would've received a terrifying wallop. It didn't bear thinking about. Grief rose inside, threatening to overwhelm her and she gulped, determined to force it down. Climbing onto the cabin top by the canvas spray dodger she inspected the boom more closely, not sure what she was looking for. Blood perhaps, or hair. Nothing obvious remained of the accident, which wasn't surprising given the rain yesterday.

She unlocked the cabin and went inside. The main saloon was tidy as was typical of her brother. The forward cabin had been slept in with the bed unmade. To her surprise one of the aft cabins had also been slept in—she wouldn't have expected Dean and Ella to sleep separately. Still, perhaps one snores or maybe it was because one was on anchor watch and didn't want to disturb the other. She shouldn't be so nosey.

Back in the galley, she packed the food into the bags she'd brought with her. Having emptied the fridge and cupboards, she'd just set to work wiping them down when she heard footsteps approaching.

"Hello," a deep male voice called. "Are you there Amy?"

"Down here." She peeled off the rubber cleaning gloves and got up to meet Frank who was clambering down the companion way.

"Nice yacht," he said, as he took in the beautifully maintained wood in the saloon. "Dean always had an eye for nice things."

"Yeah, she sails really well too."

"Did Dean take *Aurora* on an ocean passage? She appears to be well equipped."

"Yes, he got a reliever into his practice and sailed up to the islands for an extended holiday. I think it was about nine years ago, when he was still married to his first wife. She and Sara flew up to join him."

"Do you get out on her often?"

"Hardly at all these days. We used to get out a lot, however that was before Dean married Ella."

"Are you and Dean not close?"

She felt herself become defensive and picked her words carefully. "To the contrary, we were very close growing up and throughout his first marriage. I supported him through his divorce, but we haven't seen so much of each other since he got

36

together with Ella. I guess you could say he's been preoccupied with her and there hasn't been a lot of time for his extended family."

"I'm sure he would be pleased to know that you're here supporting Ella now. She must be devastated. Are they close?" He stood poised with notebook and pen ready to write down her answer.

"I think so. They always seemed obsessed with each other." Amy hesitated, wondering how much she should say.

He looked at her expectantly and waited, encouraging her to speak.

"I'm close to my niece, Sara, and she's been worried about Dean. She thinks Dean and Ella have been arguing a lot of late. The thing is she doesn't get on with Ella, so she may be overstating things. She was very affected by her parents' divorce and at the time opted to live with Dean. She was only 15 years old."

"What did Dean and Ella argue about?"

"She didn't know, but she thought it might've had something to do with money. Ella has extravagant tastes, more so than Dean's first wife, Sara's mum."

"Where is Sara currently living?"

"She's away at university in Dunedin."

His eyes dropped to her hand, which she realised was shaking badly, so she tucked it into her pocket.

"Is everything alright with you?" His voice had a softer tone.

"Yes, of course." She was embarrassed and certainly didn't want to share her news with this man. "Well at least it will be when we get Dean home."

"I wish we could find him for you, but I don't want to get your hopes up." His voice lowered and his eyes seemed to convey a deep sadness.

"Until there is absolute proof, I will never give up on Dean."

He paused, before saying, "I realise it's a difficult time for you so I don't want to take up your time unnecessarily. I'll take a look around and then I'll be on my way. Which cabin did Dean use?"

"The forward cabin."

Frank moved about the interior, looking inside each of the cabins and poking around the lockers. The head was a small room just big enough for the marine toilet and vanity, leaving enough space for your average person to comfortably manoeuvre themselves about. A beard trimmer was in the vanity cupboard and pulling a small plastic bag from his pocket, he opened the cutter-head and tipped some of its contents into the bag before putting it back.

"She's a lovely boat," he said, coming back out of the head with the bag now in his pocket. "Did Dean do the varnish work himself?"

"Yes, he loves pottering around on her and takes great pride in keeping her shining." She looked at the gleaming barometer. "I used to rib him about *Aurora*'s brass being polished more than that on any other boat."

"I can see he's taken great pride in her—he did the same with the classic yachts. He'd put a lot of voluntary hours into helping maintain them for the Trusts that owned them." He ran his hand over his balding forehead. "He was a good man."

"He is a good man," Amy corrected him.

He studied her for a moment. "You can start cleaning down here if you'd like, I've seen all I need to."

Frank climbed the steps. His footsteps could be heard overhead as he slowly walked the length of the deck before returning to examine the boom and the starboard rail. The GPS beeped and she looked up from her cleaning to watch him study the instrument, confidently pushing the buttons to go through the various menu options while jotting down notes in his notebook.

"Thanks Amy, I'll take a photo of *Aurora* and then I'll be off. No doubt I will see you again at Ella's," he called out to her.

"Bye Frank."

His footsteps receded down the jetty as she finished her cleaning.

*

Towards the end of the day, Frank steered *Deodar III* into the dock, deeply troubled after having spent the last few hours combing the water and beaches around the south and western coastline of Great Barrier Island, Coromandel and the southern Hauraki Gulf islands. Dean Hampton remained missing. The Coastguard search team had also been out looking. The search area had been carefully plotted out taking into account the tidal vectors and windage. But even so, it was impossible to pinpoint exactly where the body might be. Other factors such as the weight of the body and how much buoyancy it had could affect the drift. Over time, the search area increased, making the search even more difficult. While Frank had worked hard to make his calculations as accurate as possible, this was more art than science.

With no sightings of Dean, they were now looking for a body. To admit that there was no longer any hope—not even miraculous hope—that Dean would be found alive after all this time in the water was difficult. If the tide hadn't beached the body, the odds of finding it would increase once the internal gases were created giving it a natural buoyancy. If the body didn't surface or wasn't found, then eventually they'd have to make the call to end the search. Without a body, it would be up to the coroner to declare it an unfortunate accident and certify Dean as legally dead.

With a deep sigh and a heavy heart, he shut down the motors, stowed the gear and gathered his things. Knowing bad news was best despatched face to face, and with his personal attachment to the case, he decided to swing by the Hampton house on the way home.

The rush hour traffic was heavy as he made his way across town and for once he was grateful. He dreaded having to break the news to Dean's family that there were still no sightings and was sure they would know what this meant for Dean.

This time an extra car was parked in the driveway, so he chose to park on the street. The doorbell was answered by a tall man with a messy crop of thick auburn hair, wearing scruffy jeans and a tee-shirt that advertised Fagin Electrical.

"Hello, I'm Coastal Master Frank Smythe with the Maritime Police Unit." He extended his hand. "I've been coordinating the search for Dean."

"Terry Fagin, Amy's husband. Good to meet you." Terry's ruddy face smiled in a good-humoured way. "Come in—they're all in the living room."

As they entered the room, Ella got to her feet and walked towards him. "Any news?" She moved with a kind of sophisticated poise, keeping her emotions under control.

Frank glanced about the room. An elegantly dressed older woman with short white hair, glasses and dangly earrings stood up to meet him. She stretched out her hand to shake his and announced she was Dawn, Ella's mum.

Terry brought him a dining chair. Frank sat and smoothed his hands down his overalls.

Amy was on the couch next to a thin and frail-looking elderly woman who grinned at everyone and no-one. Amy said, "Frank, meet my mum and Dean's mum, Diane Hampton. Mum this is the policeman handling the case. He's also an old friend of Dean's."

Diane murmured a greeting and Frank nodded in her direction before turning his attention back to Ella.

He cleared his throat. "I do have news, however it's not what you want to hear. We've not been able to locate Dean and the search has been called off for today. I'm so sorry I can't bring you better tidings."

Silence.

"He's gone, hasn't he?" Ella's voice was quiet and calm.

Frank drew in a deep breath. "We can't say that, but with a head injury and no flotation aids we have to assume the worst. I'm sorry."

Ella's eyes filled with tears, although she remained composed. Amy sobbed and Terry went to her side. Next to her Diane cried silently.

Frank looked at Ella and felt deep compassion for this strong woman.

"What happens now?" Ella asked, her voice barely audible.

Carefully weighing his words, he said, "We will keep searching until we find him." He omitted to say that it was now a body search.

"What if you can't find him?" asked Terry. "At what point do we start to think about a funeral?"

Amy glared at Terry.

"We generally do find them eventually." He thought of the bloated corpses he'd found floating in the past, the production of post-mortem gases providing a natural buoyancy days after death.

"Normally in a case like this it is up to the coroner to decide whether the person is deceased and then they can issue a death certificate which enables the family to mourn the person with a funeral. Without that, the family may still hold a memorial service."

"I think I need a drink," Ella said, looking at Terry.

As Terry got up, Frank said he'd let himself out and promised to be in touch in the morning.

*

The Hampton house was quiet except for the remote hum of the traffic. Terry had left to take Diane back to the retirement home for her evening meal and Dawn had made excuses and left soon after Frank.

Amy stood in the kitchen not sure what to do next. The idea that Dean was out there, somewhere, for a second night was unbearable and all she could do was pray for a miracle. Unlike her, he had always lived life to the full and loved an adventure. Sailing had always been his passion and the ocean was his happy place.

His first marriage had ended in disaster when he'd discovered his wife was having an affair with his best friend, Simon. They always say the husband is last to know, and this was true for Dean. He really had no idea, even inviting Simon around to barbecues and the like when the affair was ongoing. The divorce was messy with Sara becoming increasingly distraught. Amy had spent many hours with Dean and Sara, helping them navigate the separation and divorce. Ella worked in Dean's dental clinic and before the ink was dry on the divorce papers, she'd moved in. Amy always felt Dean was on the rebound and Ella had virtually stalked him when he was at his weakest. Even so, she had to admit that together they made the perfect couple—both were elegantly attractive and smart. She'd always felt Ella was manipulative. Still, she couldn't imagine how difficult this must be for her now.

Unsure what to prepare for Ella's dinner, she was going to find her when she heard her voice coming from the bedroom, obviously on her phone. Trying not to eavesdrop, she turned to go back to the kitchen when curiosity made her pause.

"I know we agreed on it, but I had to call you."

Pause.

"You have no idea how hard this is for me."

Another pause.

"How about you call me in another few days."

A short pause and then something inaudible was mumbled.

It was most likely Sara, Dean's daughter, who was studying in Dunedin—there was no one else that she knew of who was close to Ella. In that moment she became aware of how bad it would look if she was caught being nosey and she hurried back to the kitchen to load the dishes into the dishwasher, loudly.

Footsteps approached and Ella entered carrying her phone.

Unable to resist, Amy asked, "Who was that?"

A wide-eyed expression passed across Ella's face before she seemed to regain her composure. Was it panic or annoyance that Amy had been listening? The look was so fleeting that it could have been in Amy's imagination. After all, Ella was under immense strain.

"It was just a friend." The colour drained from Ella's face as she looked down at her feet. In a softer tone she said, "Why don't you get going. I'm sure Terry and the girls need you at home."

"I'm happy to stay and keep you company for a while. And I can make myself useful and get you a meal."

"Thanks, but I can sort my own dinner out. I would appreciate the space to work my way through this whole mess. It's so hard to accept that they've given up on finding him."

Amy could feel the pressure building behind her eyes as the floodgates opened again and tears overflowed. Through the tears she could see Ella watching her and she was amazed at the woman's strength. Maybe she should head home and have an early night in preparation for what was likely to be a long week. She bade a hurried farewell and left for the comfort of her own family.

4

Frank was enjoying a sandwich at his desk while catching up on some paperwork relating to an alleged scuttling of a launch for a fraudulent insurance claim. The three days since Dean fell overboard had been busy, and it hadn't been easy with Frank's own emotions invested in the case. Although he was still involved in coordinating the search, it was now scaled back as they searched for a body. Central Auckland Police Headquarters was short staffed, enabling him to swing it that he kept working the Hampton case rather than hand it over.

Without a body, the coroner needed his report of the circumstances under which Dean disappeared, evidence of his untouched bank accounts and interviews with family, work colleagues and friends to show Dean hadn't been in touch. He'd been surprised to see how skint Dean had been, given how much he had to pay to see his own dentist. Still, what the Hamptons did with their money was none of his business. That file now sat ready to lodge with the coroner who could declare him legally dead if the body wasn't found so that the death certificate could be issued. In the meantime, the family were preparing a memorial service so they could express their grief in the appropriate way.

The photo of Dean he'd taken from Ella lay on top of the open file on his desk, prompting him to stare at his old mate. He was one of those people who oozed vitality and was fun to be around—such a waste of a life. It was difficult to believe how many years had passed and yet the Dean in the picture looked just like the old Dean he remembered; he'd held onto his youth well.

When he'd checked in with the family yesterday, many of the extended family were gathered at Dean and Ella's house, including Dean's daughter Sara, who'd flown up from Dunedin. Dean had been only a few years older than what Sara was now when Frank had first met him. And Sara was the female version with striking thick fair hair, a tanned complexion and lanky athletic build. Her distress had been profound, unsurprisingly so given the nature of the tragedy.

The phone buzzed.

"Frank Smythe?" A woman's voice asked.

"Speaking."

"Frank, it's Anahera Raupara. Been a long time since you left us at Central."

"Anahera, good to hear from you. I heard you'd taken a secondment with Land Search and Rescue—has it been a good move?"

Her bubbly laugh made him smile. "Yeah, the grapevine still works. I'm loving it. How about we catch up for that drink sometime? You still owe me one."

"I'd love to. Now what can I do for you?"

"I took a call today from Coromandel police. Some tourists had a nasty shock this morning when they came across a body washed up on Port Jackson beach. They described it as grisly—not sure if it'd fed some sharks, but by all accounts it's been pretty messed up. We don't yet know how long it's been in the water. I see you've been working a man-overboard case—I'm thinking the cadaver could be yours. The police photographer is there now, along with the recovery team."

"It's in the right vicinity. What can you tell me about it?"

"All I know is that it is male, the face is bearded but barely recognisable. The head has received a blow, the limbs are badly mangled with deep gouges over most of the body. Not yet fetid."

"That could be my man."

"We'll get him brought into Auckland Forensic Pathology. Sounds like dental records will be needed for identification."

"Shouldn't be a problem; my guy was a dentist."

"I'll let you know when he arrives. And about that drink, how about after work on Thursday, say 1730 at the Smugglers' Bar?"

"Yep, works for me. See you there." Frank hung up and sat back in his chair. Hearing from Anahera had lifted his spirits and made him realise how much he missed the old team. A catch up was long overdue.

If the corpse found at Port Jackson was indeed Dean, then regardless of the tragedy it would enable the family to get some closure. They would also be able to farewell Dean with a proper funeral. The thought of his friend finishing up in such a gruesome state put an end to the paperwork in front of him and he got up to brew another coffee.

Later that day he heard from the coroner's office. The Port Jackson John Doe had been transferred to Auckland by ambulance and was booked in for a post-mortem examination first thing in the morning. He confirmed he would be there. In the meantime, he owed it to Dean to extend to Ella the simple courtesy of preparing her for the possibility that he'd been found. He cleared his desk and shut down his computer before once more making his way to Ella's house.

Sara, in a black crop top over jeans, met him at the door and invited him through to the kitchen. Her blonde hair was pulled back in a ponytail. She wore no make-up to disguise her swollen eyes. Amy, wearing an apron, was busy preparing food and greeted him with a tired smile as he walked in. Ella was seated on a bar stool with a gin and tonic in hand.

"Would you like a drink?" Her words were slightly slurred.

"No, thank you." He caught Sara's eye and detected disapproval. "I've come to update you on the latest development."

A flicker of fear passed over Ella's face, or perhaps she was bracing herself for the inevitable news. He took in a deep breath and said, "A body has been found washed up at Port Jackson in the Coromandel."

A pot clattered to the floor in the kitchen. "Dean?"

Amy stood rooted to the spot, shaking with eyes wide and mouth open, the pot now forgotten. Her hand moved up to cover her mouth. Sara, tears already coursing down her cheeks, rushed around and put her arm around her aunty, making Amy look diminutive alongside her leggy niece.

The blood drained out of Ella's face and she reached for her glass. "You've found him then." It was more of a statement than a question.

"We're not sure, however I can confirm a body has been found. There will be an autopsy in the morning."

"Can I see him?" Ella asked.

"As I understand it the identification will likely be using dental records." He didn't want to mention the grisly state of the body. In a softer tone, he added, "There may be no need to put you through that."

"I want to see him." The pitch of Ella's voice became shrill.

"Ella!" Sara sounded angry. "Calm yourself, you've had too much to drink."

"Don't tell me what I can or cannot do," Ella retorted. "Dean would not permit you to speak to me like that."

The stress was palpable in the silence that followed.

Amy looked from one to the other. "Look, we are all feeling the strain. At times like this we need to look out for each other—not bicker." She paused. "Let's let the police do their job. I'm sure Frank will tell us what is appropriate and will look after our interests, for Dean's sake."

"That's right, you can count on it," Frank said, relieved to have Amy's calming influence. "I suggest you wait until you hear back from me. I'll let you know tomorrow whether we need you to come down to the morgue."

"I still want to see him." Ella's voice was much quieter this time, but it was steely all the same.

"If you need to identify him, I'll go with you as your support person." Amy cast a concerned look at her sister-in-law.

"No!" Ella spat the word with unexpected venom, before adding in a quieter tone, "Sorry Amy, it's just that this is something I need to do on my own. I feel strongly about this, it's... it's kind of an intimacy that is between Dean and I."

The interplay was odd, perhaps due to the alcohol. Frank let it go and said he'd be in touch when he knew more.

*

Next morning as Frank made his way through the early rush hour congestion, he found the usual radio traffic provided a comforting background noise to the turmoil going on in his head. The task ahead of him was going to be difficult and he steeled himself in preparation. There had been many bodies over the years he'd been in the force, but this was the first encounter with one that had been a friend. Friend or not, he would need to treat it like any other.

He parked his car in the basement of the building housing the morgue and took the stairs up to the first floor, determined to follow this through for his old crewmate.

Once through security, he met John Williams, the forensic pathologist. He was a rosy cheeked bald man in scrubs whose sunny countenance belonged more in a hospital providing light relief to the living rather than in a mortuary. They had met on several occasions in the past and Dean had been impressed by his competence.

The autopsy room contained several stainless benches, some empty and gleaming under the bright lights. John handed him a mask and put one on himself before leading him to a slab in the middle of the room where a body was covered with a sheet.

"I'll warn you, it's not a pretty sight," John said, pulling back the sheet to expose a mish mash of fleshy remains that were until recently a living being.

Frank looked away and involuntarily retched. The body was worse than he'd expected.

"Take a moment," John said. "This isn't for everyone."

Frank went over to the water cooler and took a long drink of cold water. This was something he needed to face, for Dean's sake.

John had replaced the sheet over all but the head, which was still intact. Multiple lacerations criss-crossed the face and some of it was missing. The corpse was bearded and resembled the Dean in the photo, although it was so grotesquely bloated that he couldn't be sure.

"Take a look at this." John moved the head to reveal a significant gash on the back of it. "This injury may have rendered him unconscious before he hit the water."

"I think this may be my missing man-overboard," Frank said, turning his eyes away. "Do you think the head injury is consistent with being hit by a yacht's boom?"

"I couldn't say for certain, but neither could I rule it out." He picked up a calliper and measured the size of the gash, then made some notes. "What I can say is the cause of death was drowning. He was alive when he went into the water."

"What about the injuries to his torso?"

"Again, I can't be certain, however they appear to have been sustained after death. I would hazard a guess that it was either predators or perhaps a boat propeller."

"What type of motor?"

"Again, it's hard to say for sure, but it looks suspiciously like a prop of some sort. Could be either inboard or outboard." He lowered the sheet and pointed to the gashes on the legs. "See how these are almost a regular pattern? I can't see any marks that would convince me they're bite marks. But nor can I rule it out at this stage. If the body was partially submerged, it's possible a boat ran over it and was totally unaware it was there."

"How difficult will it be to identify him?"

"I will need his medical records and his dental records to confirm the identity. This is one of those cases where it's not appropriate for the family to identify him."

"How long until you can confirm his identity?"

"I should be able to have it with the coroner tomorrow, all going well. We don't like to take too long in these cases. It's traumatic enough for the family without prolonging the grieving period."

"I'd appreciate you making this one a priority. Any chance of completing it earlier?"

"I'll see what I can do."

The smell of the lab was getting to Frank, so he hastily made his exit before he lost his breakfast, barely taking time to thank

John on his way out. Driving back to his office, he opened his window to blow the remnants of the lab away.

That afternoon Frank was on the job down at West Harbour Marina chasing some stolen gear when the call came through. The dental records had confirmed the cadaver's identity to be that of Dean Hampton. A deep sorrow settled in his heart. He regretted not having kept in touch with Dean over the years. As soon as he returned to base he'd have to go and give the news to the family. Once back he ensured *Deodar III* was shipshape before driving to the Hampton house.

*

Amy had spent the morning at home preparing food for Ella, to help cater for all the visitors expected to come and pay their respects. The memorial service was likely to be large because of Dean's popularity and his many clients, providing many mouths to feed. This was something practical that she could do to help, which she did willingly as in a way it was something she could do for Dean.

It had also given her the opportunity to touch base with work. Al had insisted she wasn't needed and urged her to take as much time as necessary, for which she was grateful. But it also made her feel dispensable, a feeling that had been nagging her since her diagnosis. These last few days had been a nightmare and she'd barely given a thought to the other cloud that hung over her. The time was coming when she would have to let work know about her Parkinson's disease. While it still felt like she was the same person, with the same ambitions, she was scared she would be treated differently and even be passed over for any promotions. To be treated like she was sick, or even as a liability or someone who was no longer capable, would be devastating. This was why she hadn't been able to share her news, nor even share her fears with Terry.

Once the savouries and sweet treats were packed up and loaded into her car, she drove over to Dean's place.

She arrived as Frank was getting out of his car, his body language telling her he wasn't bringing good news. After acknowledging each other, they walked up the path in silence and Sara opened the door before they had a chance to ring the bell.

Once more the members of Dean's immediate family gathered in the living room to hear from Frank. Amy put the food in the kitchen and took a seat on the couch next to Sara. Frank was already seated.

Ella looked ashen and her hands shook slightly as they gripped a coffee mug. "What's the news?"

Frank cleared his throat. "I can confirm it was Dean's body found beached at Port Jackson." He paused, looking around the room. "I'm so sorry for your loss."

Amy felt the wind go out of her as she struggled to take in the news that Dean was really gone. Her vision became blurry from the tears that sprang into her eyes. Beside her, Sara was quietly sobbing, so she reached across and drew her into her arms. Ella let out a long slow breath, before standing up and walking to the window where she gazed out with her back to the small gathering.

"Can I see him?" Ella asked, her voice clear and resolute.

"I would advise you not to, at least not until the undertaker has finished his work. He's suffered facial injuries and is barely recognisable." Frank spoke slowly, like a parent instructing a child.

With her voice little more than a whisper, Ella asked, "How can you be sure it's him?"

Frank shifted uneasily in his chair. "The identification was primarily through dental records."

"Oh!" Her shoulders dropped as she turned and walked slowly back to her seat. "What are the injuries?"

Frank hesitated. "He suffered a blow to the head—we're assuming it was from being hit by the boom, just as you described. He also has a series of lacerations to the face and body, but we can't be sure how these have come about. It is likely he was unconscious and drowned soon after he hit the water, so he wouldn't have felt anything."

Sara sobbed louder and Amy tightened her grip on her. Her own tears flowed freely down her cheeks. The tremor escalated and she tucked her hand under her thigh.

"Once the coroner is satisfied that Dean's death was an accident, you can go ahead and plan the funeral," Frank said gently. "If you let me know which funeral home you'd like to use, I can organise for them to pick Dean up."

The relief on Ella's face was unmistakable, perhaps because the unknown had been replaced with certainty.

"Mum, who did we use for Dad's funeral?" Ella asked.

Dawn, who had been sitting quietly in the corner, answered, "Wiley and son. As tragic as this is, it will be better to have a full funeral; it will help provide you with some closure."

"If you'll excuse me, I think I'll leave you to it." Frank looked at each of them in turn. "These times are never easy. Dean was a good man and will no doubt be sorely missed. Ella, call if there's anything you need of me. I assume you've still got my number?"

"Yes, and thanks for coming by."

Dawn walked him to the door.

The rest of the afternoon went by in a blur. The funeral home called and sent a person around who quietly went through the planning for the funeral. Ella was impressive in the way she moved from one decision to the next.

Amy struggled to function at all and felt herself go onto autopilot as she kept herself busy by providing endless food and drinks as people came and went.

*

Later that evening, Amy and Terry asked their daughters, Maddie and Tracy, to join them in the lounge. The girls were Amy's source of immense pride and gave her reason to fight the recent diagnosis. Maddie, the older at 17 years of age, was the shorter of the two, taking after Amy in height and looks. Tracy was taller at 15 years and more athletic in build like the youthful version of Terry, but had inherited Amy's thick curly hair which she kept in a ponytail.

Once they were all sitting down, Amy between the girls on the couch, Terry broke the news. The girls were understandably inconsolable. Amy hugged them to her with an arm around each. Her own emotion was rising, adding to the constant anxiety she'd felt ever since her diagnosis, yet another gift she could thank Parkinson's for.

"I can't believe Uncle Dean has gone," Maddie whispered, eyes brimming with tears. She tucked her curly bob behind her ears, a gesture that had become a habit.

"Remember that holiday on *Aurora* when he teased us with man-overboard drills? He'd jump in when we were under sail and yell out 'Man Overboard' and we'd have to keep our eyes on him while Ella brought *Aurora* around." Tracy wiped her eyes with a tissue before blowing her nose noisily. "I can't believe it's happened for real."

"I'm going to miss him, even if we haven't seen a lot of him lately—he was always so much fun." Maddie lowered her voice. "I wish we'd seen more of him after he married Ella."

"Can Sara stay with us?" Tracy loved her cousin.

"I don't think so. Ella will need her there."

"Ella's mum could stay with her," Tracy suggested.

"We'll see. Perhaps she can stay a night before she goes back after the funeral." Amy didn't want any issues, not now. She turned to Terry. "Ella is being incredibly strong. She seemed almost relieved to hear Dean's body had been found."

"I guess she's had a number of days now to prepare herself for it."

"We all have, but she is taking the news so well. Unlike me, I can't stop the tears. I have to give Ella credit, she's being a rock. As soon as Frank left, she started planning the funeral—choosing the pallbearers, the order of service and even sorting out Dean's clothing." She stopped to dry her eyes.

"She may be relieved that she's going to get the chance to farewell him properly. It would be so much harder if he'd never been found." Terry looked at Amy. "I guess we all deal with grief differently."

"She wants to scatter his ashes in the Gulf—that's what he would have wanted. I think that's nice. We're all invited to join her aboard *Aurora* to farewell him at sea. She thinks it will be sometime soon after the funeral."

"He'd want that to be his final resting place."

"It's all so..." Tracy paused. "So final."

Amy rubbed her hand up and down her daughter's shoulder, then over her thick curly hair and down her ponytail.

"Mum, are you cold? Why are you trembling?" Tracy asked.

"It's nothing," Amy lied, catching the accusing glance that Terry shot at her. To change the subject, she asked, "How about a hot chocolate?"

Hot chocolates were made, accompanied by copious quantities of marshmallows, before they spent the rest of the evening gathered around the island bench in the kitchen reminiscing about the good times with Dean.

5

Ella stood in the bedroom staring at her image in the mirror. The face that looked back at her was pale despite her tan. She hadn't been sleeping well at all and it showed in the crow's feet radiating out from her eyes and the bags underneath. Today would be one of the hardest days in her life as they publicly farewelled Dean and she wanted to honour him with elegance and grace. Fear had been her companion ever since the incident, as she'd fumbled her way through this nightmare like a blind person on an obstacle course. Alcohol calmed her nerves but left her eyes bloodshot and her brain sluggish. The drinking was becoming an issue and she determined to cut back, at least until she got through this tumultuous time. Besides, at a time like this she needed her wits about her.

She slipped into an elegant black dress and rolled black pantyhose up her slim legs. Dean loved her leggy athletic figure. She eased her feet into a pair of high stilettos that enhanced her calves.

Back studying her image in the mirror, she worked on her eyes to make them more presentable for his funeral. She would pay tribute to him with her appearance as well as her words.

Amy could be sweet and generous, but she liked to meddle and play the big sister. She was sure Amy had never really approved of her. The look Amy had given her the other night confirmed her suspicions, when she thought Amy had been eavesdropping on her phone call.

When she and Dean first got together, he'd hung out at Amy's place a lot and Amy had been like a second mum to Sara after his first marriage broke up. The way he'd depended on her had made Ella envious. Even though Dean had been completely devoted to her from the time when he'd first asked her out, she still felt jealous having to share his attention. Amy was what she would never be. She was a devoted wife and mother, a career professional and smart. But she didn't have the same genes that blessed Dean with his good looks—Amy had their mother's short stature and mousey looks with curly and unruly hair. And lately, Amy's facial features seemed unusually wide-eyed and lacking in expression.

As for Sara, Dean treasured her and as difficult as it was, Ella had to admit that she'd grown into a beautiful, intelligent young woman. Ella had encouraged her to go away to university in Dunedin rather than attend one locally as it got her out of the house. The fact that Dean had attended Otago University had helped persuade her. And now she only needed to suffer her during holiday times.

These last few days had turned the personal haven that was her house into a gathering place for Dean's well-meaning family. The sooner this was behind her the better. Her face continued to stare back at her as she finished twisting her long tresses up into a bun.

An ornate jewellery box sat on her dressing table. Inside were the stunning diamond necklace and earrings that Dean had given her last Christmas. She removed them carefully and put them on. The extravagant gift had sparked a row between them; she'd wanted them, he'd been worried about the money. In the end he'd bought them for her. Thinking of the money, she wondered, not for the first time, if the life insurance would be paid out in time to cover the funeral costs. At least with a body there should be no problem with the policy.

Lastly, she applied some lipstick, not too bright, then smiled at the image in the mirror. Dean would be proud of her.

*

Amy was having a bad day which had followed a bad night when she'd woken with the night sweats in the early hours. Call it menopause or call it Parkinson's, she didn't know and nor did it matter. Once awake her mind kept going over the nightmare that they were all living and a return to sleep was out of the question. Her anxiety was always worse in the early hours. She never expected to be going to her brother's funeral. Her tremor was a signpost that told anyone who was remotely interested that she was up tight.

She had spent the morning sorting out appropriate funeral clothes for herself, Maddie, Tracy and for her mother. She'd found her mother's clothes needed spot cleaning and ironing. At first the girls couldn't agree on what they would wear, then Maddie settled for a khaki skirt and navy blouse and Tracy a white shirt over black leggings. In between times she managed to fit in a couple of calls to work. Thankfully, Terry with his good-natured humour and steady support, took some of the stress out of the day.

Amy showered and put on a black dress that matched her mood. Normally she'd approve of the way it complemented her dark curly hair and dark rimmed glasses, but today she didn't care. Today she wore it as a sign that she was in mourning. Today she thought she might wear black for as long as it took to accept Dean was gone forever. She sighed deeply. Forever was such a long time. She decided to wear a pair of studs in her ears and keep the jewellery simple.

Her mother, in the early stages of dementia, was taking Dean's tragedy a little better. Thankfully she was a happy patient, always smiling and patiently observing what was going on around her without fully participating. Amy hoped it would mean her grief would be less severe.

It would be a long day, starting with the funeral service, during which she would be delivering a short eulogy about Dean's childhood. Hours of agonising had gone into her speech. Time and again she'd checked that her notes were in her bag. After the service there would be a cuppa and some finger food. Then the family would all troop down to the crematorium for another service. Following that, Ella would be inviting them all back to her place for a light supper. She wished she could wake up and find it was all one big bad dream.

*

Frank found a carpark 200 metres away and followed small groups of mourners to the church. The funeral was going to be big judging by the cars parked outside already—and he was 15 minutes early.

A copy of the order of service was handed to him as he entered the building and he chose a seat in the back row next to a smart looking couple who introduced themselves as the Millers and said they knew Dean and Ella through the dental practice. The picture on the order of service was the same one as the well-groomed photo of Dean that Ella had given him.

The church was capacious and already it was three quarters full, with a steady stream of people coming in. At the front and centre sat a wooden casket with shiny silver handles and a huge wreath of flowers in all the colours of the rainbow. He was thankful the Coroner's Report had come through in time to release the body, enabling the family to hold the funeral.

As the time neared, the crowd hushed as a celebrant led the family to their seats. Ella walked in, tall and upright, elegant and sombre, looking neither to the left nor to the right. She was nothing short of stunning. Sara followed with shoulders slumped, then Amy with her arm linked through her mum's, Terry had the girls on either side and lastly Dawn with a gentleman at her side.

The service began and Frank steeled himself against his emotions—this he could do well after years in the force. His knees ached from old rugby injuries, so he stretched his legs out under the pew in front and prepared for a long stay. Thankfully the family had three songs in the order of service that would help break the sitting.

When it came to the eulogies, Amy walked stiffly to the stage. She related tales of growing up with Dean who was younger by just two years. She spoke with emotion, at times overcome and having to stop to regain some composure. It seemed Dean's younger days were full of sailing and sport. Amy's hand shook badly with a tremor, far worse than when he'd seen it over recent days, and he suspected she was suffering from Parkinson's disease. A colleague had been diagnosed with the disease, forcing him to leave the police and take early retirement. Amy had the same telltale walk with one arm not swinging like the other and that wide-eyed look as if permanently stunned.

Sara shared a poem she'd written about growing up with her dad. Part way through she broke down and Amy went up to the lectern and put her arm around her, staying there until Sara had finished.

Ella, with her loss so recent and grievous, surprised him by taking part in the eulogy. She did it with poise and elegance, relating some of Dean's recent anecdotes. She said they'd shared a love of sport and she'd been attracted to his athletic ability and his intellect, to his fun-loving nature and his high personal standards. They'd enjoyed a closeness that few couples had and she'd miss her soulmate. It was a show of inner strength and character from the grieving widow.

The eulogy triggered Frank's own memories. Dean had been a very good sportsman and highly competitive. He had played a number of sports and one year he'd talked Frank into joining his twilight touch footy team. Although a social team, Dean always wanted to win and that year they'd celebrated first place honours in their grade. He was much the same when sailing the classics and was never afraid to push the laws of physics. But once the business was done, he loved to party with the older sailors and hear their stories over a rum or three, singing the best sea shanties. He was the life of any party. They were fun times and now memories were all that was left.

A dentist colleague praised Dean's professional career and the celebrant touched on the accident without labouring it before bringing the eulogies to an end. They were a great testimony to a life well lived only to be cut way too short.

After the service, people gathered in small groups sharing memories of Dean. Frank moved about the room and listened with interest. The fact that Dean was an all-round good bloke was reiterated repeatedly. He was well respected through his dentistry. A number of those he spoke with had shared regrets that they hadn't seen more of him in recent years. Seemingly Dean had lost touch with many friends after he'd married Ella.

The family were continually surrounded with people, even some queuing to speak with them and he didn't want to intrude anymore on their grief. He left with a heavy heart, satisfied the service had been a great send off for his old friend.

*

Amy stood in Ella's kitchen waiting for the jug to boil so she could make a pot of tea for the umpteenth time that afternoon. She was exhausted both physically and emotionally. The service had been a wonderful tribute to her brother and the well-wishers who crowded her afterwards spoke highly of Dean and shared lots of funny stories. Their words were a great testimony to her brother's life. Dean's life. Period. It sounded so finite when you thought about it like that. It had a start and an endpoint. As if today they'd stood off to the side, in the wings, watching it unfold one chapter at a time. As if you could stand outside time and see it all at once, see the timeline of a life. Is that how God views us? A eulogy summarises an entire life into a few key themes and significant moments, but it misses out so much of its richness. It doesn't convey the love, the laughter, the intimacy, the emotional highs and lows, decisions made, or the time spent just being alive. What is the meaning of our lives? Are we simply random matter that happens to exist for no purpose, or is there a greater meaning? She'd like to think Dean's hadn't been a random event, a life spent in vain. Death is way too final and for Dean it had come too soon and too abruptly. There was so much she'd like to have shared with Dean and now she couldn't. They could all have done with some warning, so they could've talked. But even if she'd known, what could she have said that would've been meaningful in the light of his impending death? There were no appropriate words. She loved her brother, although he'd always known that. It all seemed so meaningless, so pointless.

The kettle boiled and she emerged from her reverie. She brewed the tea and put yet more of the left-over food from the funeral on plates to hand around. Her shaking had flared up so much that she had to carry the mugs out one by one, reminding her that she couldn't put off sharing her news with the girls for much longer.

Sara was in deep conversation with Ella when she offered them some food.

"When did Dad grow the beard?" Sara took a piece of the chocolate brownie offered.

"He's been growing it for a little while now. He started it after you left for Dunedin," Ella replied.

"Any food for you?" Amy chipped in, offering Ella the plate.

"No thanks Amy. You're doing a great job. What's with the tremor?"

"Oh, it's nothing." Amy wasn't going to share it with Ella before the girls. "I remember Dean grew one years ago. He kept it closely cropped and it suited him."

"I'd forgotten that." Sara looked sad. "It was before Mum left. I thought it was smart. It didn't last long as I remember—I think he thought it unhygienic as a dentist."

"It's not so bad for the patients because he kept it under a mask in the surgery." Ella's eyes glazed over as she downed the remains of the gin she'd been drinking. "I've always liked the rugged look."

"Can I get you anything else?" Amy asked.

"A top up would be wonderful, thanks." Ella held her glass out.

Tracy came over and relieved her of the plate and Amy went to locate the gin and tonic. Terry intercepted her and took the glass from her. "Are you okay?" His concern was reflected in his eyes.

She looked at him gratefully. "I'm running on empty—it's been a huge day. Ella wants another gin; would you mind getting it for me?"

"Of course I can. How about I get you a drink too and you sit down for a bit? The girls can look after the food and drinks. Most of the visitors have left now anyway and there's not a lot more to do. I doubt anyone will want dinner as we've been snacking all day."

"I'll sit for a bit, and yes, maybe a glass of red?"

"As good as done."

Amy sank into the seat next to her mum. She looked forward to getting home and putting this day behind her. Terry returned with her drink which she sipped thankfully.

"It was a lovely service don't you think?" her mum asked.

She met her mum's eyes. "Yes, it was. Dean would be proud."

"Dean?" Diane suddenly looked confused.

Amy gazed at the face that searched hers with that faraway look. The brown eyes were cloudy with cataracts, the wrinkled skin marred with age spots. Her greyed hair was a mass of curls— the source of Amy's own unruly hair. For the first time she was thankful for the dementia that spared her mum from the full impact of the grief that came with losing a son. But watching her mum have her memories stolen and watching her slip further into confusion was heartbreaking.

In a quiet voice she answered, "Yes, Dean's gone Mum. It was a boating accident." She took her mum's hand in her own.

"Oh." Her mum breathed the word out and her shoulders sagged. Tears welled up in her eyes and ran down her cheeks. "I had forgotten."

There was nothing to say. Amy put her arm around her mum's shoulders and tried to suppress her own anguish that cut so deeply. She was learning that losing a brother was like cutting out a piece of you. But to lose a child would be unbearable. If she were to lose Maddie or Tracy it would be unimaginably painful, they were so much a part of her and had been ever since she first felt that flutter of a kick in her womb. Nobody expects to outlive their children. Her mum had already lived through as much grief as a person should have to deal with. First losing her parents and then her husband to cancer. She hugged her mum to her.

Maddie came across and joined them, a welcome distraction. "Nana, can I get you something?"

Diane sat up and, her loss seemingly forgotten, beamed a beautiful smile that enhanced the creases in her cheeks. "Thank you dear, a cup of tea would be lovely."

The numbers of those who had come to pay their respects dwindled as the evening neared. Maddie and Tracy were doing dishes and Amy was tidying the kitchen, putting left-overs into containers to help Ella deal with the on-going stream of visitors that were likely to come by over the following days. The kitchen rubbish was full, so she took it outside to the wheelie bin. As she was tipping it in, she recognised the business card that Frank had given Ella. She pulled it out of the bin and, unsure why, put it in her pocket.

Sara, Terry and the girls helped Amy finish clearing up while Ella polished off yet another gin. Everyone was exhausted and it wasn't long before they were able to bundle Diane into the car and head for home.

6

Frank was looking forward to seeing his old colleague, Anahera. Dean's unfortunate accident had shaken him and although the case was closed, he couldn't get it out of his head. Such an unnecessary tragedy. It had reminded him that life was way too short, that he needed to live more in each moment and enjoy the days he had.

This day had been a good one. With the balmy weather continuing, he couldn't think of a better place to work than out on *Deodar III* with his crew member Stephen Blackett. They had dealt with illegal trawling in a fishing reserve, a domestic that occurred on a launch anchored in Islington Bay, and they were called to ferry a prisoner from Waiheke Island into Auckland to be processed by Central. All in all it had been a normal day in the Maritime Unit.

He changed out of his police overalls into his civvies before walking over to Smugglers' Bar, getting in some much-needed exercise in the sunshine. By the time he arrived he was feeling upbeat and ready to enjoy some good company. He had to walk past the smokers and vapers to get to the door and was assaulted by the foul smell that filled his nostrils and lungs. It's hard to believe it wasn't that long ago that people were lighting up inside the bars.

Smugglers' Bar was a popular spot for folks working around the downtown area. It was packed with punters already enjoying their after-work drinks, their cheerful noise reverberating off the concrete walls and polished concrete floor. The bar, stretched along one wall of the building, boasted a wide range of craft beers as well as the usual big brands. A large pirate's chest sat at one end of the bar and various pirate regalia adorned the walls.

Anahera waved to him from a high table by the window and he weaved his way over to her through the crowded tables.

She got up and kissed him on the cheek. "So good to have that drink at last."

"It's been too long. Speights?"

"You remember, thanks."

He ordered the drinks from the bar, a Speights for her and a Corona for himself, before taking them over to their table where he climbed onto a bar stool opposite her. She was looking relaxed in a wine-coloured scoop-necked top over tight jeans.

"Cheers!" she said, holding out her bottle.

"Here's to the old unit." He tapped his bottle against hers before taking a sip. "Mmmm, that's good."

"Tell me about your man-overboard case—how did it work out?" She had to speak up to be heard over the din of the other drinkers.

"The body was positively identified using dental records as my man-overboard. The coroner ruled it as an accidental death by drowning, so the case is closed. It was a tragedy for all concerned."

"What did the coroner put the injuries down to?"

"They decided the body must have come into contact with a propeller when in the water—post-drowning." He dropped his voice. "I went to his funeral. Did I tell you I knew him?"

"No, really? That's tough." Her face showed genuine concern. "Where did you know him from?"

"We met crewing on classic yachts in the regattas. He was a top guy. He had my measure as a sailor—seemed to have an instinct about getting the perfect sail trim. I guess if he had to go then he probably would've chosen being out on the water—he loved sailing. Those regattas were fun. They were as much about the parties after the races as the races themselves—although some of the guys were pretty serious about the results. Dean could drink a rum with the best of them. And he could sing all the sea shanties." He sighed. "They were good times."

"Why did you stop?"

"I don't really know. I guess I had other responsibilities trying to fit a family life in around the shift work. You know how it is." He toyed with his bottle.

"That's tough when it's personal. I don't think I've had that situation yet—and I hope I never do." She paused and looked thoughtful. "Did he leave family behind?"

"Yeah, a second wife and a daughter, plus a sister and mother."

"How're they coping?"

"The wife is showing real strength of character and seems to be coping well—better than the sister. The daughter came up from Dunedin where she's at university and she's devastated as you'd expect."

He stared out the window thinking of the grief the family were now dealing with.

"How are you finding it in the Maritime Division?" she asked.

He returned her gaze and smiled. "Good. It's nice to have most of my shifts out on the water and I like the autonomy. I don't take my work home like I used to and I don't suffer the anxiety I had when I was at Central."

"I wasn't aware you were having issues—you kept that quiet."

"Yeah well, it's not something you want to share with your colleagues. It's not really something us kiwi blokes tend to do."

"I had wondered why you went across to the Maritime Unit. Seemed a strange move at the time, but that makes more sense." She searched his face. "How are you now, really?"

"Pretty good." He took a deep draught and savoured the taste as the cold liquid went over his tastebuds and travelled down his throat. "Now enough of me, what about you?"

"I'm doing okay, thanks. You know me, once I get my teeth into something I tend to thrive. Land Search and Rescue has plenty of challenge and the team are great."

"Getting enough life balance?" He knew this had been her weakness in the past.

"I'm working on it. Jim pulls me in line when he thinks I'm not seeing enough of our boys. And I'm regularly getting to the gym."

"What's the caseload like?"

"Enough to keep us all employed and then some." She looked around the bar before turning her attention back to Frank.

"What are you working on?"

"I've got a case where the guy's a bit of a loner. He's a self-employed computer programmer who doesn't seem to keep in touch with family and friends. A client contacted us concerned that he was overdue with some work for her and normally he always hits his deadlines." She ran her hand over her straight hair and tucked it back behind her ears.

"Sounds typical for computing—don't they always overrun?"

"Apparently not this one. It's a strange one and I'm not even sure he's missing. There's no evidence of foul play. I half expect him to turn up one day and say he's been away tramping in the bush or something. He's not using his bank cards and he hasn't withdrawn any money. And his phone hasn't been used and seems to be turned off. It appears he was a real conspiracy theorist and was prolific on Twitter, but he hasn't posted for over a week." She sat up a little straighter. "There are more than 11,000 people reported missing each year in Aotearoa and while most are found within the first 72 hours, others simply vanish."

"11,000, that's a lot in a population of five million." Frank considered this for a moment. "What about neighbours? There must be someone who knows something."

"The neighbours say they never see him. There's a property maintenance contractor who keeps the lawns mowed who says he hasn't seen him for months. The money is a direct debit, and he hasn't missed a payment." She looked pensive.

"And family?"

"They seem to be estranged. I tracked down his mother who said he's an only son and they haven't been in contact for over a year. She said it's not unusual for him to go off on his own for a time. When I asked if he had a partner or a meaningful other in his life, she thought that maybe he was seeing someone. The last time they'd spoken he was fairly coy about it. Previously he'd never shown interest in a serious relationship, preferring his own company."

"And she has no idea who this person was?"

Anahera shook her head.

"Friends, work acquaintances?"

"Nope, I've been down that route and as yet no one that's in regular contact." She paused to take a drink. "This is good."

"Well perhaps he's simply decided to take a break." He shrugged.

"The strange thing is that a month ago he reported a burglary. You could say it's a coincidence, but you were the one who taught me there's rarely a true coincidence." She smiled at him, the dimple appearing on her left cheek.

"What was stolen?"

"Well, that's the thing. Nothing that he was aware of. The flat had definitely been broken into. It's a single-story home in Parnell and the window had been prised open. There were footprints in the soil underneath—enough to show someone had been there, but not enough to get a full print. He had lots of computing gear and he thought they might have been after something there. No hardware was taken, but he was paranoid about someone stealing his client information."

"Any eyewitnesses?"

"No. The neighbours didn't see a thing—most were at work as it was during work hours."

"You said he was a loner and kept to himself. If he worked from home, how did the intruders know the place would be empty?" He finished his drink.

"Good question." She downed the rest of her beer. "The next round is on me. Corona?"

"Great, thanks."

She picked up the bottles and sauntered over to the bar, returning with the next round.

"Now where were we?" she asked, after raising her bottle to his.

"You were telling me about the burglary—how they knew the guy would be out."

"Call it luck, or perhaps they'd been watching him, or call it coincidence." Her face twisted into a wry smile. "I'm making the assumption that someone must have known what they were after and knew enough about his activities to pick the right time to go in. Or perhaps they were interrupted and fled the scene before getting anything."

"And how do you think this is linked to him going missing?"

"Well, I don't know. I'm not sure it is linked."

"Back to coincidence?" he asked.

Her big brown eyes widened as her face lit up in a broad grin.

Talking cases again with Anahera brought back the good times. She was smart and tough, a no-nonsense type. He asked, "Have you considered he may have committed suicide?"

"Yes, it's a possibility. But why would he go somewhere to do it? He had the opportunity in his own home, especially living on his own. And that would assume the burglary isn't linked." She paused to take a drink. "And that brings us back to coincidence."

"You're busting my theory on coincidence!"

They both laughed.

"Enough of work. Tell me about the family. How are they doing?" she asked.

"Margie is as long suffering as ever. Now that Brian and Jenny have left home she's gone back teaching part-time and is loving it. The hours work well for us, we seem to have a lot more time together these days. Brian is back-packing around Europe at present. He left as soon as his last exam finished. He got his results—straight A's, so he's a qualified geologist. He got his brains from his mother, that's for sure." He beamed, unable to hide his pride.

"And what's Jenny up to?"

"She's now in her third year at university and passing everything. She found a flat near campus and that seems to be working okay. In just a couple of years she'll be a qualified civil engineer. Seems like only yesterday that we were nagging her to get to school on time. Be sure to make the most of your kids now because they don't stay around for long." He paused to take a sip. "How're your family doing?"

"Rangi is at college and doing well. He loves it and all his reports are good. He's heavily into volleyball—made the rep team this year. Piri is in middle school and is also doing well. He lives for his music and seems to have some talent. I'm really proud of them both. It's hard juggling being a wife and mum with my policing, however we're making it work. Jim is fantastic—he makes up for my shortfalls as a parent."

"I can't believe you have any shortfalls. You're one of the most capable and competent people I know."

"Yeah, well you always were an ignorant bugger!" She laughed.

"No, I'm serious." He raised his bottle. "Here's to you; a great cop, a great mum and an all-round great human." He drank the toast.

"And to you." She lifted her beer to salute him.

They went on to chat about the office politics. Frank hadn't realised how much he was missing the banter with his teammates from Central and was happy to settle in for a long session.

"Another round?" He asked and emptied his drink.

She followed suit and drained hers. "No, I'd better not. I promised Jim I'd be home in time for dinner."

"I miss working with you and the others. We should make a point of catching up like this more often."

"For sure. Why don't we make it a regular Thursday evening?"

"Let's aim for that, but no pressure. Cancel anytime you need to—I understand what it's like to be pulled in too many directions at once."

They said their goodbyes and he followed her around the tables to the door, where they had a second round of farewells before splitting up. His footsteps were light and his mood buoyant as he walked to his car. After the events of the last week it had been a much-needed diversion and she'd been a tonic. He vowed not to leave it so long next time. With rush hour traffic gone, the drive home was short. The fresh air blew on his face through the open window and the stereo thumped out eighties tunes. He was more relaxed than he'd been for quite some time.

*

The day after the funeral, following some gentle goading from Terry, Amy finally agreed to tell the girls about her diagnosis. As was their habit when they had news to share, they told the girls they wanted to have a family conference after dinner. While they did the dinner dishes, she could sense their heightened anticipation of what was to come and after the events of the last week it seemed to hang in the air like a dark cloud.

They retired to the lounge where Amy took a seat next to Tracy on the couch, Terry sat in his usual recliner chair and Maddie got comfy on the bean bag. The girls looked expectantly at Amy; she was generally the one to deliver any significant news.

"Your Dad and I have some news to share."

"Are we going on a holiday somewhere?" Tracy asked.

"No, that's not it." Amy took in a deep breath. This wasn't going to be easy.

Maddie chipped in, "I hope it isn't more bad news."

"I'm afraid it is." Amy looked from one daughter to the other. "You've both noticed the tremor I have—it's been getting worse. I've been to the doctor who referred me to a neurologist."

Maddie looked at her with wide eyes. "What's wrong Mum?"

There was no other way to say it. "I have something called young-onset Parkinson's disease." To say it out loud removed any pretence or denial. She wanted to reject it with every fibre she had, but it was out now with no way of taking it back. How much more could she handle after losing Dean?

"Is that bad?" Tracy asked.

Amy dug deep and smiled at her younger daughter whose face was turned into a frown. "Yes, it's serious. It's a neurological condition that is degenerative and as yet has no cure. However, there are drugs that can help with the symptoms." She turned to look at Terry for support.

Terry added, "What that means is that it will continue to progress slowly. We may need to change our diet and Mum needs to exercise daily and minimise her stress. You girls need to help her with that—it can be a family effort."

Tracy moved across and snuggled into Amy. "Mum, what does it *do* to you? How will you be sick?"

Tears sprang into Amy's eyes, not for the first time that week. They never seemed to be far below the surface since first the news of the diagnosis and then Dean's loss. She wanted to be strong for her daughters, but right now her emotional capacity was depleted. Instinctively she knew now wasn't a great time to discuss it with them, but there would never be a good time. And there was no playbook instructing how to share this news with young teens nor how much information would be too much.

In a quiet voice she answered, "Well, it affects firstly my movements, making me shake, and then they will likely become slower and more difficult. Other parts of the body can be affected, like sleep, mood and anxiety, heart, bladder and a whole lot more. I think the trick is to manage each symptom as it comes up." She didn't tell them that the doctor had said she should be able to count on ten good years, but after that there's no guarantee.

"Will you die from it?" Tracy asked softly between sobs.

The image of Dean's coffin in the front of the church came to mind, preventing Amy from finding the words to answer.

Terry cut in, "Apparently people die with Parkinson's rather than from it. Mum can still have a good life and we can all help by focusing on one day at a time and making the most of each day."

Terry passed a look at Amy that indicated there was nothing more that needed to be said. Silence filled the space. Maddie lay on the bean bag crying quietly and Tracy sobbed in Amy's arms.

Eventually the girls would get used to the idea and it would become a family norm. On top of all the grief, this was the last straw and she resented Parkinson's for the health it was stealing from her. She would have to fight it.

Maddie broke the silence. "We can help you more with the chores."

"We can all do more around the house and share the load. I think that's a great idea," Terry said, smiling at Maddie.

"I promise to get out of bed on time and help with the chores too," Tracy added.

An overwhelming sense of warmth stirred in Amy, momentarily shaking off the deep sadness that had been hanging over her. "And I'm going to do a lot more research and will do everything I can to be as good as I can be—for all of our sakes."

"The other bit of news is that we've all been asked to join Ella and Sara aboard *Aurora* on Saturday to spread Dean's ashes over the Gulf before Sara goes back to Otago. It'll be an all-day excursion, so make sure you keep it free," Terry said.

Amy was exhausted from all the emotion of the week and the insomnia that had become her new normal. In desperate need of some pampering and me-time, she excused herself and went for a soak in the bath before bed.

7

Ella woke up to the sun shining through her curtains. It was Saturday morning, the day she was taking *Aurora* out with Dean's family. Although necessary, today would be hard—even so she was determined it would be a memorable occasion for everyone. *Aurora* hadn't left the marina since the day she reported Dean missing.

To clear her head and prepare for what was in store, she dressed in her running gear and ran five fast kilometres in the early morning sunshine. Running was her therapy and it helped build her resilience to stress.

Back home, she showered and selected a sheer black blouse over a smart pair of white shorts and took pains to get her make-up just right. She tied her hair in a simple ponytail and put it through her favourite black cap.

The arrangement was that they'd all meet at the marina after breakfast and Ella wanted to be early so that she had everything ready by the time they arrived. After wolfing down a croissant and coffee, she packed a hamper with picnic food and drinks from the fridge and retrieved a bunch of red roses from a vase, before loading it all into the car.

Lastly, she went back inside to get the one item that was the most important of all. On the sideboard sat a small urn that held the ashes, invoking a kaleidoscope of emotions that threatened to overwhelm her. She stared, mesmerised. The beautifully carved round wooden vessel was made from kauri with inlaid paua, its wooden cap enclosing its precious contents. A wave of sadness washed over her. Her life was never going to be the same again. She and Dean would never live in this house again. They could never again enjoy those lazy Saturday mornings in the bedroom they'd shared since they first got together. They could never again entertain friends on the terrace around the barbecue. There would be no more days pottering in the garden together. Or bickering over what colour to paint the house. She stifled the urge to cry and took in a deep breath. She could do this. She reached out with two hands and gently picked up the urn and carried it to the car where it rode on the passenger seat to the marina.

Once aboard *Aurora*, she stowed the food and drink in the fridge and prepared for the sail.

*

Amy instantly leapt out of bed at the first sound of the alarm. Today was going to be one of the hardest in her life as they'd be farewelling Dean from *Aurora* out on the same stretch of water that had so tragically claimed him barely ten days ago. It was way too soon, her grief was far too raw. She understood the timing was around Sara returning to university, but surely this could've waited until the next holidays when they would all feel a little more able to cope with it. Her heart was heavy as she brushed her tangle of curls back into a bob and pulled on a dressing gown.

Terry was already in the kitchen making the coffee.

"Are you okay?" His eyes studied her.

"I will be once we get through this day," she said. "I'm dreading being back on *Aurora* so soon after Dean's accident. Going out on her was always so exciting, but after everything that's happened it's never going to feel the same."

"I'm thinking the same way, but we need to put on a brave face today for the sake of the family." He passed her a mug of steaming hot coffee.

"Thanks." She sighed deeply. "It's going to be tough on us all. Did we do the right thing not including Mum?"

"I think so, it would only upset her and possibly confuse her more."

The girls came into the kitchen with Sara, who'd stayed the night. All were dressed in shorts and tees for sailing, but the normally bubbly threesome was quiet and downcast. Sara's face was drawn and pale, her eyes showing signs of too many tears and not enough sleep.

"Morning girls. Did you sleep okay Sara?" Amy asked.

Sara fidgeted with her hair that was tied back in her signature braid. "I slept okay, thanks. I feel like I've been walking through my worst nightmare."

Amy went over and gave her a hug.

"Cereal anyone?" Terry asked, taking boxes from the pantry to the breakfast bar.

"Yes, please." Maddie, her unruly mass of curls tucked under a cap, opened the cupboard to get some plates.

"I don't think I can eat breakfast—I'm feeling a bit queasy," Amy said quietly, holding her coffee mug in both hands.

"Are you okay Mum?" Tracy's face was full of concern. "Is it the Parkinson's?" She came over to put her arm around her mother and gave her a squeeze.

"No honey, I'm just not up to eating this morning." Amy looked approvingly at her daughter and gently tucked some wayward hairs that'd escaped the ponytail in behind Tracy's ears. "I think I'll take my coffee and finish getting ready." Amy left them to their breakfasts and went off to dress in shorts and top and put her things together for the day's trip.

After breakfast was over, they packed up the quiche and muffins Amy had made for lunch and loaded the car. A cloud hung over them on the drive to the marina and instead of the normally excited chatter at the prospect of sailing, there was silence.

Ella, looking stunning as always, greeted them as they climbed aboard *Aurora*. Dawn was already on board and looking smart in a sleeveless cream and navy linen dress with a navy sunhat. They stowed their gear in one of the guest cabins then checked for sun block, caps and sunnies before joining the others in the cockpit.

Ella started the motor and gave everyone instructions on casting off and exiting the berth.

"How about we all wear life jackets?" Amy asked. The dire consequences of not doing so were all too real.

"It shouldn't be necessary; it's a beautiful day." Ella's voice was unnecessarily sharp.

Terry looked from Amy to Ella. "Maybe it is best if we do, especially today of all days."

"I'll get them." Amy went below and came back up with an arm full of jackets.

The mood was sombre as they motored quietly out of the marina.

Ella looked comfortable at the wheel, her face partially hidden under her cap and dark glasses. "Amy, can you please take in the fenders?"

Amy walked along the port side and untied the three fenders that prevented *Aurora* from being damaged while berthed. She opened the port locker to stow them in their usual place. The dinghy oars were inside and one had a price sticker on it.

"Did you lose an oar?" she asked Ella.

"No." Her face was unreadable behind her glasses, but her voice had a sharp edge to it. "Why do you ask?"

"I noticed the price tag on one."

"Oh that's right, I'd forgotten. We had to replace one before our holiday."

The sticker was clean and bright white, looking brand new. Strange, but then maybe it hadn't been used much on Dean and Ella's holiday. Even so, something didn't sit quite right with Amy.

A gentle ten knot southerly breeze was blowing as they hoisted the sails and set course for North Head before turning left along the shipping lane to the northern side of Rangitoto Island. Ella had decided that it would be a good area to spread Dean's ashes. As *Aurora* cut through the slight chop, the sparkle on the aqua water and the sun's rays on their skin helped lift their spirits ever so slightly. With the motor off, you could hear the gentle sound of water lapping against the hull, only interrupted by the occasional high revving buzz of a passing motorboat. Dean loved to sail in these conditions. Amy blinked hard to avoid tears and maintain her calm.

The three girls were sunning themselves on the foredeck. Sara sat hugging her knees to her chest with Maddie next to her. Tracy lay sprawled out on her tummy beside them, safe inside the lifeline netting. Ella remained on the wheel while Dawn, Terry and Amy sat in the cockpit.

Amy stared at the sea. Her thoughts, a collage of memories of happier times sailing with Dean, were now shrouded in deep sadness. Her reverie was only broken by the intrusion of an occasional sea bird. She'd never had a fear of the sea; for her it had always been a place of peace and reflection. However today the sea seemed ominous and unforgiving. Everything had changed and nothing would ever be the same again. Somewhere out here Dean had lost his life, the sea had stolen him from her, and he would never come back.

As they crossed the shipping channel west of Rangitoto, Ella asked, "Drinks anyone?"

"I'll make them," Amy said, thinking the distraction would do her good.

"I'll help," Terry offered, immediately taking the orders before joining Amy in the galley where she was putting the kettle on.

"Terry, there's a brand-new oar in the locker that can't have been used as the price sticker is unmarked. Ella denied it at first, as if she could've forgotten buying an oar. Then she said they replaced one before their holiday, but don't you think that's odd?" Amy asked in a low voice so as not to be overheard.

"Why would that be odd?"

"Well, surely the oar would've been used if you're out for a few days and if so the sticker wouldn't stay pristine."

"Not necessarily, they could've used the outboard."

"Really? Dean always liked to row ashore. I just feel something's not right."

"I think you're reading too much into it. You're in mourning and probably seeing things where there aren't any. It will look differently in a week or so, you'll see." He looked at her gently and said, "You've never really liked Ella and you need to be careful you don't allow that to colour your thoughts."

Amy had to admit he had a point. Feelings of anger over losing Dean were only just below the surface and she wanted someone or something to blame. She made herself a promise to be nicer to Ella. After all, she had lost her soulmate and was now having to face life alone. How would she cope if she was in Ella's shoes and had lost Terry? And poor Ella, being there when Dean fell overboard and not being able to save him must be a terrible burden to live with.

"Are you going to tell Ella the news about your Parkinson's?" Terry asked.

"No, I can't face that today. And I don't really want Ella to know... not yet anyway." She looked up at him and softened under his warm gaze. "Soon, I promise."

Terry took the coffees out to save her any embarrassment over her tremor and she climbed back up with some sweet treats.

Offering the food to Ella, she asked, "How have you been since the accident?"

Ella smiled. "I'm doing okay, thanks for asking. How about you?"

"Still shocked but okay. I admire you for being so strong."

Ella looked surprised. "Thank you Amy."

"Would you like me to take the wheel for a bit while you have your coffee?" Terry asked.

"That'd be great, thanks Terry."

"What's your plan for today? How do you want to go about things—are you planning a kind of ceremony?" Amy asked.

"I haven't really given it too much thought. Perhaps we could sit on the transom to empty the ashes into the water. I brought some flowers to spread with them—maybe the girls would like to do that? And I thought we could all share some happy memories of Dean. What do you think?"

"I think that would be just lovely," Dawn spoke up.

"I do too," Amy agreed. Not feeling sociable, she turned away to watch the patterns made by the breeze on the water. A flock of fluttering shearwaters were disturbed by *Aurora,* taking to their wings and reconvening on the surface a few hundred metres away.

"Look!" Tracy yelled from the forward deck. "Dolphins!"

The splashes visible in the distance were getting closer. Ella climbed up onto the deck and gracefully moved to join the girls.

Dawn and Amy followed, leaving Terry on the helm. A large pod of common dolphins with white splashes along their sides swam around and under them. The girls were delighted and chattered excitedly as the dolphins frolicked alongside. They didn't seem to be in a rush to go anywhere and for a while they provided an escort. As one came alongside Amy, it eyeballed her as if conveying a message that it understood her pain. These beautiful creatures were guardians of the oceans, keepers of the secrets of the depths. Their special bond with humans left her wondering if perhaps Dean hadn't died alone after all.

The dolphins had better things to do than spend all day with them and they left as quickly as they'd arrived. In their wake, the gloomy spell that had been over *Aurora* was broken and the sound of chatter once more filled the quiet.

They anchored at their destination north of the island and everyone gathered in the cockpit for the picnic lunch. Amy wasn't hungry and put only a small amount on her plate, but it tasted so good that she found her appetite and helped herself to a second plateful. The dread she felt about the ceremony to come couldn't be shaken and she just wanted it to be over.

After the lunch was cleared away, Ella invited everybody to join her on the stern. She brought up a beautifully made wooden urn with inlaid paua, its colour intensified in the sunshine, as well as a couple of bunches of red roses. Amy couldn't take her eyes off the container of ashes, Dean's ashes. Despite the day's warmth, a chill filled her, sending a shiver up her spine. She forced herself to look away. The small group of mourners stood expectantly on the stern as Ella unwrapped the flowers, laying them loosely on the transom.

Ella held the urn and cleared her throat. A single tear found its way down her cheek. "As you know, Dean loved *Aurora* and he loved the sea. I think he would be happy to know that we were out here today to celebrate him and to scatter his ashes over the Gulf. In fact, I know that's what he wanted. He was a wonderful husband and my soul mate, and I never doubted his love for me. I think we had something truly special that few couples experience. I will miss him." She looked at Sara. "And he was a wonderful father and really cherished you."

Sara cried and Amy, trying to hold back her own tears, put her arm around her. On her other side, Tracy was crying so Terry moved closer to comfort her. Maddie also placed an arm around her sister.

Ella dabbed her eyes under her glasses with a tissue and continued. "I don't want to have a big ceremony today. I just thought it would be nice if we scattered the ashes and each of you could take some roses and cast them in as well."

Ella lifted the urn and paused, staring at it, before kissing it lightly and opening its top. This was too much, reducing Amy to tears. Through them, she saw Ella hold the container out over the water and tip it upside down. Grey ash fell out over the surface of the water before slowly sinking out of sight. She then picked up three of the roses and scattered them after the ashes, watching as they floated away from the boat. Amy led Sara onto the transom and they each picked up some roses and gently dropped them in the water. Dawn followed next and then Terry with Tracy and Maddie. The random array of roses slowly floated away.

"Terry, would you mind going down and getting the bottle of rum from the saloon and some glasses. It's Captain Morgan, Dean's favourite. I thought it would be appropriate to toast him with it—I know he'd approve of that." Ella looked from one to another. "And it would be nice if we all share some stories of the good times with him on *Aurora*, because she really was his special place."

They sat in silence while Terry and Maddie retrieved the bottle of rum and glasses. Ella was looking almost relieved, possibly because the hardest part was now over. Terry handed out the token glasses of rum and Amy swirled hers around the glass, watching the dark liquid wash up the sides. Memories emerged of lazy evenings spent in the cockpit with Dean, a rum in his hand and a care-free grin on his handsome face, telling yarns or putting the wrongs of this world to right. The tears welled up again and she hastily dabbed her eyes, not wanting to set the others off. But looking at her family she could see they were already upset.

"I learned to sail with Dean—it was a big part of our relationship," Ella began. "We spent so many happy times aboard *Aurora*. We've sailed up to the Bay of Islands and down to Tauranga and everywhere in between. I caught my first fish on board *Aurora*." She smiled at the memory. "You know how competitive he was, well my first fish was larger than anything he'd caught up until that point and I could see he was a little jealous so I couldn't resist rubbing it in. And I've reminded him of it many times when he was crowing about out-fishing me. Our dream is to... was to sell up and sail around the Pacific islands, perhaps even circumnavigating the globe. It was something Dean always wanted to do." Her voice trailed off and she took another sip of her rum. "He would make me laugh by putting on a pirate voice and telling me pirate stories or singing sea shanties at the top of his lungs as we were sailing along."

"What about you Sara? What's your favourite memory?" Dawn asked, her voice somewhat detached.

Sara looked up and took off her glasses to chew the arm. Tears glistened in her eyes. "Gee, I don't know. I have so many good memories of Dad. Growing up was kind of special with most of our spare time spent aboard *Aurora*. Dad was always so patient teaching me how to sail, how to use the dinghy, daring me to swim further or climb the mast or generally to go a little bit more out of my comfort zone. A lot of my confidence comes from those times." She looked apologetically at Ella before continuing. "*Aurora* always reminds me of the happy family holidays with Mum and Dad before things turned sour."

"Do you remember the time I flipped the dinghy and Uncle Dean had to clean the salt out of the motor to get it going again? He was so cool about it." Maddie, her wild hair framing her face under her cap, smiled at Sara.

"That was the first time you used the outboard and I don't think we let you use it again for quite some time." Terry reached over to gently tap her on the head before taking a sip of rum.

Dawn held up her glass. "I think it's time we toasted Dean. To his memory... he was a good son-in-law and a good man."

They all partook in the toast. Maddie and Tracy screwed up their noses and gasped as the liquid burned its way down their throats.

"How can anyone like this? It's disgusting!" Tracy said, breaking the tension. They all laughed.

Amy savoured the strong slightly seasoned liquid in her mouth before swallowing. It wasn't that she was a rum lover, rather it was because it held a memory of Dean.

Tracy, smiling at a memory, said, "Do you remember the time Uncle Dean took us out to Great Barrier? We sat on the beach watching the sun go down while eating fish and chips. By the time we rowed back to *Aurora* it was so dark we struggled to find her amongst the other boats anchored in the bay and we nearly boarded the wrong one."

Maddie, also getting into the spirit of it, said, "I remember when we were little, we would be allowed to row ashore on our own with Sara and we'd collect lots of coloured pebbles and shells. But when we got back to *Aurora* Uncle Dean would always say we were only allowed to keep two each and we'd have to try and choose our favourites and throw the rest away."

"It took you hours to choose." Sara, her eyes now hidden behind her sunnies, spoke softly with affection.

Amy added, "My special memory would have to be visiting Tiritiri Matangi and spotting the native birds. Dean knew the names of all of them and could recognise their songs. We'd sit and listen for ages—it was like going to a special orchestra. One night Dean took us ashore for a bushwalk in the dark and we had red cellophane over our torches. Do you remember, girls? It was really very special because we saw kiwi and tuatara and ruru and even a little blue penguin walking up through the bush. Dean was always so passionate about the endangered species and conservation." She took another sip to force down her rising emotions. "I just wish he were here now to share these memories."

They continued to relate precious stories about Dean. Despite her doubts, Amy had to admit Ella had been right to do this now as it was a special time and provided the tonic they needed. The girls even tried to imitate Dean singing a sea shanty which made them all laugh and helped ease their pain. Dean would've loved to see them all out here remembering him with so much love.

8

Amy tossed and turned, her body moving stiffly between the sheets. Outside it was dark and quiet; the early morning traffic hadn't yet started. It wasn't unusual to be awake at this hour and she knew that insomnia was yet another symptom of Parkinson's. But something was eating her; she'd harboured an uneasiness in her spirit ever since the day she'd learnt that Dean had drowned.

The business of the new oar bothered her. Ella had almost certainly lied to her. Having spent enough time sailing with Dean she knew it would be unusual not to use the oars when out on *Aurora* for more than a few days. And even if they had used the outboard as Terry suggested, the oars would have been in the dinghy and surely a little white sticker would have shown some wear and tear. Instead, the sticker looked like it had only just come out of a shop.

She had felt troubled about the whole accident even before seeing the sticker yesterday. It started that first evening with Ella when she'd felt she wasn't hearing the whole truth. It had been odd that Ella had omitted to tell her about the change of plans, which came up later when questioned by the police. She conceded it was a minor point, yet it was strange.

Part of her uneasiness came from the fact that she couldn't believe that Dean of all people would make the mistake of getting in the way of the boom during a jibe. Sure, it can happen so fast that it takes you off guard, but Dean was experienced enough to not stand in the way of the boom. He was always watching the wind in the sails and tweaking the way they were set to maximise *Aurora's* sailing speed. And she'd seen how he would take extra care when sailing on the point of jibe to prevent it happening and always preferred to manage it in a controlled way to minimise the wear and tear on the gear.

She wondered if Dean and Ella were having problems. Although Ella claimed they were soulmates, it was just her perspective and not necessarily true. They had seen so little of them in recent times that she didn't know how solid their relationship was. Sara had made the comment that they argued but then perhaps that was down to their personality types; after all they were both strong-willed. Two cabins on *Aurora* had been used with two beds made up, but there could be a host of reasons why that might be the case. It didn't mean there were problems.

Another memory surfaced and she visualised Ella's guilty look when Amy had asked her about the phone call when she was helping to get her dinner. Was it possible she was having an affair? That might not be surprising given Amy suspected her relationship with Dean had begun as an affair.

Her imagination was beginning to get away on her and things always seemed worse in the early hours. Even so she wondered if she should take it up with Frank—she could call him as she'd kept his business card in her wallet. Or was she blowing it up into a big thing when its parts were simply innocent pieces? It would be best to talk it over with Terry in the morning.

She tried in vain to focus on work and determine how she would break her Parkinson's news, but her thoughts kept returning to Dean. Unsettled, she wrestled with these doubts for some time. The first of the early morning cars passed by. The first birds sang their dawn chorus. And finally, she dozed off.

The alarm aroused her from sleep and beside her Terry stirred. He hugged her to him and asked, "Sleep alright?"

"Not really, same old. I spent several hours awake worrying about Dean and Ella. Something doesn't add up."

"If you're thinking about the sticker, I think you're wrong. There's bound to be an innocent explanation for it."

"It's not just that, it's a combination of things. I have this feeling in my gut that something isn't right. What if Ella murdered him?"

"Come on Amy, you are going too far." He removed his arm from her and sat up on the edge of the bed. "This sort of talk isn't doing you or anyone any good. Things always seem worse in the night, but you need to accept that we lost Dean through an accident and nothing more. If there was any doubt the coroner would have said so."

"You may be right, but please hear me out for a minute." Amy sat up and put on her glasses. "Remember I told you how Ella had omitted to tell me about their plans on that first evening and it felt like she was making it up when questioned by the policeman?"

Terry shook his head. "We went over that—it sounded to me like an innocent omission."

"Yes, but they'd apparently used separate cabins."

"Again, there could be many reasons why. You yourself have slept in the guest room when you said my snoring was keeping you awake."

"And I heard Ella on the phone, talking to someone in tones that didn't add up, especially the way she reacted when I asked her about it."

"Again, likely you read her the wrong way." He sighed. "Amy, you are anxious and upset about Dean. I think you need to let it go. All these things likely have innocent explanations. You've enough on your plate just now—we all have."

"I think I should talk to Frank, the policeman, all the same."

"That's your call, although I think you would be wasting his time." His voice became gentler. "Amy honey, there is no case to investigate; Dean had an unfortunate accident and died from drowning. You heard what Frank said."

"But what if they're wrong. I need to pass on my concerns for Dean's sake. Otherwise, I'd be doing him a disservice."

"And do you think Dean would be happy to know you want to point suspicion at his wife, to implicate her as a murderer?" His eyes bored into hers and his voice took on an insistent tone. "Think about it Amy, this is serious."

"All the same, everything just feels off. Frank is a good man and a friend of Dean's. Perhaps I could pass on what I know and let him decide if he wants to investigate it further."

"You know I would never try to stop you doing something you feel strongly about, however I really think you're wrong."

"You may be right, but my gut says otherwise." She went over and kissed him lightly on the lips. "Please trust me on this."

*

Frank's day couldn't have gotten any worse. After a restless night, Margie's car wouldn't start meaning he was up for a new battery. The time it took to charge it enough for her to drive it meant he'd left home when rush hour traffic was peaking. Then there was a road closure along Quay Street making him even later for a meeting with the Area Commander that had been scheduled in for some time. The not-so-unexpected news was cutbacks to the Maritime Unit staff due to Auckland-wide staffing shortages and how this would affect him personally was still unclear. They already ran on a shoestring with minimal staff. Potentially he might have to move back into Central or float between the two. And then to top it off, there had been a further spate of burglaries from moored craft.

Before taking *Deodar III* out he decided to grab a break in the fresh air. The effects of the countless mugs of coffee he'd consumed were starting to take hold and he left the office and strolled along the waterfront towards Okahu Bay. As he walked along looking out at the moored yachts, he thought once more about his old sailing buddy Dean Hampton. What a waste of a life and one that had been lived to the full. How foolish to not be wearing a life jacket, especially on the passage between the southern end of Great Barrier and Auckland where it could cut up rough at times. Not a friendly stretch of water at all and Dean should have known that. He wouldn't have taken him for a fool.

The bearded photo of Dean was a classic and he'd barely recognised him—in fact he could have walked right past him on the street. He grinned, recalling the time he'd tried to grow his own beard and Margie had complained bitterly, threatening to sleep in the spare room until he'd shaved it off. His impression of Ella was a woman who valued appearances and who obviously took pains with her own presentation, so he was surprised she'd tolerated it.

He was still thinking of the Hamptons when his phone rang. "Frank Smythe," he answered the caller.

"Hello, it's Amy Fagin here, Dean Hampton's sister."

"Hello Amy, what can I do for you?" His curiosity was aroused.

"Frank, would it be possible to meet? I would appreciate a chat." Her voice was hesitant.

"Yes, of course Amy. What's on your mind?" he asked, thinking of the pile of papers on his desk.

"Dean's accident." She paused. "It might be nothing, but there're some things I'd like to pass by you... just in case you think they are of interest."

Now she had his full attention. "Would you like to come into my office? When suits you?"

"I'm back at work, so in my lunch hour would be good. And yes, I can come to your office." Her voice had a nervous edge to it.

"What about 12 o'clock tomorrow? Do you know where the Maritime Unit is based?"

"I can google it. Thanks Frank, I'll see you tomorrow." She ended the call.

Having enjoyed the sunshine for long enough he wandered back to face the workload, intrigued by what it could be that Amy wanted to pass on.

*

Amy hung up the phone and was overcome with doubts about whether she was doing the right thing. Terry clearly thought not, and she always trusted his judgement. To go against Terry was unusual for her and rarely did she take a course of action he disagreed with. On the other hand, she had to consider Dean and he no longer had a voice or the means to fight his corner. And if there was a need for justice then justice would be done. The appointment had been made and she'd go through with it. If Frank thought she was being paranoid and wasting his time, then that's where it would end with nothing lost. She sighed and turned back to the set of accounts she'd been analysing.

That night Terry didn't raise the subject and for that she was grateful.

The next morning, she felt apprehensive as she worked though her schedule of meetings and a full inbox while keeping an eye on the clock so she wouldn't be late. She still hadn't told her workmates about her Parkinson's and had promised Terry she'd have that chat, but she was continuing to procrastinate. It was another point of disagreement about which she knew she'd need to do something soon.

The sun was bright and the skies clear, so she decided to take the extra time and walk down to the Maritime Unit. After a poor sleep followed by a hectic morning, she found the fresh air cleared her head and by the time she arrived, her mood had improved.

The Maritime Unit was in a small non-descript office building near the port. Inside, the reception area was small and dingy with the reception desk unmanned. Frank, dressed in the Maritime Police blue overalls she'd come to expect, came out to greet her. They exchanged pleasantries and he led her through to a small office with his name on the door where he gestured for her to take a chair in front of a desk strewn with paper and next to two old metal filing cabinets sitting side by side. He took the recliner office chair behind the desk. She realised she hadn't really seen him at Dean's, she was too wrapped up in her grief. He had a kindly face with a generous nose and short grey hair that was thinning on top.

"So Amy, what is it you want to discuss?" He leaned forward.

Her tremor was increasing with her heartrate, so she tucked the offending hand under her leg to hide it.

"It's about Dean. I have this gut feeling that something isn't right and I can't seem to shake it off. You may think it's nothing, Terry does, but I felt I should talk to you." She paused. "I don't want to waste your time. I know you must be busy, however it would be good to get it off my chest."

"Of course, I'm happy to hear you out." He opened his notebook and picked up a pen. "What exactly is on your mind?"

"Well, each of the things I'm going to tell you could have an innocent explanation, but together they add up to something that seems suspicious. And if I'm right, then I want to make sure justice is served for Dean's sake."

"Go on." His hand was poised over a blank page in his notebook.

"Well firstly there was the jibe. Ella told me they were heading for home after an uncomfortable night in Whangaparapara with westerlies. She said they were under full sail when *Aurora* jibed. When you asked her about that, she said they'd changed their minds about heading for home and were heading towards the western Coromandel when the jibe happened."

"And what makes you think this is odd?" He watched her intently.

"I would have expected her to tell me that, instead of leaving me with the impression they were on their way home." She paused and took a deep breath. "That's not all."

"What else Amy?" His tone was friendly and encouraging.

"Well then there was the oar."

Frank sat up even straighter, leaning forward over his desk. "What about the oar?"

"Ella took us out on *Aurora* on Saturday to spread Dean's ashes on the Gulf. I was putting the fenders away in a locker and noticed a new oar. It still had the price sticker on it. When I asked Ella about it, initially she denied it before saying they'd replaced one before their holiday. The sticker looked brand new and the oar didn't appear to have been used—I thought that was odd, especially as Dean would often row to shore. Terry says maybe they just used the outboard, but it seems strange to me."

"That's interesting. Is there anything else you've found odd?"

"I'm not sure." For the first time she felt uncertain of her suspicions. If she was wrong, and Terry was right, she'd be doing Dean a terrible disservice. But she'd come this far...

"Tell me anyway and let me judge if it's relevant." He regarded her thoughtfully.

"It's probably nothing." She hesitated before continuing. "I accidently overheard Ella talking to someone on the phone. It was late afternoon on the day after Dean's drowning. Please don't think I eavesdrop. It sounded intimate and when I asked her who it was, she said a friend."

"What made you think it was suspicious?"

"I'm not entirely sure now, it was something she said."

"What was that?"

"Something in her voice sounded intimate to me. And it was the way she reacted to me when I asked her who she was talking to. I wondered if maybe she was having an affair. Sara has mentioned Dean and Ella fought a lot. Two beds were made up on *Aurora* and it seemed that Dean and her may have been using separate cabins, but then again it could have been for any one of many reasons."

Frank looked up from his notebook. "How do you think Ella is dealing with losing Dean? Do her actions seem in line with her character?"

"Ella is a difficult person to read. I've never been able to get close to her. She's being incredibly strong and seems to keep her emotions in check."

"Is there anything else on your mind?"

"I don't think so." Her answer was slow and pensive. It all seemed so innocent now and maybe she was being foolish; perhaps this was a mistake after all.

A long pause ensued while she waited for him to finish his notes.

"How long have you had Parkinson's?" he asked.

She was taken aback. "Not long. How do you know?"

"I guessed from your tremor and the way you walk with one arm not swinging, also from your facial expression." He paused, his look kindly. "I've seen similar signs before with a colleague who was diagnosed with young-onset Parkinson's disease."

"Is it that obvious?" she asked, feeling slightly panicked.

He replied in a soft voice, "Probably only to those who know someone with the disease."

His genuine concern encouraged her to talk. "I've only known a few weeks and so far I've just told my immediate family. I don't want to be treated differently just because I have this..." She paused, struggling to find the right word. "This curse. I'm worried it will affect my position at work and my future career. I'm also embarrassed by it and feel too young to have an old people's disease. And I'm scared I will become a burden on Terry and the girls." Out loud it became more real and tears welled in her eyes. She pulled a tissue out of her bag and dabbed up the moisture.

"Amy, you shouldn't be afraid or embarrassed. I think you'll find a lot more acceptance these days towards people who have health challenges like this. I suspect that in general the workplace is far more accommodating. And as for your family, they seem very supportive. Look I'm no doctor, but I would've thought you're a long way off being disabled and losing your independence."

It felt good to be talking openly about it, even with this stranger. Maybe he and Terry were right. Maybe she should confront it head on and tell her work. After all, she wouldn't be able to hide it for much longer—if Frank had recognised it so too could her colleagues.

"I'd better be getting back to work. Thanks for the chat. And I do appreciate the advice. I just hope I haven't wasted your time." Amy stood up and extended her hand.

Frank came around the desk and shook it. "Thanks for coming and sharing your concerns regarding Dean. I promise to investigate it some more."

"Please be discrete—I would prefer Ella doesn't know I've been in."

"Certainly. And thanks Amy."

Amy walked back into the sunshine, feeling lighter in her step like a load had been lifted. She warmed to Frank's easy manner and was confident that he would investigate Dean's drowning further. If there was anything to find, he would find it.

Enough of her feeble excuses for procrastination. From now on, she would work hard at accepting the idea of coexisting with this disease that was invading her brain. She vowed to schedule a meeting with her manager, Fran Byers, to come clean about the Parkinson's. She could do this.

After Amy left, Frank leaned back in his chair, his elbows on the chair-arms and his fingertips touching, tapping, staring at the whiteboard that filled the wall opposite but without focusing. There could well be innocent explanations for the matters Amy raised. However, if her suspicions were justified, then he'd failed Dean and the family. He had always prided himself on his innate ability to see through the lies and determine the truth—so if this was more than an accident, how had he missed it? He berated himself for being careless. His personal involvement with the deceased may have led him to overlook crucial evidence, which would be unforgiveable.

Was Amy reliable? Was her own motive simply to find the truth and see justice done or was there an ulterior motive? Perhaps her grief had given rise to anger and a desire to blame someone for her loss and Ella could be a convenient scapegoat. As an older sister, Amy may be over-protective of her younger brother, leading her to look for problems where there were none. Alternatively, her motives could be less than honourable with her actions driven by jealousy or some other negative emotion. After all, she and Ella hadn't been close. During his time policing he'd seen all these situations play out, and this time his instinct told him that Amy was being sincere about her concerns. And if she was right, then there was something that needed to be investigated.

His impression of Ella was of a good looking, elegant and educated woman, who came across as calm and strong in her grief. One who by all accounts loved her husband. Ella did admit to having had a disagreement with Dean on the day of the accident.

And although Amy thought they were a tight unit, she claimed Sara was worried they were arguing more in recent times—but Sara may be oversensitive being the stepdaughter. After all, the odd spat is commonplace in most marriages.

To believe that under Ella's calm exterior lay a cold and calculating killer, as Amy had insinuated, was hard. As someone who'd witnessed a tragedy that no wife should have to experience, Frank's empathy for her may well have displaced his objectivity. Perhaps he had been too trusting. If so, how could he have made such a mistake? His normal default was a suspicious and inquiring mind. Could his friendship have thrown him that far off his game?

Regardless of his own feelings, Amy had told him enough to warrant delving into the facts behind her claims, starting with the accident itself and the oar. Any inconsistencies in either narrative or behaviour almost always led to a guilty party. His observation and listening skills were key, they had rarely let him down. In this case, he acknowledged he'd readily accepted the facts at face value. Although he had a lot of cases on the go at present, he owed it to Dean to take another look at the circumstances of his drowning. If he could find evidence of any inconsistencies, then he would open a formal investigation into Dean's death—it was never too late.

The Hampton file was buried in the pile of folders on his desk and he shuffled through them until he found it. Inside, the coroner's report sat on top. Skimming through it, the narrative was fairly straight forward. Dean had received a blow to the back of the head consistent with the boom hitting him during a jibe and this was largely based on the assumption that Ella's account was true. His death was through drowning—a fact. He'd been alive when he hit the water. Post death, his body had sustained injuries consistent with those of a propellor—an assumption based solely on the nature of the injuries and the fact the body had been in the water when the injuries were received. Identification had been through dental records—no argument here.

Reading the report reminded him of the grisly sight on the slab in the autopsy room. Poor Dean, such a terrible way to end up. Overcome with sadness, he got up and went to the small kitchenette and made himself a strong coffee.

Back at his desk, he flicked through the pages in his notebook until he found the notes relating to his initial interview with Ella and read through them. Then he reread them. Ella had said they initially started out in Whangaparapara Harbour and headed for Westhaven Marina, that would mean a southwest course. She also said the wind had enough westerly direction in it overnight that small waves were coming up the harbour making it an uncomfortable night.

He turned to his computer and pulled up the MetService weather information. Scanning it, he found what he was after. On the morning in question, the actual wind averaged 22 knots nor'west. A jibe could only have happened if *Aurora* was pointing downwind, that is to the southeast.

He went over to one of the filing cabinets and leafed through a drawer of marine charts and pulled out one of the Hauraki Gulf. He cleared his desk and laid it out. Using a parallel ruler, dividers and a pencil, he marked the potential course on the chart. He then added the leeway and tidal flow vectors to get a rough estimate of the course they would have had to steer. It confirmed that they could not have jibed on this course. Ella said they pulled the sails up once they left the harbour and he would've expected them to reef the mainsail if sailing this course in those conditions. Reefing the mainsail decreases the amount of sail area to avoid being overpowered by the wind, but you wouldn't reef the sails when sailing downwind. It's likely they took the reefs out when they changed direction—that could account for it. He would ask Ella about this.

When he'd initially questioned her on this point, she'd said they had changed their minds and had decided to head for the west coast of Coromandel. An odd decision, based on the wind direction and the fact that there are few bays sheltered from the westerly wind. After one rough night, he was fairly certain they'd want to ensure they had a quiet night at anchor in a bay on the leeward side. However, there were a couple of anchorages that would likely have been okay.

He moved the ruler along the initial heading to establish the point at which they would have changed course if heading to one of those Coromandel anchorages with a downwind heading where the jibe would be possible. While this wasn't conclusive, he pencilled in the line and noted the direction. He checked his notes again for the position of *Aurora* when the mayday was received. The point he'd derived was well south of the mayday coordinates. It could be that Ella, in searching for Dean, had moved significantly further north from their original course and that could explain the position she gave Coastguard. It would be worthwhile getting a techie to take a look at the GPS to see if any tracking data was retrievable.

Something else was bugging him, so he took another look at his account of the discussion with Ella. This time he read his notes slowly out loud and mulled over each sentence. He abruptly stopped mid-sentence and sat upright. Then he read it again. Ella had said Dean was standing on the cockpit seat on the starboard side and she was sitting on the port side when the jibe happened. The wheel was located in the centre of the cockpit on *Aurora*. If sailing on the verge of a jibe, normally someone would be on the wheel to avoid an unplanned jibe. Most autopilots perform poorly in these situations—a human is better to anticipate the swells and prevent the jibe. It was possible Dean had left the wheel only briefly to get up on the cockpit seat to do something and was unlucky that the jibe happened at that moment. This was something that Ella could verify.

Frank stretched and sat back in his chair. There may well be more to Dean's drowning than he first thought, although he'd need to keep an open mind as there could still be valid reasons for each situation. On these points alone they wouldn't have enough to pull Ella in for questioning and certainly not enough to open a formal investigation. And at this stage he didn't want to alert her to any further inquiry. But his interest was piqued. A visit to *Aurora* would be worthwhile to follow up on the oar, but he'd need a warrant to look into the GPS.

*

Amy picked up a coffee-to-go on her way back to work after her meeting with Frank and was turning on her computer when Al popped his head in.

"How's your day so far?" he asked, grinning good-naturedly.

"Going fairly well." This was the moment and she steeled herself. "Hey Al, there's something I want to tell you. Come in and shut the door if you don't mind."

"This sounds serious."

"It is."

"I'd better take a seat then." Seeing her cup, he asked, "Did you get me a flat white too?"

"Huh? Oh no, sorry, I didn't even think. I've been a bit distracted."

"How's the family doing?"

"They're fine, thanks. It's all been a bit of a nightmare, but the girls are coping well. They are back at school." She sighed. "Life just goes on."

"What's up?"

She took a deep breath. "I've been diagnosed with Parkinson's disease."

There, she had said it once more and it wasn't so hard. Perhaps after all the events of the last week it paled into insignificance. She watched Al's face for a reaction, but he remained passive.

"That doesn't sound great. I thought Parkinson's was a movement disorder affecting old people?"

"They say I have young-onset Parkinson's. You must have seen my tremor?"

"Yeah, although a lot of people have a tremor and it doesn't seem to be a problem."

"There are other causes, but mine is Parkinson's and it's degenerative—with no cure. Eventually I will lose the ability to walk normally and use my motor skills. I could also be affected in a whole host of other ways, like speech, sleep and cognitive issues."

"How fast will it progress?"

"No one knows for sure." She hated the insecurity of not knowing. "I'm going to fight it and do everything I can to slow it down. It shouldn't affect my work."

"Have you told Fran yet?"

"No. I'm going to try and see her this afternoon. How do you think she'll react?"

He hesitated. "I honestly don't know—there shouldn't be a problem, what with your track record. You'd never know with her." He grinned cheekily. "She's so driven and focused on her own career that all she wants from us is to make her look good to the senior partners."

"I know what you mean. I guess that's what's behind my procrastination."

"Don't sweat it, you'll be fine. You're the rising star—she needs you!"

"I'm not feeling stardom just now. Anyway, I'll let you know how it goes."

They went on to discuss the latest tax legislation changes and Amy felt the burden lift. Once Al left, she called Fran's assistant and made an appointment to see her later that afternoon. The time dragged by until she was knocking on Fran's door.

"Come in." Fran was sitting behind her large wooden desk. As was her custom, she was dressed to slay the corporate giant in a skin-tight grey top that revealed some cleavage. Her hair was cut short, a diamond stud protruded from her nose and her nails were manicured. In her mid-thirties, she was a stereotypical Gen Y—self-important, self-absorbed and she often treated her elders as having already lost much of their relevance. Not that Amy had a problem with Gen Y; after all, Al was one and he was a great work colleague. In fact, she wondered just what percentage actually fit the stereotype. Fran interrupted her thoughts, asking, "Are you okay?"

"Yes...um...sorry Fran. Thanks for making the time this afternoon," Amy began. Her shake had worked itself up and so she tucked her hand under her leg to hide it.

"I was sorry to hear of your loss. In fact, the partners asked me to extend their condolences. Did you receive the flowers?"

"Yes, thanks, they were really appreciated. It's been a hard couple of weeks." Amy felt herself relax.

"I was meaning to ask you to come in for a chat, so your timing is good. I'm really pleased with your results so far this year—you should be in for a reasonable bonus. It's too early to say exactly how much, but you're exceeding target on all your key performance indicators. Well done."

"Thanks."

Fran rarely praised her staff and Amy was encouraged to open up about her Parkinson's. "I was..."

Fran cut across her. "Before you begin, there was something else I wanted to give you a heads up about. As you know, our revenue has been down this past year largely as a result of Covid. We've been taking a close look at our productivity and we're considering making some changes. You should be fine—your results speak for themselves. We will be making the announcement within the week. In the meantime, I would ask that you keep this to yourself." She stopped and sized Amy up. "Now what was it you wanted to see me about?"

Amy took in a deep breath. "I have been to see a neurologist about the shake in my left side and he diagnosed Parkinson's disease." She'd said it and she couldn't take it back.

Fran frowned. "Isn't that an old people's condition?"

"Not exclusively. Many people under 65 get it. It is the fastest growing neurological disease and over 12,000 kiwis suffer from it."

"What exactly is it?"

"It's a progressive neurological condition that is caused by the loss or degeneration of nerve cells that produce dopamine in the brain. As at this time there is no cure, however there are some treatments that help manage the symptoms."

"You say it's progressive?" Fran looked pensive.

"Yes, but it won't affect my ability to do my job, at least not for a long time." Amy was feeling panicked. She could see Fran watching her with a curious gaze and wondered if she'd sealed her fate in a potential round of cutbacks.

"Well, thanks for coming and telling me. If you are having any issues, let me know." Fran dismissed her.

"Okay, thanks." Amy got up and left the office feeling somewhat downcast.

Al was hovering in the hallway when she got back to her office. "How did it go?"

"I'm not sure—I didn't expect any empathy. She made it clear she's pleased with our results."

"That's something. You'll be fine Amy. Just let me know if there's anything I can do to help—any time."

The anxiety that had plagued Amy for the last little while returned and gnawed at her as she worked through her accounts. She couldn't wait to get to the sanctuary of her home.

*

Frank decided to have a chat with the Coastguard volunteer who had brought *Aurora* in after Dean went missing. He wandered upstairs to the Coastguard office and got the contact details for Pete Drury. Back at his desk he dialled the number.

"Pete Drury? It's Frank Smythe of the Maritime Unit."

"Hi Frank. How can I help you?"

"I just want to ask you some questions relating to a case I'm reviewing. Do you have time now? It shouldn't take long." He opened his notebook.

"Sure, now is good. What's it about?"

"Do you recall the man-overboard situation with the yacht *Aurora*? I believe you went on board and brought her back to Westhaven. The wife, Ella Hampton, was on board."

"Yeah, that's right. Bit of a sad case. What is it you want to know?"

Frank consulted his notes. "Was there anything that was out of place or unusual on board?"

"No, not that I can recall. I had a look around, but everything was well-stowed and my impression was that she was a well-loved craft."

"Did anything strike you as odd?"

"Not really. I did see that two cabins had been used, but that's not that unusual. Come to think of it there was something, a minor thing. I remember that morning the wind was westerly turned nor'wester. The wife said they were sailing home with full sail when *Aurora* jibed, which couldn't be right on that heading. When I asked her about this, she said they'd changed their minds as her husband wanted to go to Coromandel. I had thought they were a bit far north for that heading, but then she'd been searching for him for a while and so I thought no more about it."

Frank finished jotting his notes. "How would you describe Ella Hampton's behaviour?"

"Well, I noticed that she's a real stunner!" He chuckled, then went quiet. "I'm sorry Frank—that was a bit flippant. Seriously though, I thought she was grieving cos' she seemed so sad and melancholy. She was taking it all fairly bravely—she didn't lose it or anything like that. She perked up a bit when we had a cuppa and gave me a bit of her life story. She certainly shed some tears if that's what you want to know."

Frank thanked him and said he'd get back to him if he needed anything else. He hung up and looked at his notebook. Grabbing the pencil he drew a circle around the notes pertaining to the heading. A visit to *Aurora* was warranted, but he wanted to gain access without Ella knowing that he was beginning to suspect things weren't as straight forward as they'd seemed.

10

Amy was in the kitchen preparing a lasagne for dinner when Terry came home from work. He walked around the breakfast bar, put his arms around her from behind and kissed her on her neck.

"How was your day?" he asked.

"Okay, I guess. I finally came clean and had a chat with Al and told him about my diagnosis. I met with Fran and told her."

"Good." He went to the pantry and helped himself to some biscuits. "How did they take it?"

"Al was fine—it was all very low key. But I'm not so sure about Fran. She told me they're doing a so-called productivity review, insinuating that I'd be okay based on my performance to date. She was hard to read when I told her about my Parkinson's." Amy picked up the saucepan of cheese sauce she'd been stirring and turned to face him. "I don't trust her."

"You'll be fine, don't worry. What could she possibly do? You're just as capable now as you were before you were diagnosed. Nothing's changed. You know you're a valuable employee."

The spoon clattered against the side of the pan as her tremor increased. "I hope you're right. I might be over-thinking it because I'm feeling exhausted. I wish I could sleep through the night—at least for more than three to four hours."

"Why do you think this is? You used to be a good sleeper."

"I guess it's related to Parkinson's. I sometimes wake up with the night sweats and then I lie there worrying about what lies ahead. I don't want to be a burden for you and the girls. I can't bear the thought of you sitting for hours by my bedside or helping me with my personal cares. I worry I won't be able to fully enjoy the girls' lives, to see them grow up, have careers, get married. What if I can't hold my grandchildren?" Tears welled in her eyes, a common occurrence of late. "Everything is so bleak in the early hours. And all this business with Dean hasn't helped. I get overwhelmed with anxiety and once awake, it's so hard to get back to sleep."

He came and gave her a hug, before asking quietly, "Do you think you should go back and see your doctor?"

"What use will that be?" She broke away from his embrace to pour the last of the sauce over the layers of pasta, vegetables and meat.

"Maybe she can prescribe you sleeping tablets or something to reduce the anxiety."

"I don't want any more tablets—I have enough now with the Parkinson's drugs."

"I still think you should talk to her. You can't go on like this and keep doing all you're doing. You need a good night's sleep to function well."

"Maybe you're right. I might see how I go over the next week. It hasn't been that long since we had Dean's funeral and some of it may be exacerbated by grief. I'm worried about Mum too; I think she's slipping rapidly and now I don't have Dean to help with her."

"Dean wasn't doing much for her before he went missing, that's the truth. It was all you. He's had little time for the family ever since he married Ella. He was totally captivated by her."

"It was like she had a spell over him. And what red-blooded male wouldn't be smitten by her?" It came out as a snipe and Amy immediately regretted it.

"Me for one, I've got the girl I want." Terry grinned. "Would you like a wine before dinner?"

"Thanks, it may help me sleep."

Terry poured her a wine and got himself a beer from the fridge while Amy put the casserole dish in the oven.

"I think I'll go around to Ella's on Saturday and see how she's doing. Do you want to come?"

"Not really." He gave her a wry smile. "You're not going to start playing detective, are you?"

"No. Although if I get a chance to look around, maybe I'll find something that'll help Frank."

"Now don't you go snooping about where you have no business to be. Really Amy, don't destroy the relationships this family has—Dean wouldn't want you to alienate yourself from Ella, especially after what she's just gone through."

Amy let it pass without further comment. At that moment Maddie came in looking for a snack and the conversation moved on to her day at school.

*

Frank was looking forward to his weekly catch up with Anahera. He called Margie to remind her that he'd be late home and decided the numerous reports he needed to finish could wait. He chuckled as he thought about the conscientious detective he used to be— perhaps all this time on the water was giving him a better perspective.

Going off duty, he replaced his overalls with a blue shirt, sports jacket and casual trousers. The drive down to Smugglers' Bar was short, but rush hour, combined with the difficulty of finding a park near the Viaduct, took time and he found he was once again running late. Anahera was already waiting at the same table as last time when he rushed in through the crowd of patrons.

"Sorry, I didn't mean to be late. Finding a park around here is hopeless at the best of times." He hitched himself up onto the bar stool opposite her.

"You should be in traffic management." She chuckled. Getting up from her seat, she asked, "Is it my round?"

"Stay there, I'll get the first round." He felt in his pocket to check he had his wallet. "Same as always?"

"Yes, thanks." She sank back onto her seat.

Frank went to the bar and came back with a Speights and a Corona and slapped them down on the table, saying, "Some things never change."

"You're right there." She raised her drink. "Cheers!"

"Cheers!" They both took a sip.

They chatted for a while about what her boys were up to, like old friends do.

"How have you been—what with your friend dying and all?" Anahera looked at him with a solemn expression.

"Yeah, good. It was a bit of a shock though—such a waste." His eyes roved the room before staring into his bottle. "The sister came to see me. She had some interesting things to say. She thinks there are some inconsistencies in the wife's story and she also saw a brand-new oar on board."

"How did she know it was new?"

"It still had a new-looking price tag on it. Although I've yet to see it for myself."

"And do you think it could've been used in the man-overboard?" Her eyes were wide with interest.

He sighed. "At this stage, I really don't know."

"Is Central investigating it?"

"No, I want to do a little digging myself first to see if there's anything to the claims. And if there is, I intend to get the investigation handed to my unit given my background with it already."

"Good luck with that—you know how sensitive the DI is to patch boundaries. And you have a conflict of interest being a friend."

"Well, hardly close friends—I hadn't seen him for years. I want to continue with the case as I now know the players. I had thought a team approach might work—I could ride point and work with one of the detectives at Central." He grinned at her. "Like maybe you, one for the old days!"

"That might work, especially as we're understaffed right now." She looked thoughtful as she drew her hair back from her face. "It would be great to team up again."

"I will need to argue that I can balance the time on this case with my ongoing unit work. We're also short staffed—we barely have enough qualified skippers now to cover if one of us is off sick. And it doesn't sound like that's going to change in a hurry as there are none currently undergoing the training. But I'm keen to carry on with it." He stopped and drained his beer. She followed suit.

Anahera stood up and picked up the empties. "My round."

Frank watched her go to the bar. Dressed in casual work-out clothes, she looked like she'd come straight from the gym. It was admirable how she always seemed to fit everything in and cope well with whatever was thrown at her. She was a survivor.

Even here, the Hampton case was top of mind. Tomorrow he'd look into the business of the oar and if he still felt there was a need for further investigation, he'd call his old Detective Sergeant at Central and square it away with him.

A Corona was thrust at him.

"Thanks." He reached out and put it to his lips in a single movement. This time he took only a small sip, conscious of the need to slow down his drinking.

"Do you think the wife pushed him in?"

"Well, there were only the two of them on board at the time. It was either an accident with the boom hitting him on the head in a jibe manoeuvre, or she clobbered him and somehow got him over the side. Before talking with the sister, it looked like a straightforward and very tragic accident."

"If it was the wife, what do you suppose her motive was?"

"That could have been an accident...they could have been having a heated row and one thing led to another. I saw no evidence of it when I looked over the boat. Or maybe she was having an affair, but she's given me no reason to doubt she was the typical bereft widow."

"Was there a life insurance payment?"

"To be honest, I haven't looked. Although come to mention it, when I checked Dean's accounts for the coroner's report, I was surprised to see he has considerable debt."

"Interesting." She looked thoughtful. "Have there been many man-overboard cases where they turned into a murder investigation?"

"As far as I can recall there's only ever been the odd one—it's certainly not a major problem." He paused. "It's a tricky scenario because it's difficult to prove without hard evidence and there's unlikely to be an eyewitness if it's done away from land. By the time they're reported, the offender has had plenty of opportunity to clean up the evidence, making these cases mostly circumstantial."

"Makes you think you don't want to have a domestic on a boat."

"That's for sure." He cupped his hands around the cool bottle and toyed with the condensation. "How's your caseload at the moment?"

"I'm juggling a number of missing person cases at present. I seem to be seconded full-time to the Land Search and Rescue—I'm not complaining as I'd rather this work than chasing gang members or ram raiders."

"What happened with the missing person case you were telling me about? The one where you weren't sure he was really missing?"

"It's a low priority for me at present, so no real progress at my end. Probably still living off the grid somewhere." She screwed up her face. "Did I tell you he's heavily into conspiracy theories and sees himself as a version of Mariner from Waterworld?"

"There seem to be more and more conspiracy theorists about, especially after Covid."

"His phone is still not active." Looking more animated, she added, "By the way, I did go through his recent payments and saw one to Hampton Dental Services in Newmarket. That wasn't by any chance your dentist friend, was it? I was meaning to ask you."

"Yes, it is Dean's clinic, or I should say 'was' his clinic. That's interesting—I guess we all need a dentist at some time. A bit of a coincidence though." Frank took a sip of beer.

"You and your coincidences." They laughed as they shared the old joke.

"Hey, you wouldn't believe what happened to me the other day. I had a call out to Waiheke Island to pick up and deliver a woman in labour to the city. When the pain had got too much, she'd decided that maybe a home birth wasn't for her after all. We were halfway across between Motuihe and Rangitoto when I heard a cry. She'd popped out a healthy baby boy!"

"I hope she called him Frank."

"Not this time. I suggested they call him Motuihe or Rangitoto. Anyway, the mother and child were fine, so we turned around and took them back to Waiheke. The *Deodar III* crew were left with a mess to clean up."

"You get some interesting cases...while we at Central do the real policing."

He chuckled. "Don't go that way."

They drank in silence for a bit. Frank mused about some of the strange things the Maritime Unit had been called to do.

"What are the worst cases you get to deal with?" Anahera asked.

"Definitely the suicides. They leave you sick to the core—you never get used to them. They are such a waste. It makes you think that there are not enough interventions in place for mental illness in this country. We call it *God's Own,* but it clearly isn't if you look at how those stats are increasing."

"I've had a few of those too—some of the missing persons have ended up being suicides. It's grim alright. I feel deeply for the ones they leave behind." She played with her earring and took another sip.

They chatted some more about interesting cases until they'd both drained their drinks. The time had come to hit the road to their respective homes. Before they left they agreed to catch up again the following week.

*

Next morning Frank had not long been at work when he took a call to investigate some petty theft down at the Westhaven Marina. Stephen Blackett was rostered on as his crewman for the day. *Deodar III* had been left ready-to-go at the end of the previous shift and they grabbed their kit bags and took her around to Westhaven.

Once they'd interviewed the first complainant and Frank saw that the offences were minor, he left Stephen to gather statements from the other two complainants. Frank's hunch was that it was the work of kids. He took the opportunity to wander down to where *Aurora* was in her berth. She was looking sleek and beautiful, her paint gleaming in the morning light. No one was around, so he climbed on board and looked about the cockpit. He wondered how Dean had spent his last moments, what he might have been thinking and feeling as he went to his death. Or did it happen so fast that there was no time to think. Frank would never know.

He stepped up onto the starboard cockpit seat and noted that the height of the boom was lower than his head height. In fact, if it swung around now it would clip him on his shoulder and not the back of the head—that is, unless Dean was partially bending over. If memory served him right, Dean was a couple of centimetres taller than him meaning if he had been standing up it would have been marginally lower against him. There was a topping lift, the rope that lifts and lowers the aft end of the boom, that could be adjusted to lift the boom higher. However, lifting it would not be normal procedure when sailing downwind as that would cause the sail to be less efficient. This was another point that could be checked out with Ella. Pete Drury would also know if it had been adjusted while he was on board and Amy would know if it had been used when they went out to distribute Dean's ashes. He was also assuming that *Aurora* hadn't been out at any other time since the incident. He noted these things in his notebook.

The cockpit had a locker on either side and neither of them was locked. The first locker had the black water tank and spare fenders in it but no oars. He hit the jackpot with the other locker, finding two oars and the dinghy seat among other items. On closer examination, he found one oar had a price sticker on it just as Amy had said. It was clean and showed no sign of scuff marks or any sort of wear and tear. He pulled out his mobile phone and took a photo of it. The retailer was a local chandlery chain whose manager, Graeme Morris, he knew well.

He searched in his phone for the number and placed the call.

"Can I speak to Graeme Morris please."

"One moment please."

He listened to the voices in the background and then heard someone say, "For you."

"Hello." The voice was loud and clear. "Graeme Morris speaking."

"Graeme, it's Frank Smythe here. Do you have a minute?"

"Sure Frank, what can I do for you?"

"I would like to send you a photo of a price sticker on an oar that is of interest in an investigation. I would appreciate you finding out when it was sold and if possible, who purchased it. I'll send it through as soon as we hang up."

"Not a problem. We don't sell too many of those. I'll get on to it straight away."

"And I know I don't need to explain to you that my inquiry is confidential."

"Of course, understood. I'll get back to you within the hour."

"Thanks Graeme, talk soon."

Frank pushed the button to end the call and sent the photo attached to an email. Before leaving *Aurora*, he took the time to look at the other locker contents. He found the usual gear you'd expect on a recreational yacht: spare ropes, spare anchor and chain, spare steering gear, cleaning equipment and more. A locker in the transom contained the fishing gear.

He left *Aurora* and wandered back to find Stephen. Cruising about marinas looking at the boats was a favourite pass-time that never failed to put him in a good mood. As he reached him, his phone chirped.

"Hello Frank? Graeme Morris here."

"That was quick Graeme. Do you have the information?" Frank asked.

"I looked it up on our system and I see we've only sold three in the last two months. What time period are you interested in?"

"Just the last month."

"Two of the sales were in the last month. The first was a visa sale three weeks ago and the other was a cash sale ten days ago. I can give you the transaction details for the visa sale and the exact timing for both. Can I email them to you?"

"That would be a big help, thanks Graeme."

"No problem."

"Any chance you have the CCTV footage for them?"

"You're in luck—we keep it at head office for a month. Can I get them to send it over to you at the Maritime Unit?"

"Thanks, I'd appreciate that."

The call ended and Frank breathed a long sigh. As soon as the information was available, he would be able to verify exactly who the purchaser was and when the purchase was made. He was hopeful it would tie the purchase back to *Aurora*.

Within minutes Frank's phone alerted him to an incoming email. At the top of his inbox was one from Graeme with the date of both sales and the visa card details. Unfortunately, the name for the visa card transaction was not Ella Hampton. That left the possibility of the cash sale. With a bit of luck the CCTV footage would be clear enough to identify the purchaser.

It seemed like a long day out on *Deodar III* before he returned to base. He left Stephen to refill the diesel and water tanks, to wash her down and get her in a ready-to-go state for the next shift.

A small courier package was waiting for him on his desk from the chandlery retailer. Inside was a USB storage stick which he plugged into his computer. He checked the time of the cash sale on the email he'd received and fast-forwarded the video footage. He pushed play and watched. The footage was a wide-angle view of the counter. A woman resembling Ella Hampton came into view holding an oar which she placed on the counter. He watched as she opened her bag and pulled out some cash, then waited for her change. He rewound the video and played it again, freezing it on a frame where the woman's face was unobstructed. He enlarged it and the image was clearly that of Ella Hampton.

"Gotcha!" he exclaimed.

The timing confirmed Ella purchased the oar after Dean went missing. There could still be an innocent explanation, but things were not looking good for Ella. Why would she lie to Amy unless she had something to hide?

The fact he'd missed this during the initial investigation was worrying. The incident had looked so much like an accident. He was filled with renewed determination to see justice done and if Ella was guilty then he would see she paid for it. It wasn't only a matter of doing his job, he was also compelled to look after Dean's interests.

With further investigation now warranted, he decided to have a chat with Detective Inspector Brad Smart at Central. Given the circumstances around the incident, he thought it would be best if he provided him with an update in person. Assuming a formal investigation would now be opened, he'd argue that either he leads it out of the Maritime Unit with support from Central or he be given a secondment back to Central for the duration of the investigation. He didn't mind which, but with the shortage of skippers his preference was to run it out of Maritime.

11

Saturday morning was normally a sleep-in for the Fagin household. Amy had woken up in the small hours and had tossed and turned while desperately wanting to get back to sleep. With the daylight apparent through the curtains, she crept out of bed and put on her dressing gown before going downstairs.

While waiting for the coffee to percolate, she stood at the window. The day was grey and dismal outside. The backyard garden was lost behind the blur of the water running down the windowpane. The rain droplets were mesmerising as they streaked and merged across the glass forming an ever-changing pattern. Right now, she felt as inconsequential as a raindrop with no control over the things that mattered in her life. Her health, her mother's health, Dean's death; these were things she cared about deeply and she was unable to fix any of them.

The more she thought about Dean and his terrible drowning, the more she believed Ella had had something to do with it, making her more determined than ever to find out the truth. She made up her mind to visit Ella that day on the pretext of updating her with her own news about the Parkinson's diagnosis and finding out how Ella was coping on her own.

The doubts surrounding the so-called accident had consumed her thoughts when she should have been sleeping and she needed to find some clue as to why Ella might have wanted to be rid of Dean. At this stage she had no idea what she could do. But no matter what, she'd need to take care not to alert Ella to her suspicions—that was for Frank to do if he indeed believed there was a case to answer.

The coffee brewed and she poured some into a mug and sat at the breakfast bar with it cupped in her hands, enjoying the warmth. What could she possibly hope to achieve by visiting Ella? How could she get access to Ella's comings and goings, her conversations, her actions, her relationships? If this was a movie, then she would arrange to bug her home. Or she could employ a private investigator. Or maybe spy on her from a neighbouring window. Or send a drone over. Even a satellite. She smiled at the silliness of it all.

She raked her hands through her hair and smoothed it down. It had always been a mess, but whenever she'd tried straighteners, Terry had complained it wasn't her. He liked her the way she was.

What possible reason could Ella have had to get rid of Dean? If she was having an affair, divorce would be a lot less risky than hitting Dean over the head with an oar. Maybe Ella had an anger problem, perhaps they were fighting on board when she grabbed the oar and hit him, accidentally killing him before destroying the evidence by throwing him overboard. But it would take a lot of strength to get a man over the side of *Aurora*. Maybe she needed money and was after his life insurance. Or it was all part of some grisly game on the black web—she'd heard about those types of games where murder was performed live for perverted gamers who'd watch to get their kicks—then again that may have been a fictional story she remembered like a horror film on Netflix.

On the other hand, what if she was wrong? Maybe Dean had been hit during a jibe as per Ella's story and it was all just a terrible accident. That was possible, nevertheless something felt off about the whole nightmare. And she was convinced that Ella was hiding something with the oar going missing.

Maybe she could carry out a little detective work of her own. The first step might be to get access to Dean's study, although that could be problematic. Nor did she have any idea what she might be looking for. In the movies they'd probably swipe Ella's mobile phone and go through the call log or look through her files and correspondence on the computer. But this wasn't the movies where things were simplified for the sake of a good yarn. Devices are more likely to be locked with password protection or some other thief-proof means.

The worst-case scenario would be to get caught snooping red-handed. How would she explain that one? *I got lost* or *I must have picked up the wrong phone* or *I got confused*. Amy laughed out loud. Maybe the latter cap fits best, or she could blame it on the Parkinson's—it must be good for something! No, sneaking about wouldn't be easy and she didn't possess the stealth and cunning needed to be a private eye.

Terry was right in that she'd need to be careful not to damage family relationships. For Dean's sake, she would continue to act normal towards Ella—and that she could do. An outright accusation wouldn't help, that was Frank's job. With luck Ella would let something slip in conversation or an opportunity would arise for Amy to learn something while she was visiting, like overhearing a phone conversation, and this time she wouldn't forget the details.

Amy made the decision to call Ella and ask if she could visit her later that day after the girls' matches. Netball season was beginning and both Maddie and Tracy were playing for school teams. Amy loved to watch their games.

She finished her coffee and realised she'd barely tasted it. Kicking off the day with a coffee was a habit she enjoyed, so she poured herself a second cup and this time she savoured each mouthful. The rain continued to fall like a curtain across the window.

Soon the kitchen was alive with activity and noise as Terry and Maddie joined her for breakfast. The fears of the night no longer had a hold over her and she joined in with their banter. Tracy had not yet emerged, which wasn't unusual as her youngest child liked her sleep-ins. It became a typical Saturday morning in the Fagin house.

*

Amy turned the car into Ella's driveway with a sense of anticipation—of what she wasn't sure. Maddie and Tracy bounced out of the car as soon as she'd pulled on the handbrake. They were dressed in green and white netball clothes, representing the school colours, although Maddie was in a short sleeveless dress and Tracy wore shorts and top, depicting their team seniority. Both girls had their surname plastered across their backs.

By the time Amy got to the door, Ella had already opened it to the girls and was greeting them with a smile.

"Come on in. How did your netball go?" Ella asked, looking from Maddie to Tracy.

"We won, 32 to 26." Tracy's voice was full of exuberance. "I played Goal Attack for the full game and scored nearly half of the goals."

"We lost, but we played last season's winners. It was only a grading game anyway." Maddie's voice was a little more down beat than her sister's.

"What position did you play?" Ella asked.

"Wing Defence, but the coach only played me for two of the quarters." Maddie sounded annoyed.

"Never mind, I'm sure you both played well." Ella looked at Amy for the first time. "And how are you Amy?"

"I'm fine." Amy drew in a sharp breath. "Actually, that's one of the things I wanted to see you about."

"Coffee?" Ella asked, as they followed her to the kitchen.

"Yes please," Amy responded.

"What about you girls? I have some juice in the fridge."

"I'll get it," Tracy said, walking to the cupboard where the glasses were kept.

Ella got to work making the coffee. She was dressed in jeans with a navy and white striped tee-shirt and her fair hair sat loosely over her shoulders. Her eyes were expertly made up with natural hues behind dark rimmed glasses and they no longer sported the red tired look she'd had after Dean went missing.

Ella got out some biscuits and put them on a plate while Tracy chatted to her and gave a blow-by-blow account of her game, Ella providing noises of encouragement whenever Tracy paused for breath. Amy watched their interaction closely, looking for anything and nothing. She didn't think Ella was showing any signs of grieving—but maybe she was being too hard on her.

Ella passed a mug of steaming hot coffee to Amy, saying, "Shall we take it to the living room?"

Not trusting her shakes, Amy took extra care not to spill the coffee as they followed Ella through to the other room where Ella sat in an armchair and Amy sat on the couch between Maddie and Tracy.

"How are you coping Ella?" Amy asked, once they were all seated.

Maddie got up and passed the plate of biscuits around.

"I'm muddling through, thanks. There's nothing else you can do really—life must go on." Ella paused to take a biscuit. "What was it you wanted to tell me?"

"I thought you should know I went to the doctors just before Dean went, um, you know." Being here, sitting in Dean's house, brought her emotions back to the surface and she couldn't bring herself to say the words.

"Go on," prompted Ella, obviously unaware of the silent struggle going on inside Amy.

Amy followed her urge to get it out. "I've been diagnosed with Parkinson's disease." Those awful words brought a lump into her throat.

"Oh no, that's terrible. But isn't that an old people's disease?"

There it was again—people's perceptions made her feel embarrassed and inadequate. Amy immediately went onto the defensive, her voice sharper than she'd intended. "No, that's a myth. More and more younger people are getting it. The neurologist called mine young-onset Parkinson's and it's apparently not that uncommon."

"So, what's the prognosis?" Ella's tone lacked emotion.

Amy went on to explain what Parkinson's disease was and outlined her symptoms, finishing up by explaining how the future was now uncertain and they would live day by day and try to manage the symptoms as best they could.

"Will you have to resign from your work?" Ella asked.

"No, I can continue to work as I have been doing, no problems. My cognitive ability hasn't been affected. I need to manage any stress because that makes it worse." Amy decided to change the subject and probe Ella in the hope she might reveal something of interest. "What about you? What will you do now with Dean's dental practice?"

Tracy cut in. "Can we go out and throw the netball around? Mum, please can you give me the car keys? Come on Maddie, it's stopped drizzling."

Amy passed her younger daughter the keys and Maddie followed Tracy out the front door. After watching them leave, Amy turned back to Ella. "I was asking you about your plans regarding the practice."

Ella looked at Amy, her face a beacon of calm. "Yes, as soon as the lawyer has finished winding up the estate, I plan to place it on the market. I don't expect it will take long to sell—as a going concern it's a thriving business."

"What will you do?"

"I think I will resign from the practice—it's too hard without Dean there. Too many reminders." She looked away from Amy and gazed out the window where the girls could be seen throwing the ball to each other. "I'm also thinking about selling this house."

This was a surprise. The house was a goldmine with its location in a swanky street in Auckland. "Where will you go?"

Ella looked back at Amy. "I'm not sure, but I'm thinking of living aboard *Aurora* for a bit. I'd feel closer to Dean there."

"Really? What will you do with all your things?" Amy looked about the room at the tasteful and lavish furnishings, the knick-knacks and expensive artwork that adorned it.

Ella pulled her knees up onto the couch and hugged them into her chest. "They can go into storage, at least for now."

"Do you feel capable of handling *Aurora* on your own?"

"Of course I do," Ella said somewhat testily. "Do you doubt it?"

"No of course not. It's come as a shock, that's all. I'm sure you'll manage just fine living on board."

"I had a good teacher," Ella said smiling, her tone now moderated.

"He was. I remember him showing amazing patience with the girls when he taught them to sail." Amy couldn't bring herself to mention Dean by name. Then realising her faux pas, she added, "I didn't mean he needed patience with you. I'm sorry, that all came out wrong, but you know what I meant."

Ella smiled. "I think so."

Sitting in this room reminded Amy of the day Dean had his alleged accident and of the papers she had sorted. It had completely slipped her mind, but now her curiosity was once more aroused. "Were you and Dean into cryptocurrency?"

Ella looked surprised. "Why do you ask?"

"I happened to see a paper about it that day of the accident."

Ella maintained her poker face. "Well yes, we did invest some money in Bitcoin." She checked her watch.

"I don't know much about the crypto markets—and I'm surprised Dean would have been interested. I do know that people bold enough to speculate in the early days made a killing." She waited for Ella's response.

"And some people have lost a fortune." Ella picked up her mug and stood up, signalling the discussion was over. "More coffee?" She turned her back on Amy and marched out of the room before Amy had a chance to answer, leaving her intrigued and wondering which camp Dean and Ella were in with their investment—the winners or the losers? Amy followed Ella, determined to find the answer.

In the kitchen Ella was making more coffee. "Was that a yes from you for another cup?"

"No, thanks. One is more than enough for me. I seem to be developing poor sleep habits and I really should avoid too much caffeine." Amy decided to pry a little more. "So, were you and Dean lucky with your crypto investment?"

"It's really a personal matter and I don't think Dean would want us discussing it." She looked at her watch again.

Amy thought Ella was using the 'Dean-card' to shut her up and she had to respect that their business was their own no matter how curious she might be. Regardless, she was left wondering whether this could be related to a motive. Maybe she should let Frank know—he would have the resources to investigate it properly. Satisfied that she'd at least gleaned something that might be of interest, she changed the subject to safer ground. "I thought the way you arranged our time sprinkling the ashes was really well done and I wanted to thank you."

Ella looked appreciatively at Amy. "Thanks Amy, that means a lot. How's your mum doing?"

Amy chatted about her fears for her mum's health and then they discussed the state of the nation until it was time to go. As she left, she kissed Ella on the cheek and told her how good it was to see her looking more like her old self and to hear she was making plans for her future. She stepped outside and called the girls who bade their own farewells before piling into the car.

The girls chattered happily in the rear seat while Amy thought about all she'd learned. Snooping about at Ella's was not something she could do as there were no credible reasons why she might be in the study where she assumed anything of interest might lie. Having even considered trying to sneak into the study to rifle through private documents was absurd. No way would she be able to get access to the house when Ella wasn't home. No, she'd have to leave the investigation to the professionals. Her foolishness made her laugh out loud.

"What's the joke?" Maddie asked.

"Oh nothing." She turned on the radio and soon they were singing along to the 80's Rock Station music.

Later that afternoon, the girls were in the lounge watching a movie when Terry arrived home and joined Amy in the kitchen.

"Would you like a red wine?" he asked.

"Mmmm, that would be nice." She placed her arms around his neck and held him tightly to her.

"What's this for?" he asked.

"Just because I love you. Do I need a reason?"

He pulled away, chuckling. "No, best you don't wait for a reason."

She put some nuts into a bowl and Terry poured a generous helping of wine into a crystal stem glass and passed it to her, before getting a beer for himself.

"How was the netball?" he asked, taking a sip.

"The girls played well for pre-season games. Tracy especially played some good netball; her passing and shooting were much better than last season." Amy chomped on a handful of the nuts.

"Did you see your mother?"

"No, I'll go round tomorrow. We did visit Ella after the game and I told her about my Parkinson's." She sipped her wine. "You'll never guess what Ella told me."

"No, I don't suppose I could."

"She's selling up, both Dean's dental practice and the house and she's going to live aboard *Aurora*."

His eyes widened. "No, really? Now that's a surprise."

"I know—who would have thought? It's not really an Ella thing to do. She's so neat and has always surrounded herself with lots of beautiful things. I can't imagine her living a life as a gypsy, let alone one on the water. It doesn't fit with her personality."

"Do you think she's capable of handling the boat on her own?"

"She seems to think so." Amy ran her fingers through her hair, combing it down.

"Perhaps it's the grief talking. She may think differently in a week or two."

"We'll see. But there's more." Amy took another sip and let the velvety liquid linger in her mouth before swallowing it. "She and Dean invested in cryptocurrency."

"I hope you weren't snooping among her things."

Amy looked down at the glass in her hands and felt guilty about the thoughts she'd had. "No, of course not. She told me."

"What they do with their money is none of our business." Terry took a handful of nuts.

"Just imagine if they bought in the early stages when the Bitcoin was relatively cheap, when you could buy it for something like a few hundred. If they cashed it in during the heady days when investors went mad, sending it climbing in value to something like fifty thousand or more, Ella could be sitting on an absolute fortune."

"Well, she wouldn't want to be holding on to it now that it's fallen through the floor." Terry took a drink.

Amy picked up her phone and tapped the screen. She said, "In 2013 Bitcoin was worth around 200 US dollars and it climbed to 65,000 US dollars in 2021. Currently it's worth around 26,000 US dollars."

"It was a fairly risky thing to invest in."

"It sure was, but it paid off for a lot of people. We were talking at work about some investors who'd lost everything. It's password protected and the passwords are the most important thing—you can't redeem it without the password. If you lose that, as some have, you're stuffed. You can literally kiss goodbye to your investment. It would be heartbreaking."

"That's terrible. Hopefully that didn't happen to Ella and Dean. Anyway, what's for dinner?"

They worked together to prepare the meal and once more Amy was grateful for her husband. Having Terry at her side made all her concerns about what might lie ahead so much easier to deal with.

12

Frank had spent the weekend in the backyard constructing a small retaining wall and back-filling to create a garden along with installing some new garden lights that Margie had picked up in a sale. The work was backbreaking yet both satisfying and relaxing at the same time. Its physicality helped shake off his unease over the Hampton case. He was bitterly disappointed that there appeared to be more to Dean Hampton's early demise than he'd previously thought, giving him a severe case of the guilts. His muscles ached when he returned to work on Monday morning, but nothing sharpened the mind like a little pain making him more determined to find the truth.

The A Team, as Stephen liked to call Frank and himself, was rostered on. Stephen was a good crewmate who had been in the police for just over a year. Having grown up with boats, he found the job appealing and he loved nothing more than to be around them. In his mid-twenties, he was single and living life to the full. When not at work he liked to spend a lot of his own time out fishing in a small run-about that was his pride and joy.

The Gulf was quietening down after the summer activity. People were back at work, school terms were underway, and only the retired and those still on holiday were out and about on their recreational boats. Over the coming weeks they could expect it to get increasingly quiet as the colder weather arrived. However, to balance this trend, shipping was busy with the container port running at capacity and the cruise liner season still underway. The call-outs at the port were usually fewer than those of the recreational fleet. And in the quiet times they were expected to back up the Central Police Unit by providing on the ground assistance around the Viaduct area. This not only helped the over-stretched Auckland Central police but was a logical fit with the unit as the Viaduct housed a lot of super yachts, commercial charter vessels and classic boats. The sector was always busy, having become a popular area for events and recreation, well catered for by its many restaurants and bars.

Frank took a call from the Waiheke Island police to transfer a prisoner to Auckland. He and Stephen decked themselves out in their wet weather gear and checked *Deodar III* before setting off for the island.

The day was grey and drizzly with poor visibility, and not a breath of wind disturbed the water. Sea temperatures had already started to drop with the changing season. And as the northerly flow of warm air coming down from the tropics cooled over the colder ocean the relative humidity increased resulting in the sea fog that hung over them. There would be even fewer boats out today in these conditions.

Deodar III made steady progress through the calm water. Because of the fog Frank kept an eye on the radar, searching for any vessels that might be in their path. The stretch of water between the port and Waiheke could be busy with the port traffic and the frequent ferry service. By the time they neared the Motuihe channel, the fog was lifting and visibility had increased.

As they passed the Motuihe reef, Stephen called over the noise of the engines, "What do you make of the Hampton case. Do you really think the wife could've done it?"

"I honestly don't know, but it looks like she lied to her sister-in-law about the missing oar and her story about the jibe doesn't entirely add up." He sighed. "I really hope there's an innocent explanation for it all."

"If she's guilty, what do you think her motive was?" Stephen pushed his beanie further up his forehead, revealing some of his ginger hair. "Do you think she was having an affair?"

"Possibly, although it's a fairly radical way to end a marriage."

"What's her history? Did she have previous partners?"

"Good question, and one worth following up on." Frank made a mental note to do just that.

"Could it be another domestic violence case?"

Frank didn't answer immediately, allowing the thought to sink in as he hadn't considered this as a possibility. "There's been no mention of it—she certainly didn't have any obvious signs of injury. It's possible of course, but the Dean I knew was a good-humoured gentleman."

"I'd wager a bet that the guilty ones aren't always the obvious ones." Stephen paused. "Are we thinking about this the wrong way around? Have you considered it might be him that was having the affair and that she was jealous? She could have been upset to be cheated on and clobbered him in a fit of rage."

"I hadn't thought of that angle." Had he been so blinded by his loyalty to an old friend? He vowed silently to put what he thought he knew about Dean aside and to treat this inquiry like any other. No more assumptions based on the past. Time can change a person.

"What's your next move?"

"I'm hoping to get over to Central this afternoon to get a formal investigation underway and to plead the case for keeping our involvement with it."

As a breeze rippled the water surface and dispersed the last of the sea fog, their destination loomed ahead of them. Frank skilfully brought *Deodar III* into the wharf and Stephen leapt off with the mooring line in hand to secure her to the dock. Frank turned off the engines, removed his life jacket and climbed onto the wharf. A squad car was there to meet them and a local policewoman, Sue Jamieson, came towards them wearing the uniform of the NZ Police. Beside her was a sorry-looking man in dirty holey jeans and a scruffy tee-shirt, wearing His Majesty's bracelets. Frank exchanged a few words with Sue and accompanied the hand-cuffed man back to *Deodar III*, where he cuffed him to the rail before setting off for home base where they would transfer him to the Central lock-up.

No sooner had they delivered the prisoner than they were called out again. This time a local resident at Takapuna beach had been walking his dog when he saw a boat anchored in the zone where oceanic fibre-optic cables are laid on the seabed connecting New Zealand to the world's internet. The newest of the cables runs along a 15,000 kilometre route from Takapuna to Australia, Fiji, Kiribati and to California. Anchoring and fishing are banned in the zone around the cables.

A large triangle was visible on shore clearly indicating the anchoring ban area so the boatie's lame excuse that he didn't know was not met with sympathy. Frank got the launch skipper to haul his anchor chain up by hand to check they hadn't interfered with the telecommunications cable. Thankfully, it wasn't caught on anything, so he let them off with a warning that next time they could be fined a minimum of 20,000 dollars. That was infinitesimal compared to the cost of repair to the cable should it be damaged.

With *Deodar III* back at base, Frank left Stephen to scrub her down and make her ready to go for the next shift while he made his way down to Central headquarters. Before moving to the Maritime Unit, he'd worked under Detective Inspector Brad Smart who was a good cop and an all-round nice guy, with the right balance of being insightful and fair while tough and politically savvy. More a player coach than a team player. To his credit, he had rapidly been promoted up through the ranks and was the youngest inspector in the region.

Frank found Brad in his office at a desk laden with papers. Brad was a bear of a man; tall and muscular, built like a prop forward and with the cauliflower ears that came from seasons of scrapping in the rucks and mauls of senior rugby. Brad looked up and smiled as Frank knocked and entered.

"Good to see you Frank. What brings you here?"

Frank provided a brief update on the Hampton case, explaining why he now doubted the incident was as straightforward as it had initially appeared. He took Brad through the inconsistencies around the alleged jibe and the missing oar.

Brad had listened without comment. Now he asked, "So you're telling me you want a new investigation opened?"

"Yes, and I want to stay involved. I have the history and things are starting to quieten down in the Unit with the change of seasons. I think I can juggle this case with the Unit's case load, but I'd like full support from Central with clearance to pull in another detective should we need to up the horsepower."

"Did you have anyone in mind?"

"Anahera Raupara—you'll remember we've worked well together in the past. Between us we can get this one cleared up."

Brad cleared his throat. "I can't see why in principle you can't be involved in the case. As I see it, there are two options; either you are seconded to Central and run it from here, or one of our detectives heads it and you assist working out of Maritime. Either way this case is worked from here. What do you think about being seconded to Central for a while? If this is a murder investigation, I would prefer you full-time on it and based here under my command."

"I'd agree to that, but I'll need to run it by my boss. You'll be aware we're also running pretty thin on the ground with barely enough qualified skippers as it is." Frank scratched behind his ear. "There is one other thing you should be aware of."

Brad cocked his head slightly to one side. "And that is?"

"I knew the deceased. Not well, or at least I hadn't seen him for years. We used to crew on the classic yachts together. I don't see it as a conflict of interest—as I said it was in the past. If anything, it makes me keener to discover the truth for his sake. I thought you should know."

"Did you know the wife?"

"No, it was before they got together."

Brad stared at him, his face unreadable. Moments passed and Frank waited. "I guess I can sanction that, so long as you are sure it won't affect your judgement. But if at any time during the investigation you feel you are compromised because of it, you'll back away. Got it?"

Relieved, Frank said, "Yes, thanks. I will be needing to file a request for the Hampton phone logs and bank accounts. That's my next move—I don't want to alert Ella Hampton to our inquiry until such time as I'm confident she has something to answer."

"Understood. I'll have to clear the secondment with my superiors—that one's above my pay grade." Brad chuckled. "I'll let you know as soon as I get an answer. And I will check out Anahera's availability. I've got her working Land Search and Rescue at present, but I'll see what I can do." Brad made a note on the pad in front of him.

Frank returned to base satisfied that he would be able to continue to work the case, provided he could get released from

Maritime. He didn't expect the secondment would be long for as soon as the evidence was gathered, he'd confront Ella with it and with a bit of luck she might just confess to any wrongdoing. If he had to place a wager, he'd give it just a week until they made an arrest; that's assuming they found it wasn't an accident.

Stephen was washing the decks on *Deodar III* when he got back.

"All quiet?" Frank asked.

"Seems to be." Stephen stopped and leaned on his brush. "I was thinking about the oar. Why not give Sea Cleaners a call and ask if one of their crews has found one during their clean ups."

"That's a great idea—I'll go and give them a call now." Frank turned and went to make the call from his office.

Sea Cleaners was an organisation that took crews of volunteers around the Waitemata Harbour and Hauraki Gulf removing rubbish from the water, the estuaries and beaches. He knew the skippers, having regularly seen them out and about on the Gulf, and he dialled the number for one of them.

"Stuart? Frank Smythe here."

"Hi Frank. What can I do for you?" The voice spoke loudly over the noise of an outboard motor.

"Stuart, I wonder if you'd mind asking around the crews to see if anyone has found a wooden oar in your clean-ups?"

"Why would the police be looking for an oar?"

"All I can say is that it might help us with an investigation. I won't know unless we find it."

"Where and when was it lost?"

"I'll text you the date and last known coordinates where we think it may have been lost. Roughly speaking we think it could be somewhere in the area between Barrier, Coromandel and eastern Waiheke. Given how lightweight they are it could have washed up pretty much anywhere, or it could still be adrift in some flotsam."

"I'll give the other skippers a call."

"Thanks Stuart. It's a long shot—who knows, we might just be lucky."

"No problem, happy to help anytime."

Frank hung up and checked his notebook before punching in the text message and sending it off. He sat and stared at the window where passing rain squalls were delivering curtains of water onto the pane. If they found the oar he'd get Forensics to examine it, although the chances of finding something that'd link it to *Aurora* and Ella would be remote. Still, it was worth a shot.

The next thing he needed to do was clear his potential secondment to Central. His immediate superior, Andy Johnston, was a likeable man who was vastly experienced, having been around the force for over 40 years. What Frank liked about Andy was that he left his skippers to work largely autonomously, which was important when you were working out of *Deodar III* more hours than not. Andy had even allowed them to be the first Maritime Unit in the country to sleep on board, which was great for the guys on night shifts when all was quiet.

Frank gave him a call and provided a comprehensive update of what he knew so far, including his own personal relationship with the deceased.

Frank concluded, "I'm afraid we may now be looking at a case of manslaughter and possibly murder. Whichever way, Ella Hampton knows more than she initially led us to believe."

"I appreciate the heads-up Frank, you have my support. We'll miss you for sure, with the lads thin on the water now. But we'll make it work—after all it should only be for a few weeks at most."

Frank thanked him and hung up. The wheels were now in motion.

The rain continued to fall and consequently the remainder of the afternoon was thankfully quiet. He thought about Ella, puzzling over how someone who came across so well could be hiding something so terrible and he hoped he would find her innocent. It was easy to think of criminals as being gang members or fitting a certain stereotype, however Ella wasn't close to fitting the bill. Years on the job had taught Frank that people are often not what they seem—and they never ceased to surprise and disappoint him. He wondered whether she had a criminal record and how her previous relationships ended. A quick check on the police database found no trace of her.

He placed a call to Amy.

"Amy speaking."

"Amy, it's Frank Smythe. Have you got a minute?"

"Yes, now is good." She sounded formal so he assumed she was at work.

"I wanted to get some background from you. Did Ella have any serious relationships prior to Dean?"

"Yes, she'd been twice married. What does this have to do with your investigation?"

"Just filling in the picture. Did you ever meet her ex's? Was she on good terms with them?"

"No, I didn't meet them. I don't know how amicable the breakups were. Sara may know more. How's the investigation going?"

"I'm sorry, I'm not at liberty to discuss the investigation. But you can be assured that I am looking into it." He picked up his pen. "Would you be able to give me Sara's number?"

"I will text it to you."

"Thanks. And I assume she's back in Dunedin?"

"Yes, she went back the week after the funeral." A sharp intake of breath. "I went around to Ella's on Saturday. She told me she is putting Dean's business and the house up for sale and is planning to live aboard *Aurora*."

"Interesting. I wouldn't have taken her for the live-aboard type." He made a note in his notebook.

"None of us would have."

"What about her work?"

"She's resigning from the dental practice. Says it's too hard without Dean there."

"I can understand that. Well thanks Amy, you've been a big help." He was struck by another thought. "One other thing. Did you adjust the topping lift on *Aurora* the day you took her out to spread Dean's ashes?"

"No, why do you ask?"

"Just checking a few facts. Thanks Amy."

"Call me if you want anything else. Bye for now." The line went dead.

Frank leaned back in his chair and put his arms behind his head. So, Ella Hampton was going to sell up and live aboard *Aurora*. That puzzled him. It did seem entirely out of character, leading him to ponder her motivation. If her decision was driven by grief, not wanting to be reminded of Dean in all the things they had shared, or an inexplicable desire to put her life with him behind her, then she'd hardly want to live aboard the boat he cherished. Or perhaps that was why she wanted to be aboard, to be constantly reminded of him through the care he'd obviously put into maintaining *Aurora* to such a high standard. Alternatively, could it have something to do with her being guilty? But why that could be the case wasn't obvious. It did mean Ella would be mobile, having completely uprooted herself, leaving him feeling the need to rapidly progress the investigation should she be planning to disappear.

The worst-case scenario would be for Ella to leave New Zealand before the investigation had progressed enough for him to confront her and potentially charge her. They could easily monitor the airports, but there was also *Aurora*. Any New Zealand registered boats wanting to leave New Zealand waters must first go through a number of safety and administrative matters before they could depart, including holding a current Category One safety certificate. Frank had noted that *Aurora* was already equipped with a number of the safety features required, including the lifeline netting. She also had a wind generator and a desalination plant necessary for ocean voyages. It would be surprising if Ella was capable of solo ocean sailing. However he couldn't rule anything out at this stage.

His thoughts were interrupted when Stephen appeared through the doorway.

"I've completed the handover with the next shift. If there's nothing more you want, I'll head off home. See you tomorrow Skipper."

"Thanks Stephen." Frank looked at his watch. "I think I'll call it a day too."

He hoped he would get the opportunity to focus fulltime on the Hampton inquiry starting tomorrow.

13

Amy was completely immersed in a set of accounts when her phone alerted her to a new e-mail. Fran was requesting a meeting with all the departmental staff that very afternoon. No sooner had she read the e-mail than Al came into her office.

"Have you seen the e-mail from Fran?" he asked, his face drawn into a serious frown.

She nodded. "I just saw it."

"What do you think it's about?"

"I'm guessing she's going to announce the cutbacks she's been hinting at."

"Everyone's been talking about it. Some are scared they'll lose their jobs and with home mortgage rates on the rise and the increasing inflation, now's not the time to be without work."

"The good thing about the meeting being today is that it will put an end to the uncertainty and gossip. There's nothing worse than being in a workplace where the future's uncertain and job security is on the line. It only creates an atmosphere of negativity and it doesn't help productivity."

Al smiled. "Spoken like one who ought to be in senior management."

She laughed, easing the tension. "I have no desire to be promoted. I like doing what I'm doing now and wouldn't like to be the one looking to make the cuts. She can keep her job and her salary—she earns it."

"Well, I'm sure your job will be secure with your track record. I wish I could be so sure about my own." He frowned again. "I guess I'll find out this afternoon."

"You'll be fine Al, you've no need to worry about it. You're an integral part of this team and we've performed well this year-to-date. They wouldn't dare dismantle a well-performing team like ours."

"I hope you're right Amy," Al said, leaving her to wonder what would be in the announcement.

Amy had come to respect and care for her colleagues and she didn't like the idea that some of them would be getting their marching orders. They were all dedicated to the company and worked long hours. She was quietly confident that she'd be okay after her chat with Fran last week. And Al was right in that now was a bad time to be without work, especially if you had bought a house when the market was peaking in the last few years. Many were now servicing a mortgage at ever-increasing interest rates, with some on interest-only terms just to survive. Food prices were increasing, along with all other necessities including the cost of getting to work. The economy was looking grim. If there were layoffs today, it would be a very sad day in the history of the company. And she doubted Fran had the personality or the experience to do it well. Worrying wouldn't help her colleagues and Amy turned her focus back to the spreadsheet in front of her.

*

That afternoon Amy and Al followed numerous other staff down to the lift and took it to the eighth floor which housed the conference room. The place was already abuzz with hushed chat as staff waited for Fran to arrive. As there were not enough seats for everyone, Amy and Al joined those who were already standing around the walls.

The venue was typical of the corporate meeting room. It had windows that looked out at the building next door along one side and windows into the hall along the opposite wall with vertical blinds for privacy. At one end was a screen that was rolled up with a projector placed strategically on the ceiling in front of it. At the other end was a large whiteboard that virtually filled the wall space. The room was furnished with fashionable wooden tables and the chairs were high backed and adjustable for comfort in the long meetings. In one corner sat an empty coffee percolator and mugs sitting upside-down on their saucers. The furnishings were more to impress their corporate clients than benefit the staff.

Fran arrived with a folder under her arm followed by her personal assistant close on her heels carrying a box. The room quietened in anticipation.

From the front of the room Fran cleared her throat and began. "Thank you all for coming today. The partners have been faced with a very difficult situation where it has become increasingly apparent that we can no longer afford to continue in the way we have been going. If it hadn't been for Covid-19 things may have been different. Now I know that you have all worked hard and the decision has not been an easy one. In fact, we have agonised over this for quite some time and have looked at all the possibilities to be able to carry on with the full complement of staff that we have today. However, we are all agreed that it has become necessary to make some cutbacks for the good of the company going forward. To this end we have scrutinised the productivity of each department and have had to make the tough calls." Fran was continually scanning the room, careful not to look at any individual.

Gesturing to her assistant, she continued, "I have with me a series of envelopes with a letter to each one of you. The letter will outline the future for you in this company. For some of you, it will be business as usual. For others, the letter will outline an offer for a new position within the firm. And that brings me to the last group. It is with sincere regret that I have to inform you that your time with this company is coming to an end and there will no longer be a position for you. We have done our best to offer you what we believe is a fair termination package and as is company policy, we would ask that you clean out your desks at the end of this meeting and that you finish up today. On behalf of the Partners and senior management group, I would like to thank you for all that you have done while in our employ."

A murmur went about the room.

"If I could have your attention for another minute." Fran's voice rang out over the noise.

Amy could feel the tension in the air as a hush settled over the room.

"When I call your name please come up and get your envelope and return to your office."

"Bloody hell, that's a bit tough," Al muttered under his breath. "Easy for her."

The noise level in the room steadily increased as Fran called out the names and one-by-one those present went up and collected their letter from Fran's personal assistant.

"Amy Fagin."

Al said, "See you back at your office."

Amy went forward, received her envelope, then left the room. Small huddles of people were milling about outside the lifts, some comforting colleagues who'd obviously received bad news. Eager to see what was in her own envelope but wanting to do so in private, Amy made her way back down to her office without interacting with anyone.

With a deep sigh and a shaky hand, she tore open the envelope and skimmed the letter. At the word regret, her eyes pricked with the tears that threatened them. She was to join the third group. They had dared to make her redundant—she could hardly believe it. After all the long hours and successes of the past year, they were cutting her off. The words on the paper blurred as her eyes filled and overflowed with tears, but she continued to stare at it. Unseeing. Stunned.

A knock at the door interrupted her thoughts.

"Amy?" Al looked concerned.

"I'm being scrapped." It was all she could say.

"You? No, how could they?" Al waved his envelope at her. "I guess that must mean I'm going too."

Amy looked around her office for something to pack her personal items in to avoid watching Al get his news—that was more than she could cope with just now. She couldn't see anything suitable to carry her things home in, not that there was much, only the usual photo frames, personal pens and bits and bobs.

"Woohoo!" He waved the paper before stopping to look apologetically at her. "I'm sorry Amy. It's just that I didn't expect to be staying, but it looks like I'm keeping my job after all."

Amy tried to sound positive. "That's great news—I'm really happy for you."

"What I don't get is why you're being made redundant if I'm staying. You've had such a stellar year. It should be you staying and me going."

"I wonder if it has something to do with my Parkinson's diagnosis."

"Surely Fran isn't that cold-hearted!" He paused. "You might be right though—we've been led to believe the redundancies are performance related. There must be another reason for you. If it's the Parkinson's, then she's a cow! I'm not sure I want to stay on and work for a company that'd make a star performer redundant because they have a health issue—it's not like it affects your work."

"Al, how on earth am I going to get another job when I have to front up with Parkinson's?" Amy pulled out a tissue and dabbed her moist eyes, trying not to smudge her mascara.

"It's so unfair. I'm truly sorry Amy," he said sincerely. "Tell you what, let's head down for a drink. I'll round up some of the others."

"Good, but first give me a minute will you? I need to call Terry."

"I'll go and find you a box, then I can help you pack up."

Amy picked up her mobile phone to call Terry. In a shaky voice she told him the news and the silence that followed told her he was as stunned as she was.

"Amy I'm so sorry. Looking on the positive side, we're in a reasonably good position and can make do without the salary coming in." In a gentle voice he asked, "Are you okay? Do you want me to meet you?"

"No, I'm fine. I'm going to go down to a bar with Al and some of the others for a drink before coming home."

"Well try not to worry, we'll be okay. And don't worry about dinner, the girls can help me cook tonight."

"Thanks Terry—I'll call when I am on my way home."

At that moment Al came back in with a box and packed up the items as she placed them on the desk. Once packed she took one last look around her office, then picked up the box and followed Al out the door, closing it behind her.

*

Later that evening when she and Terry were clearing up after dinner and the girls were in their rooms doing their homework, she said, "I'm thinking they've laid me off because I told Fran about my Parkinson's. I thought I saw the look in her eye when I told her my news."

"Surely they wouldn't lose a good accountant because of that. You've said she has been impressed with your performance."

"That's what she said, and this is what I was worried about, why I procrastinated over telling her."

He paused as he filled the sink to wash the dishes. "Perhaps this has a silver lining."

"How so?" She was gutted. Tonight she couldn't see past the fact that she'd been dumped. This bad news had come so soon after losing Dean that she felt her world was crumbling.

"You said stress makes Parkinson's worse—well this is making you de-stress your life. And we've talked about the need to exercise more, but it's always time that stops you. Now you'll have the time."

"That's called retirement and I'm too young to be retired. I love my career."

"What about looking for part-time work?"

"Maybe—but look at me!" Amy held up her hand that was trembling badly. "Who would want to take the risk and employ someone like me, when they don't know what I'm capable of?"

"You should get a good reference." He dried his hands and placed them around her. "It's not the end of the world. Use some timeout to get into good habits for your Parkinson's and take the time to work out what you want to do. You don't have to work if you don't want to. Over the years you've more than pulled your weight for this family and my business is going well. We're now in the privileged position that we don't need the money."

From tomorrow she'd have time on her hands. What Terry said made sense. That she and Ella would now both be out of work was odd. Perhaps this was the opportunity she needed to spend some more time with her. With a bit of luck she might be able to work out exactly what happened to Dean, but rather than air her suspicions again with Terry and risk a disagreement, she decided to keep this to herself. Fate may have given her the space to try her hand at being an amateur sleuth.

*

Frank looked around his new office. It looked more like a utility room, lit by artificial light with no external windows. A whiteboard complete with pens was fixed to one wall. There were two desks perpendicular to each other crammed into the space which would normally house one, however they were adequate and the chairs comfortable. Each had a computer and phone that were standard issue and a couple of paper trays. The space was uninspiring when compared to the office he used in the Maritime Unit, but it was functional and that was all that mattered.

His secondment had been rubber stamped and Central would be his home for the next week or two, or until they'd wrapped up the case. He'd swapped his regulation overalls for an open-necked white shirt, the sleeves of which he'd already rolled up, and blue trousers. Anahera had expressed her eagerness to work the case provided she could be released from her current work, which Brad had seen to, and Frank was looking forward to partnering with her again. He placed the few items he'd brought with him out on one of the desks.

"Welcome to the dream team!"

Frank recognised the voice before he saw her.

A wide grin was plastered across Anahera's face. "Look at you! Quite the detective now you're out of those ugly overalls."

He grinned back and said, "Just like old times. How will Land Search and Rescue cope without you?"

"Much like the Maritime Unit will cope without you." Anahera dumped a small box of things on the other desk. "Is this desk mine? I assume we won't be here in this broom cupboard long."

"Hopefully not. If I'm right about this case, we should be able to close it soon. And if not, then we'll be dropping it equally as fast."

Anahera removed her jacket and draped it over her chair. "How about you take me through what you already know?"

Frank walked over to the whiteboard, picked up a pen and wrote *Dean Hampton* in the centre and drew a circle around it. He chose the clean-shaven photo of Dean, because that represented the Dean he knew, which he stuck above the name with some Blu Tack® that he found in the desk. "As you know, Dean Hampton's body was washed up after allegedly being knocked over the side by the boom during a jibe manoeuvre on his yacht *Aurora*. The coroner ruled death by drowning. In addition, the body had incurred injuries consistent with those of a propeller."

"And the prime suspect?"

Frank wrote the name *Ella Hampton* out to the left of Dean's name. "His wife, Ella Hampton, was the other person aboard the yacht at the time and reported the man-overboard."

"And what makes you suspect this is more than an accident?"

Frank wrote a bullet point under Dean's name and the word *Jibe*. "His sister, Amy Fagin, came to me with concerns regarding Ella's story. The first related to the jibe incident which I have since determined was unlikely to have happened in exactly the way Ella first described it due to the conditions at the time, as well as the direction they were allegedly travelling in."

Frank jotted a second bullet point under the first with the word *Oar*. "The second inconsistency is the date a replacement oar was purchased. Ella told her sister-in-law it was purchased before the holiday she and Dean were on and I have verified it was purchased after Dean had his accident."

"And you're thinking the oar may in fact be a murder weapon?"

"It's possible."

"Any idea of motive?"

Frank picked up a different colour pen and wrote *Motive* Under Ella's name. "I'd like to find the motive before we bring Ella in for questioning. I'm hoping our scrutiny of phone logs and bank details will help us discover it."

"What do you think we are looking for?"

"Anything to suggest Ella might have been having an affair. The sister-in-law overheard a phone conversation that sounded both secretive and suspicious. Or perhaps the motive relates to financial issues—I've yet to investigate whether she's due any life insurance payout. Alternatively, Dean may have been the one having the affair and her actions were driven by jealousy or rage. Can you think of any other obvious motives?"

Anahera tucked her hair behind her ears, a habit she had when deep in thought. "Could Dean have been an abusive husband?"

"We can't rule anything out at this stage." Frank added the possible motives to the board as bullet points. "How about you start by logging a request to access the phone records of both Ella and Dean, as well as bank records and a full credit check?"

Anahera made a note. "I'll get a techie onto it. And what about the relationship between the deceased and his wife?"

"The sister-in-law thought they were close and went so far as to use the word obsessed. Apparently, Dean's daughter from his first marriage had concerns that they were arguing." Frank wrote *Sara Hampton* out to the right of Dean's name. "She's at university in Dunedin and I was going to call her for a chat—I think it's best I talk to her since I met her when she came up after Dean went missing."

"And we know Dean was a dentist, right?"

"Yes. And Ella worked for him in his surgery."

Anahera continued to ask questions and Frank filled her in on the background until he was satisfied that she was completely up to speed.

"Let's take a caffeine break and get started." Anahera stood up and pulled on her jacket.

"You sound eager. Shall we grab a decent one from a barista?"

They wandered down to Anahera's favourite café and ordered flat whites. Once back at their desks, Frank put a call through to Sara Hampton.

"Hello, Sara speaking."

"Sara, it's Frank Smythe, with the Auckland police. I met you when you were up after your dad's accident."

"Frank?" She sounded surprised. "What's the matter?"

"My apologies for the delay in contacting you. I wonder if you would mind answering a few routine questions? I need to wrap up some loose ends around your dad's case."

A short pause followed, before she answered, "Okay,"

"Is now a good time? And please know that whatever you say will remain confidential."

"Yes, now is good."

"Firstly, would you mind if I record this conversation?"

"I guess I don't have any objection to that." She sounded hesitant.

Frank started the recording. "Sara, how much time did you spend at home with Dean and Ella?"

"I lived at home with them for the first four years after Ella moved in, then for the past three years I've spent my university holidays at home."

"How would you describe your father's relationship with Ella?"

"They were close, they did everything together. I think he was infatuated with her." She paused and he waited for her to gather her thoughts. "Ella can be feisty—in the early years Dad just took it like a lap dog. Then over the last year they seemed to be arguing more."

"Would you say it developed into a volatile relationship?" Frank asked.

"Yes, that would probably sum it up. I'm not sure what it was that would set them off—they were always fairly discreet in front of me. But from the odd comment that I overheard, it might have been over money or investments."

"Did you ever witness any type of abuse?"

"Abuse? Not at all. Never." Her voice was firm. "It wasn't like they were arguing all the time—Dad still adored her. It's just that they never used to argue and then something seemed to have changed."

"When was the last time you were home, before the incident?"

"Before the start of the semester, around six weeks prior. Why are you asking all these questions? Do you think Ella had something to do with Dad's death?"

"Like I said, we are obliged to tie up a few loose ends." He paused. "What do you know about Ella's previous relationships?"

"Only that she'd been married twice before."

"Do you know if they ended amicably?"

"I truly don't know—it was never talked about. To my knowledge there were no children, and I don't think she kept in touch with her ex-husbands." She paused. "Why?"

"Just wanting to complete the picture. You've been very helpful, thanks. If I need anything else, is it okay If I call you back?"

"Sure."

"And please keep this conversation to yourself."

Frank hung up and shared what he'd learned with Anahera.

Having listened intently, Anahera said, "It sounds like something changed that caused them to start arguing. That's usually the way, when the going gets tough and all that."

"You're probably right. And I'm guessing the motive is related to whatever that pressure point was."

"So, we need to find out what that was. Hopefully the phone records and bank statements will turn something up." Anahera looked up at the whiteboard. "Is there anyone else who was close to them who could both verify Sara's account and know what their issues were about?"

"From what I understood from Amy, they pretty much kept to themselves." Frank thought for a moment. "It might be worth talking to the other dentist in the dental practice—maybe Dean had shared with him."

"Good idea. I'll keep chasing up these records."

Frank called the surgery and was able to get a time to see the dentist between patient appointments. Anahera was left to the task of accessing the data while he drove across to Dean's practice.

14

Frank parked in front of a neat white weatherboard house which had two signs outside: one advertised *Hampton Dental Services* and the other *Newmarket Dental Care*. Two receptionists sat behind a high wooden partition with gleaming wood grain, each intent on the screen in front of them.

As Frank approached, one looked up and gave him a pearly white smile. "Can I help you?"

"I'm Frank Smythe and I have an appointment to see David Fairweather."

"Please take a seat and I'll let him know you're here." She indicated to his left.

The waiting room was otherwise empty, allowing Frank to choose a comfortable looking chair that gave a view down the hall. Magazines were stacked on a small table and Frank selected one on boating. He was thumbing through it when a short bespectacled man approached. "Frank Smythe?"

Frank stood up.

"I'm David Fairweather. Please come on through."

Frank followed him down the hallway and into a room that had a dentist's chair in the centre and a sink at the side, a coat stand, a small desk laden with a computer and two large screens, and a couple of leather chairs. He indicated one of the leather chairs for Frank then sat at the desk in the corner of the room.

"I really appreciate you seeing me at such short notice," Frank said, sitting down. "As I explained on the phone, I'm with the police and I have a few questions for you regarding Dean Hampton. I shouldn't keep you long."

David looked at his watch. "That's okay as this is my lunch hour and my next patient doesn't come in for three quarters of an hour." He raised his eyebrows. "Why the questions? I thought Dean had had an accident."

Frank opened his notebook and pulled out a pen. "I'm just tying up some loose ends."

"I don't see how I can be of any assistance." David had a nervous disposition with eyes that flickered when he talked.

"How well did you know Dean Hampton?" Frank asked.

"We were colleagues, however I wouldn't say we were close. Apart from the odd social occasion when we got the staff together, we didn't tend to socialise. We were very different people with different interests. Dean was gregarious and I, well I'm not really the social type."

"Before Dean's holiday, did he seem upset to you? Did you notice any change in his demeanour or moods in recent times?"

"No, I can't say I did. Like I said, I really didn't know him that well at all. I took over my practice eighteen months ago and Dean had already been here for years. We each own our businesses although we share rent and reception staff plus some of the other overheads."

"What about his relationship with Ella? Were there any changes in that?"

"No, I can't say I noticed anything out of the ordinary. They always seemed like a close couple." He paused. "I did walk in on them having an argument not long before the holiday. That was unusual as they were always very professional when at work."

"Did you happen to hear what it was over?"

"Well yes, it was hard not to. I believe it was something about mortgage payments."

Frank made a note in his notebook. "He and Ella were having money problems?"

"I'm really the wrong person to be asking as I don't know anything about his private affairs. I liked to keep it that way." He hesitated again and appeared unsure whether to continue.

Frank waited patiently.

"There is something, although it's probably nothing. Dean wanted to cut one of the staff in reception, not Ella you understand. He thought we should save on costs, but that just wouldn't work well at all. We need someone manning the front desk at all times. Our patients expect that from us, and Lord forbid if I wasn't unrelenting on that one." He smiled, as if wearing the last statement like a badge of honour. "He wasn't usually one for budget cuts you understand."

"Is there anything else that you think might have been unusual or out-of-character?"

David looked at his watch. "No, that's pretty much it. Sorry I can't be of more help."

"Any interest in the sale of the Hampton dental business?"

"I believe it's nearly under contract." He looked towards the door.

Frank got the message. "You've been very helpful, thanks. And I'd appreciate it if you could please keep our conversation to yourself." Frank pulled a business card out of his pocket and handed it to David. "If you think of anything else, you can call me on this number."

They both stood and shook hands. Frank said, "I can find my own way out. Thanks again for your time. I realise it was an inconvenience and I appreciate you seeing me in your lunch break."

*

The drive back to Central had Frank replaying the conversation with the dentist. What was becoming evident was the Hamptons were having significant money problems. This theory was in part supported by the poor state of the bank balances he'd seen when preparing his report for the coroner.

He parked the car and took the stairs two at a time before going up to the office where he found Anahera staring into her computer screen.

She sat upright and crossed her arms. "How did it go?"

"Interesting but he didn't know a lot; claimed he didn't really know Dean. It does seem like Dean and Ella were having money issues." Frank opened his notebook and proceeded to relate the key points in more detail.

"I'll dig into their mortgage situation," she said.

Frank moved to the whiteboard and put a red line under the word *money* beneath *Motive*.

"We need to check if there was any life insurance as well."

"I'll check my emails to see if I have the credit check and bank statements yet." Anahera tapped her keyboard. "Good, they're here. Take a look at these."

Frank moved behind her to peer over her shoulder at the screen. Anahera opened a document and scrolled down; numerous transactions moved up the screen.

"Tell you what, how about I print this lot out and I'll go through it and highlight anything of interest." She looked at him with a good-humoured grin. "I know how you hate trolling through databases."

"Sounds good to me." Frank resumed his seat.

Anahera returned her attention to her screen.

Frank's phone chirped.

"Frank Smythe."

"Stuart, Sea Cleaners. I think I might have found what you were looking for."

Frank leaned forward. "The oar?"

"I can't say it's the same one you're after, but one of the lads did pick up a wooden oar last week. It had washed up on the eastern end of Waiheke Island."

"What did he do with it?"

"He took it home, thought it might be useful. I asked him to drop it into the Sea Cleaners base. It's here now if you want to pick it up."

"That's good news. I'll come down right away."

Frank hung up and grinned. "We may have had our first real stroke of luck. That was a contact at Sea Cleaners who said they've found a wooden oar. There can't be too many oars lost. I'll go and pick it up now and take it over to Forensics."

"See you in a bit." Anahera turned back to the task at hand.

Frank's mood was cheerful and optimistic as he travelled to the Sea Cleaners depot. Stuart was leaning against the wall in the reception area with his arms folded over his lean frame, chatting with Elaine, the office lady.

"Hey Frank, that was quick." Stuart unfolded his arms and stood up.

"Hi Stuart, how goes it?" Frank reached out and shook Stuart's hand.

"Things are going well here. I was just saying we have a full complement of volunteers at present—it's pleasing to see the growing interest in cleaning up our harbour and waterways. We're wanting to do more in schools to increase awareness there." Stuart regarded Frank thoughtfully. "Now what's this I hear about you moving off *Deodar III*?"

"It's a temporary secondment. I don't expect to be land-based for long."

"The boys will miss you—I gather skippers are an increasingly rare breed in the Maritime Unit."

"That's true. Ever think about joining the police?"

Stuart laughed heartily. "Not my thing. Now you'll be wanting that oar. I'll just go and get it—won't be a tick." Stuart disappeared through a door and returned holding a wooden oar. "Does this look like what you're after?"

"It could well be. I'll have to get Forensics to determine that."

"I'm curious about what you want with a discarded oar?"

"It may have something to do with a case we're working on." Frank pulled a sheet of plastic from his pocket and wrapped it around the oar.

Watching him, Stuart said with a wry smile, "It will have my fingerprints all over it, so don't go thinking I'm the guilty party. I promise I had nothing to do with whatever it is you're investigating."

Frank chuckled. "Don't worry, I think we can rule you out of this one."

He thanked Stuart and drove straight to the Forensics Lab, hoping against the odds that they could find some evidence to link Ella and Dean to it. It was a long shot given the time it had been in the water. If only they could find something, perhaps some DNA in the grain, they might have their first tangible piece of evidence.

The current waiting time for DNA testing was around a week to ten days. As oars come in many types and sizes, they would need to match it to the original oar aboard *Aurora*. While Frank couldn't be sure that an oar hadn't been replaced previously, meaning they were odd to start with, he decided to visit *Aurora* again to measure up the original oar.

*

Amy arrived outside Ella's house to pay her an impromptu visit. A large *For Sale* sign was on the berm beside the driveway with photos of the interior and a picture of an attractive real estate agent at the bottom.

She walked up the path and rang the doorbell. Ella answered looking lovely in a cotton button-through dress that accentuated her curves.

"Amy, what a surprise," Ella greeted her.

"I thought I'd drop by and see how you're doing."

"Come in. Coffee?"

"Please, I'd love one."

Amy followed Ella to the kitchen where Ella busied herself making them coffee.

"When did the *For Sale* sign go up?"

"Only yesterday."

"Is it going to auction?"

"No, I was advised to sell by negotiation."

"Are you still serious about living aboard *Aurora*?"

"Yes, I'm planning to give it a go."

They lapsed into an awkward silence that was soon broken by the sound of percolating coffee, its aroma heady and enticing.

Handing a mug to Amy, Ella asked, "How come you're here at this hour?"

"I've been made redundant. The firm had to make cutbacks after Covid and I was one of the ones to go," Amy answered levelly, trying to mask any emotion in her voice. "I'm still reeling a bit from the shock. My results have been good, especially over the past year and my performance reviews didn't indicate any issues, so it was unexpected."

"I'm sorry to hear that Amy. You've been having a few shocks of late, what with the news of Dean and your diagnosis. What are you going to do?"

"I don't know. I guess I'll take the time to work out what's next. In the meantime, I have time on my hands to make some healthy lifestyle changes. Exercise is good for fighting Parkinson's and I certainly need to do a lot more. I never had the time when I was working, but now I've no excuse. I'm also researching intermittent fasting and low carb diets as they seem to be the new thing for dealing with neurological problems." She paused to take a sip and was struck by an idea that was pure genius, giving her a practical way to get inside Ella's house to look for clues. She looked at Ella and smiled. "Hey, I've had an idea. How about I help you pack up? I'm available and I'm sure you could do with some help."

Ella looked uncertain. "I don't know. There's no rush—the house isn't under contract yet."

"I'd love to help you—I'm sure Dean would've wanted that." Amy wasn't sure if she'd overplayed her hand mentioning Dean's name, however Ella didn't seem to mind. "We could get some boxes and pack up the contents that you won't be needing and leave the furniture for the potential buyers to see."

"I guess it would be good to have someone helping me. The real estate agent told me to declutter as it makes the rooms seem more spacious. I thought she had a cheek, after all my house is hardly cluttered." She paused. "There are some things that I won't be needing. And I need to work out what is going to the tip, what goes to a charity shop and what I want to keep in storage. I had planned to start in the office. It's full of Dean's files and pretty much anything that needed a place to be stored."

"I can pack while you sort."

They drank in silence for a few moments.

"How about I buy some packing boxes for you? I could bring them over in the morning. This is such a beautiful home that I wouldn't be surprised if it's sold in no time at all."

Ella smiled at Amy. "Thanks Amy, I truly hope so."

They finished their coffee and Amy promised to be back in the morning with the boxes. She left feeling more than a little pleased with herself. Helping Ella pack gave her the perfect opportunity to have a good look about and perhaps discover the reason why Dean drowned.

*

The sun was shining as Frank walked down the marina to the pier where *Aurora* was berthed. Thankful that no one was around, he climbed aboard and opened the cockpit locker that housed the oars and found they were in exactly the same position that they'd been in on his last visit. It would be important to ensure the oar found matched *Aurora*'s oar. The easy way to do this would be to take the oar with him, but he didn't want to alert Ella just yet and so he decided to use measurements to establish if they were the same type.

Lying the original oar next to the newly purchased one they appeared to be identical, so he tapped the retailer's name into google on his phone and found the specifications. To be sure he had what he needed, he pulled a tape measure out of his pocket and measured the length of the oar, the length and width of the blade, the circumference and length of the grip. Each measurement was jotted in his notebook.

With the oars returned to their locker, he left *Aurora* as he'd found her. The drive back to the office was surprisingly slow for the time of day with some of the roads closed around building sites.

Anahera looked up as he walked in. "Did you forget the coffee?"

He laughed and sat down. "Anymore and you'll be dangerous. How are you getting on with the accounts?"

"Good. I'm ploughing through it all now; there's a lot of data. What about you?"

Frank filled Anahera in on the development with the oar before turning on his computer to send an email to the forensics technician detailing its specifications. Anahera was deeply engrossed in her computer screen.

"Bingo!" Anahera exclaimed.

Frank looked up and asked, "What do you have?"

"The Hamptons were having severe money issues. They have a separate account for Dean's business from which they took their salaries, as you'd expect. The business was trading okay, so no obvious issues there. They shared joint personal accounts. Looking at these, they use a revolving credit account which is running in the red by more than 100,000 dollars and that figure has been increasing. They had a first mortgage with their bank on their house which they topped up by 250,000 to one million dollars. But get this, they took out a second mortgage of 500,000 dollars on the house in 2021 with a second-tier mortgage lender. They must have been getting desperate with the interest rates doubling over the past two years."

"What caused them to get into that much debt?" Frank asked.

"I'm still working that through. There were three big chunky withdrawals of 250,000 dollars each in 2021 to an organisation called Pliotrade. As far as I can make out it is registered in Barbados, although I'm struggling to find more information on it. The mortgages must have been taken out to enable them to make these payments, whatever they were for."

169

"Were there any assets to show for it?"

"Not that I've found so far. Only the house, the boat and of course his business. And like I said, he appeared to keep the business separate."

"The boat is hardly a super yacht and besides, Dean has owned her for years, so we can rule that out. What about real estate? Are we sure they weren't operating a portfolio of rentals or into property development or any other type of trading?"

"I've run a title search under their names and no other properties come up. Nor do their names come up in a search on the Companies' website other than his dental business. There's no evidence of regular rental payments either. Six months ago, their credit rating took a dive because on the credit report a note states a loan application was declined. The revolving credit has spiralled rapidly into negative balance in recent months."

"Could it be a gambling problem?"

Anahera shook her head. "I don't think so. If it were gambling, you wouldn't expect to see three large withdrawals in 2021. A gambling addiction would likely show a drip feeding of debt. If the withdrawals had gone into a gambling fund, it would question the purpose of the Pliotrade company."

"Drugs?"

She shook her head again. "Possibly, but again you'd expect more purchases of smaller amounts."

"Interesting. That sounds like big time to me. Enough to make somebody desperate."

"Does it sound like something the Dean you knew would do?"

"No, not at all. I would have had him pegged as conservative when it came to business and investments." He sighed. "It makes you realise you don't always know a person or what they're capable of. However, we don't know it was Dean's fault they found themselves in that sort of debt. It could have been Ella."

"True."

"So, Ella is in financial trouble." His inflection inferred a statement rather than a question.

"It appears that way. I searched the statement data for payments to the insurance company and it seems like they had all their insurances with the same company. I'll need to find out what the life insurance premiums were and see when the policy was started, or if it was increased," Anahera sat back on her chair and stretched her arms up over her head.

"Let's go over what we know." Frank stood up, walked to the white board and picked up a pen. He rubbed out the word *money* in the bullet point under *Motive* and replaced it with the words *large debt* in red ink. "Dean and Ella were in substantial debt to the tune of..."

"1.6 million dollars, in round figures," Anahera finished his sentence.

Frank wrote the amount on the board. "Could it be that Dean's death was motivated by collecting insurance money to clear the debt?"

"She'd have to be an extremely callous woman to take his life for that," Anahera said in a flat voice.

"Could Ella have placed them in debt for reasons unknown and when Dean found out he got angry and they started fighting over it and eventually in the heat of the moment, she hit him with the oar and he drowned?"

She paused, looking thoughtful as she contemplated this. "That scenario is plausible. Accident or premeditated?"

"Could be either. In a fit of rage, perhaps accidental. Or else she could have planned it to get the life insurance payout." Frank rubbed his right temple.

Anahera said, "Alternatively, Dean could have been the one to place them in debt and again this caused arguments until that final one where she hit him over the head."

"Again, it's entirely plausible." Frank perched on the side of the desk. "We need to know what the nature of the debt was and who was responsible for it—him or her."

"And what his life insurance was worth and when the policy was taken out. That may be key to whether it was premeditated," Anahera added. "I'll send an email now to get the policy information."

Frank smiled. "I think we're making good progress."

"I hope so." Anahera turned her attention back to the screen.

Frank stared at the picture of Dean, muttering under his breath, "Poor sod."

"How about we take another coffee break to clear our heads and fire up the neurons," Anahera suggested.

The café was bustling, so they chose a quiet corner table to sit and wait for their coffees.

"Did you manage to wind up the cases you were working on in Land Search and Rescue?" Frank asked.

"Not entirely. I had to hand them over to my replacement."

"I'm honoured that you chose to come and work with me on the Hampton case then." He grinned. "Did the conspiracy-theorist guy that you told me about turn up?"

"Not up until the time I handed it over. It had been a low priority as you know, but he recently used a debit card from Great Barrier Island and I'm guessing that by now they will have located him. It's the perfect place around Auckland to disappear and go bush. Imagine not being missed by anyone, sad really."

The coffees arrived and they chatted about the latest endeavours of their respective kids before heading back to the office.

15

Frank and Anahera had been called to a meeting in Brad's office to discuss the case. They had just updated him on the dire financial state that the victim and his wife were in and the possibility that the missing oar had been found and was with Forensics.

"You still don't have enough to persuade a judge to issue a search warrant. How soon can you get the information on the life insurance?" Brad asked.

"Today," Anahera said.

"What about the phone records?" Brad sounded frustrated.

"Not as yet, but they're next on the list," Anahera answered defensively.

"I want to know what the cause of the financial problems was and if the life insurance was a motive for murder. This should be your top priority." Brad let out a long sigh. "Without it, you almost certainly won't get a warrant and I want the search done when you interview the suspect."

"I'm hoping the oar will turn something up that may help get the warrant," Frank said.

"I would have thought that would require a stroke of luck after the time it's been in the water, so I wouldn't be counting on that at this stage," Brad shot back.

Frank shifted uneasily on his seat.

"Look, I need you two to wrap it up soon. Concentrate on getting the facts together so you can get the search warrant and pull the wife in for questioning." Brad paused before looking at Frank and continuing in a quieter voice. "I'm getting pressure from above to return you to Maritime. They are apparently feeling

173

the squeeze without the full complement of staff. And we could do with some positive PR right now, so I want to put out a media release."

Frank and Anahera had left Brad's office feeling somewhat dejected. It was hard not to take it to heart. They didn't speak until they were back in their small office sitting at their desks.

"I feel like I've been to the principal's office," Frank said.

"Don't let him get to you. Those guys all live under constant pressure."

"That's why they get the banquet and we get the crumbs," Frank said with a smirk.

Anahera got up and went to the whiteboard, picked up a marker pen and tapped Ella's name. "What do you think the bare minimum is for us to have enough to question Ella?"

Frank looked at the board. "We need some evidence to catch her out on her lies. We have nothing concrete to suggest it wasn't an accident as she's claimed. If we're right, the motive looks like it's to do with their debt, but I'd like us to be clearer on whether it's premeditated or not. The timing of the life insurance policy will be critical to that, so we'll need to get that information."

"It would be helpful to know what it was that got them into trouble in the first place." Anahera sighed. "And getting to the bottom of that Pliotrade company won't be easy. We may need some help with that."

"Unless we can get it out of Ella when we question her. That's got to be our best hope," Frank said.

"We'll stand a better chance of getting the truth out of her if we can demonstrate that we see the holes in her story about the jibe and the purchase of the oar."

Frank considered that for a moment. "We can tell her we've found the oar from *Aurora* and it's being processed forensically, even if we don't yet have the results. That might help open her up."

"I think you're right. That's a card worth playing given we don't have a lot to go on right now. It's all circumstantial."

"We're going to need her confession," he said emphatically. "I recall a similar case where a suspect chartered a launch and his wife drowned after falling overboard. They had been having marital problems and he hadn't been a boatie at all. After the alleged accident, he didn't call it in for a couple of hours. It was all very suspicious, but we had no evidence and no confession, so we couldn't nail him. He got away with it, however I'd swear he was as guilty as sin."

"I think we just about have enough to confront her with during questioning, so it may be time for the search warrant. The answers will almost certainly be there in her computer."

"Let's aim to get a warrant by end of play tomorrow. In the meantime, I think I'll call Forensics and see if I can hurry them along," Frank said, picking up his phone. "Brad's right. We're going to need more evidence if we want to convince a judge that there are solid grounds to issue a search warrant for her property. I don't think we're close to passing that hurdle as yet."

"Must be my turn to get the coffees." She stood and picked up her jacket. "I'll chase the life insurance information when I get back. And the phone records—not that I'm expecting them to show us much."

As Anahera left the office, Frank punched in the number for the Forensics Laboratory.

"Cyril Williams, Forensics."

"Cyril, it's Frank Smythe here. I'm calling about the oar for the Hampton case that I left with you yesterday. Has anyone had time to look at it yet? We're under a bit of pressure on this one."

"Everyone is under pressure. But just a minute Frank, while I go and check."

Frank drummed his fingers on the desk as he waited.

"Are you still there Frank?" Cyril asked.

"Yes, I'm hoping you've got some good news for me."

"You're in luck. A hair was found wedged in a small crack on the edge of the blade and we've sent it off to ESR for DNA processing. Any evidence of foul play such as blood is long gone, unsurprisingly given the time it has been in the marine environment. However, it is our opinion that to be wedged in the blade like that there must have been considerable force involved. In the very least if it's a match for your victim then it will link it to the boat in question. We will need to get a sample of the deceased's DNA so we can match it."

"That's not a problem. I scooped up some clippings from a beard trimmer on board the yacht on the off chance it might come in useful. I'll drop the sample bag over to you now." Frank looked across at the file in which he'd stored the small plastic bag should it be needed. "How long until we get the results from ESR?"

"That's out of our hands I'm afraid. The good news is that of late the waiting time has improved to less than one working week. Not often I can say that of a government entity."

Frank let the comment pass. "What about the physical measurements of the oar. Does it match the ones I gave you?"

"We did check it against the measurements you provided, and they do match. If you could bring us the other oar, we could give a higher degree of confidence that they are a matching pair."

"I should be able to do that in a few days' time, once I've secured the warrant." Frank thought for a moment and added, "I will need an opinion around how the hair could have become wedged in the blade, should this go to trial."

"That sort of testimony would best be supplied by ESR since they're independent from us. They're highly respected as a Crown Research Institute with world class forensic investigators."

"Okay, but I shouldn't get ahead of myself. Let's get the results and see what we have. I'll bring down that sample for DNA testing in the next half hour. Thanks." Frank ended the call, opened the file labelled *Hampton case* and pulled out the envelope that contained the small plastic bag with the clippings he'd retrieved from the beard trimmer. He was labelling it when Anahera walked in with two coffees.

"Good news," Frank grinned. "The dimensions for the oar aboard *Aurora* are the same as the one found by Sea Cleaners. And Forensics have found a hair in a crack in the edge of the blade on the oar and have sent it away for DNA testing. I collected a sample from Dean's beard trimmer and I'm going to drop it off for them to match the DNA." He held up the envelope.

Anahera smiled in return, the dimple in her cheek prominent. "At last, some positive news. Here." She thrust the coffee at him. "Drink this before you go."

"Thanks. I've been thinking about the meeting with Brad this morning. Hell, it was hardly a pep talk," Frank said. "He never used to succumb to pressure like that."

"I'm not letting it worry me, although I did feel he was being unreasonable. It's not like we're being sloppy with our inquiries and we're hardly going to manufacture evidence, so what more does he expect?" Anahera sipped her coffee.

"I suppose I need to cut him some slack. After all, there's a lot more pressure on him now with the staffing shortages and the increase in violent crimes. The current wave of ram raids is the last straw—those kids should be home doing homework, not out causing mayhem."

"You're not wrong there." She stared at the whiteboard looking puzzled. "I can't help but think we're missing something here. If the insurance money was to prevent a mortgagee sale, why go to all that trouble of committing murder to get the payout and then sell up?"

"Unless it wasn't about a mortgagee sale at all. We need to keep digging." Frank downed the remainder of his coffee and stood up. "I'll get going then. Hopefully you'll have more good news on my return."

He left the office with the envelope firmly in his hand.

*

Ella opened her front door and dropped her gym bag in the foyer while she removed her shoes. The gym had been busy. She'd exhausted herself pumping more weight than she'd ever lifted in the past, finishing up with a fast 30 minutes on a gruelling incline on the treadmill. The punishment was for overindulging in gin and tonics—they were becoming a problem, especially when, on mornings like today, she'd wake up barely able to remember getting into bed.

After showering and putting her gym gear in the laundry, she made a sandwich and a strong coffee. Caffeine was essential to chase the last of the night's terrors away and clear her head. It was important to stay on top of her game.

Ever since the incident, she'd been suffering anxiety and insomnia. Unless she drank herself to sleep, she would lie awake for hours. If she nodded off, then as often as not she'd wake in the middle of the night fuelled with fear, leading her to pace the floor like a lioness trapped in a cage looking for a way out.

In the past, she'd always been strong and decisive. Dean had called her his shrewd and clever wife, only she knew she possessed

178

a side that he didn't see; he had trusted her and was absolutely besotted with her. Like most men he'd been easy to bring around to her point of view. She didn't like what she'd become.

Men had always been easy to manipulate. As a child she had enjoyed the benefits that came with being the only one, and a daughter at that, of a doting father; rarely did her father ever say no to her. Her first two husbands were easy to influence and after a while she got bored with them. Perhaps if they'd just occasionally stood up to her, she might have respected them more. Men seemed to find her attractive and too often thought with their loins.

Paranoia was becoming a problem. Like this morning, when she'd suspected someone was following her as she drove to the gym. But then when she pulled into the carpark, the car carried on.

Taking her sandwich and coffee with her, she went into the lounge and sprawled out on the couch. Her body needed a rest before she attempted the packing task ahead of her. Clearing out the last of Dean's personal items wasn't going to be fun, nonetheless she'd decided to dispose of them at a charity shop.

She worried that even her carefully made plans would fail. Should the house or Dean's business not sell then she wasn't sure what she would do. The insurance money would be a help, but she'd need it to clear debt and she'd always known that she would need the money from the sale of their assets.

The real estate agent was nosey and Ella didn't want her snooping about. Letting strangers through to view the home was bad enough, although a necessary evil if she wanted the sale.

And then there was Amy. Her offer of help could've been made out of kindness, curiosity, or even out of suspicion. She had always been the protective big sister type. That day they'd taken the ashes out and Amy had seen the new oar, she looked like she hadn't believed Ella when she'd answered her by saying it had been replaced before the holiday. There was a risk that Amy could start digging into things that didn't concern her. Ella would have to keep an eye on her.

There was so much to do to get away from here. Contemplating leaving made her smile. The thought of walking away from it all was liberating, like shaking off the old and walking away into the sunset, or in her case sailing away into it.

Managing *Aurora* and sailing solo was going to have its challenges, but it wouldn't be for long. While she'd never actually gone solo before, she had loads of experience sailing with Dean and he'd been a good teacher. She could do this. She had to do this.

*

Having dropped the beard trimmer clippings off at Forensics, Frank returned to the office and found Anahera looking upbeat.

"I've got the insurance information," she said in a voice that betrayed her excitement. She paused, maximising the impact.

"And?"

"I thought you'd never ask." She wrinkled up her nose. "Dean's life insurance cover was for 1.5 million which would nearly clear the debt. But get this, the policy was increased from 800,000 dollars just five months ago. Suspicious or what?"

Frank whistled. "Who takes out that much life insurance? I certainly couldn't afford the sort of premium that would buy me that much cover on my salary."

"Me neither!"

"Interesting. It would make sense if they'd upped it because of their debt situation," Frank said, sitting at his desk.

"That's what I thought, but the increase in premiums when they were slowly going out the back door only added to the burden of debt, that is unless they, or at least one of them, thought it might be cashed in." Anahera's exuberance was infectious. "But wait, that's not all."

"Okay, so what else do you have?" He leaned forward in his chair with his elbows resting on his desk.

"I've started going through Ella's phone records. They appear normal with no calls from Dean's phone since the day of the accident. What's interesting is that three calls were received since that day from a pre-paid phone that's not registered to anyone. And the odd thing is they were pinged off a tower on Great Barrier Island." She looked pensive. "What do you make of that?"

"From a burner phone? Now that is strange. Could there have been a third party involved? Maybe a lover?"

"It's an angle worth considering."

"Amy overheard a conversation the day after the incident. Does that marry up?"

"Yes, one was made around 1700 hours that afternoon."

"Maybe it has something to do with the Pliotrade payments."

"Quite possibly. It does sound a bit shady." She played with a paper clip looking pensive. "I wonder what they were up to?"

"That's the 60-million-dollar question."

"Perhaps she simply wanted to clear the debt and be free of Dean to take up with a lover. If so, he could be on Great Barrier."

"It's plausible." Frank got up and moved to the whiteboard, picked up a pen and wrote *GB mystery caller* in a space with a line linking back to *Ella*.

"Have you found anything out about her previous relationships?" she asked.

"No, not as yet. We may have to track her ex-husbands down, however that can wait until after we question her. I don't want them contacting her before we do."

"So, we're talking about two alternative scenarios that might warrant someone using a burner phone. The first is that Ella has been having an affair with someone who has recently been on Great Barrier and the phone has been used to keep it secret. The second is that whatever she was involved with that resulted in her and Dean going into serious debt is dodgy. So dodgy that someone is using a burner phone from Great Barrier to hide their communication with Ella. Are there any other obvious scenarios?"

"Blackmail?" he asked.

"So why kill Dean?"

"Maybe someone knows what she did, an eyewitness perhaps, and now they are blackmailing her." Frank wrote the word *blackmail* under the motives.

"So, she murders Dean to get the insurance payout and clear the debt but is seen by an opportunistic blackmailer based out at Great Barrier." She shook her head from side to side. "Sounds too unlikely to me. Besides the timing doesn't add up."

"Or whatever dodgy dealings they were into had something to do with blackmail, causing her to become desperate enough to go after Dean's life insurance money as a way out."

"It's possible. It would account for the large payments."

"It's another angle we hadn't considered." Frank sat back down. "Great Barrier seems to be significant. I think I might give Dave Watson a call. He's the local cop on the island and there's not much that goes on out there without Dave knowing about it."

"Must be the dream police job."

"I've often thought that. There're no gangs and no ram raids on Barrier." Frank picked up his phone.

"I want to finish going through these phone records," she said, looking at the screen in front of her.

Frank dialled and put his phone to his ear. "Dave? Frank Smythe here."

"Frank, how's it going?"

"Not too bad. I'm currently land-based and working a case at Central. We had a man-overboard incident a few weeks back and it's now looking suspicious."

"I heard about that. I believe they'd left Whangaparapara Harbour that day. What was the name of the yacht?" Dave asked.

"*Aurora*. Have you seen her around? She's a Beneteau Oceanis 43-foot with dark blue hull."

"I can't say I remember her. What was it you were wanting to know?"

"I'm curious to know if there were any sightings of anyone else having contact with them out there. Bit of a long shot, but there've been calls to the widow from Barrier using an unregistered phone."

"Sorry, but I can't help you with that." He hesitated. "However, I can put you onto someone who may be able to help. He's a bit of a hermit, lives in Whangaparapara up a remote track above the wharf. Has a telescope and spends his time watching the goings-on in the bay. If there was anything to see it would be unlikely to have escaped him."

"Thanks Dave. I think it might be worth the trip over. I'll give the Maritime boys a call and get a lift with them."

"Let me know your arrival time and I'll be there to meet you."

"You've been a great help, thanks." Frank hung up.

Arrangements were made for the *Deodar III* crew to ferry Anahera and himself out to Great Barrier the next morning. The thought of having the ocean under his feet again cheered him up and any despondency left after the morning meeting with Brad dissipated. Tomorrow was going to be a good day that would hopefully see some real progress made.

16

Amy had completed a Pilates class and finished it off with a run. Running had never been her thing, not because she couldn't run but rather it always seemed such hard work. Although not a fitness fanatic, she'd read that cardio exercise was good for Parkinson's and she was determined to slow down its progress any way she could. Now with more time on her hands she was trying to juggle cardio exercises with flexibility, balance, strength, cognitive tests and new movements that challenged her neurons to make new pathways. That was the theory. It made her feel like an exercise junkie, something she'd never been.

The hot water from the shower nozzle felt good on her body and she luxuriated under it for longer than she needed. Her wet hair was slimy with conditioner as she massaged her scalp. The water ran over her face and dripped down her body.

Exhausted after her workout, she felt alive and good despite her illness, more vital than she had for a long time. It was early days and yet her fitness was already beginning to improve, resulting in energy levels that she hadn't experienced since her thirties. Now with her redundancy, she had the time on her hands to take care of herself. It was ironic that the loss of her job turned out to be a precious gift, enabling her to truly battle this disease that was trying to steal her health.

Eventually she turned off the faucet and stepped out of the shower, wrapped herself in a large bath towel and prepared to go to Ella's home to help with the packing.

That Ella fully intended to sell Dean's house and go through with living aboard *Aurora* was a surprise, especially as she was going solo. How long that would last was anybody's guess. Amy would give it one month or maybe two—as winter approached it wouldn't be nearly as much fun. There had to be a reason why Ella was making such random plans and Amy was determined to find out what it was. Her hunch was that it was somehow linked to the motive behind Dean's death. Not for the first time she wondered if Ella had a lover, but surely divorce would have been easier; after all she'd been divorced twice before. If Ella had killed Dean it must've been an act of desperation, or else it was an accident. What could possibly have caused her to become that desperate was hard to imagine, like a cornered animal forced to lash out. Amy needed to find a clue and today was her opportunity.

Once her hair was dry, she put on her jeans with a favourite pink shirt. The back seat of her car was piled high with bundles of packing boxes, along with some rolls of tape that she'd bought. As she drove to Ella's, she thought about how strange it was that she'd made this trip more in the last few weeks than in the whole of the previous year when Dean was alive. She parked close to the front door and carried her bag and a couple of the bundles up to the door. The doorbell sounded as she pressed its button, footsteps came closer and Ella opened the door.

"Amy, oh how nice of you to bring the packing boxes." Ella was immaculately made up, her hair tidy in a braid and wearing skin-tight jeans and a white top.

"I said I would and I'm here to help. There're more bundles in the car, but these should do for starters. You'll need to direct me to what you'd like me to do." Amy walked past Ella and into the house.

"Shall we start with coffee?" Ella asked.

"That would be great, thanks. Shall I put these boxes in the study for now? I can bring the rest in while you make the coffee."

"Yes, the study would be good. I have a real estate agent bringing potential buyers through for a viewing later today, so I want to keep the other rooms tidy."

As Ella went to the kitchen, Amy went the other way through to the study. Although only the size of a single bedroom, a large window that looked out onto the backyard made it light and airy. Along one wall was a storage cupboard. A full bookcase with spines of all colours and sizes stood opposite. A large mahogany desk with a high back leather chair was positioned against the adjacent wall, cluttered with the usual office equipment including a computer, printer and two trays overflowing with papers.

Amy resisted the temptation to start going through the trays of documents, knowing she'd need to be sure Ella was suitably distracted to give her the time she needed. The computer was of more interest, but getting past any password protection would be difficult. The cupboard was likely to have files stored inside and that was another possibility. She would need to look for an opportunity during the day.

She placed the bundles and tape next to the desk and went back to the car to get another load before joining Ella in the kitchen.

"How is the house selling going?" Amy asked, accepting a mug of steaming coffee and sitting on a bar stool.

"There've been some potential buyers, which is pleasing as it hasn't been long. The agent thinks it should sell quickly. There's been one open home so far and she said there was some real interest, not just tyre-kickers." Ella sat next to her at the breakfast bar, cradling a mug in her hands.

"That's lucky. By all reports the market is fairly flat at present."

"This is a sought-after location and the house is in good condition, so the real estate agent's confident it will sell."

"It's a pity you've missed selling up when prices were still peaking."

Ella gave her a look that clearly said *butt out*.

Changing to a safer subject, Amy asked, "How have you been since the funeral?"

"Fine, thanks. Of course, I miss Dean terribly. And what about you with your illness?"

"It's work in progress. I'm focussing on exercise and am changing my diet to try and help slow down the progress of the disease. At least that's what I've taken out of the research I've been reading."

Ella didn't comment and they sipped their coffees in uneasy silence for a while.

Wondering how she could gain access to the study alone, Amy asked, "Do you have a plan for the packing today?"

"I thought we could start on the study and also the knick-knacks in the lounge," Ella said. "Did you happen to bring some tissue paper for the breakables?"

"It's in the car." Amy drained her coffee. "I'll go and bring it in."

Amy left Ella to put the mugs in the dishwasher while she brought in the tissue paper and the last of the bundles of boxes. When she got back, Ella was in the study constructing a packing box and taping the end in place. She got up and opened the cupboard doors where two shelves were lined with storage boxes, each neatly labelled.

"I thought we could start by packing these archive boxes," Ella said. "Perhaps you could begin with those while I sort the loose papers."

"That's an easy place to start," Amy said, moving to the cupboard. "I'll make up some more boxes first."

As Amy made the boxes three pings came from somewhere down the hall.

"That would be the washing machine. I'll just hang it out—I won't be long." Ella left the room.

Amy could barely believe her luck. Sounds of activity came from the direction of the laundry followed by a door opening and closing. Silence. The washing line was on the other side of the yard and out of sight from the study, giving her the privacy she needed. For now. If Ella were to walk past the window she would almost certainly catch her snooping. She'd have to work fast.

Without thinking of the consequences should she get caught, she moved across to the desk. The loose papers might be the best place to start. With a last check out the window, she started to rifle through them. Her heart was pounding in her ears. There were receipts and some copies of work memos on top of one tray. On top of the other tray were emails expressing sympathy for Ella's loss and a dozen or more sympathy cards. Under those was an envelope with the lawyer's logo in the corner. With badly trembling hands Amy opened it and pulled out its contents. Dean's will. She quickly skimmed it. Surprisingly, all his assets went to Ella with no mention of Sara, his only child. Amy stared at the page aghast before quickly replacing it in the envelope. Why would Dean not provide for Sara in his will? The Dean of old would never have agreed to such a callous omission and she had to assume Ella was behind it.

Under the envelope was a letter from an insurance company that confirmed Dean's life insurance cover was for 1.5 million dollars. The paper waggled in Amy's trembling hand as she tried to take in the amount. It was more than double what either Terry or herself were insured for. The policy wasn't with it, nor could she tell when it was taken out. Regardless, it was clear that Ella benefitted financially from Dean's passing. Maybe this was what had precipitated Dean's death.

To her relief all was quiet and still no sign of Ella out the window. The thumping of her heart reverberated noisily inside her head—so loud it was a wonder Ella couldn't hear it out at the clothesline. Her hands continued to shake as she flipped through the other papers, but there was nothing more of interest in the trays.

Adrenalin was pumping as she shifted her focus to the archive boxes in the storage cupboard. The top shelf was full of boxes of photos, each with a year indicated on the label and even one called *Negatives.* Beneath those were boxes of documents, their labels indicating their contents related to travel, insurance, education, medical, certificates, tax and so on. The boxes that were of greatest interest were those of investments and there were several of these with time periods marked on their spines.

With another check out the window, she opened the first of the investment boxes and found it contained manilla folders of papers. They were mostly statements and tax certificates from managed funds and a host of bonds and shares dating from before they were married. Having dropped the first box into the packing box, she opened the second box and found more of the same. It appeared Dean had managed a diverse investment portfolio prior to getting together with Ella, which they'd continued to grow over the early years of their relationship. The next box was labelled 2021 and looked similar, but as she thumbed through it she came to a section where the brokers' statements showed that the investments had all been cashed in. Interesting. What had happened to the money?

The last box was only partially full and the folder on top was marked *Bitcoin*. Inside was a statement from an exchange trader called Pliotrade showing three large purchases totalling 750,000 dollars. An involuntary whistle escaped her lips, causing her to nervously glance out the window—thankfully all was clear. The timing for the purchases was mid-to-late August 2021, when Bitcoin was still on the rise but nearing its peak. She couldn't see any evidence that they'd cashed it in. If that were the case, then they stood to lose a significant amount to the order of 500,000 dollars. Her earlier assumption that they'd made a killing on Bitcoin was wrong—very wrong. They'd lost a fortune buying near the peak and holding on to it after the collapse. Maybe they were among those who'd lost their passwords. Somehow this new information was related to Dean's death, of that she was sure. Her mind reeled, struggling to make sense of it. Dean and Ella had exchanged a solid investment portfolio for a speculative gamble on Bitcoin and may have made themselves insolvent. The fact the life insurance money was nearly enough to cover their losses seemed more than a coincidence. Now, with the sale of the house and business, Ella would be financially secure.

Amy was so engrossed in the documents that she almost didn't register a door bang. She hastily replaced the papers as she'd found them and was just putting more of the archives into a carton when Ella walked in. Her hand shook violently displaying her stress, so she sat on it to hide her guilt.

Ella looked at Amy and frowned. "You haven't made much progress. What have you been doing?" Her voice was sharp.

Thinking fast, Amy said, "Sorry, I've been on the phone."

"Oh, okay." Ella seemed satisfied and started leafing through the loose papers and sorting them into piles.

"Ella, did you want to file any of those papers before I put these boxes in the cartons?" Amy asked, trying to sound innocent.

"Good idea. Perhaps you could hold off for a little while until I finish sorting them."

"Shall I bring in a rubbish bag?"

"Thanks, that would be helpful. You'll find one in the bottom drawer of the island bench in the kitchen."

Amy went out to the kitchen and came back with a bag. "How about I start packing the pieces in the lounge while you finish here?"

Ella showed Amy where she wanted her to start and left her to it, giving Amy some much needed relief from Ella's watchful eye. Before her was an array of china figurines, a collection of small Limoges dishes, some old fine bone-china cups with saucers and some crystal glasses. With the pile of tissue paper at her side she sat on the floor by the cabinet and carefully wrapped the items one by one placing them in the packing box.

A mobile phone rang in the other room and she heard Ella answer it.

"Hello?"

Pause.

"You shouldn't be calling me."

Another pause.

"Soon, I promise. Someone is coming for a second look today."

A door shut and Amy couldn't hear the rest, but she was convinced Ella was hiding something. Maybe she'd been having an affair and was waiting until the appropriate time to come out publicly so she wouldn't be suspected of cheating on Dean. Then again, Amy could just be acting like a paranoid big sister.

The pieces of the puzzle were mostly there, but she couldn't quite put them all together. Ella had appeared to change her story about the jibe and Amy was sure she'd lied about the oar. Ella and Dean had lost money on Bitcoin and Dean's life insurance would mostly make up for the loss. And it seemed plausible that Ella had been having an affair. The only benefit from killing Dean over divorce was the life insurance money. That had to be it.

The best course of action was not to confront Ella but to pass what she'd learned onto Frank and let him deal with it. The packing could wait—this was more important.

She finished wrapping the trinkets in the tissue paper and carefully packed them into the carton while she waited for Ella to emerge from the closed study.

"How's the packing going?" Ella asked, entering the lounge looking worried.

"All done. You have some beautiful pieces; I especially love the figurines."

"Why thanks Amy."

"Ella, I'm going to have to get going. I can come back tomorrow if you'd like more help," Amy said.

"That's okay. I probably need to pack the study myself and there's not a lot more I can do until I get a contract on the house. I'll call you when I need some help." Ella's smile appeared forced. "I appreciate your help today."

Amy drove down the street and pulled into a supermarket carpark where she picked up her phone. She pulled Frank's business card out of her wallet and punched the number into her mobile.

"Frank Smythe," he answered.

"Frank, it's Amy. Do you have a minute to talk?"

"Yes, what's on your mind?" He sounded polite but businesslike.

"I've been helping Ella to pack ready for her move and I found a couple of things that I thought you might be interested in."

"Go on."

"In 2021 Ella and Dean invested 750,000 dollars in Bitcoin through an organisation called Pliotrade just before it peaked. I couldn't see any evidence to suggest they'd sold it. They must've lost a significant amount when Bitcoin crashed."

"How did you find that out?"

Embarrassed, Amy hesitated. "I have to admit I did look inside some paper archives at the house today."

"Thanks for letting me know."

"There's something else," Amy added, no longer sure she should be telling him. She drew in a deep breath. "Ella is the sole beneficiary of Dean's will; Sara isn't even mentioned. And Ella will receive a large life insurance payout of 1.5 million dollars."

"Is that so?" Frank sounded thoughtful.

Amy considered whether to tell him about the phone call and decided she had nothing to lose. She felt like a snitch although she'd already crossed that line. "Look I don't know if this is anything, but while I was there Ella received a phone call that sounded..." Her voice trailed off. "Frankly, it sounded suspicious. She shut the door so I couldn't hear it all, but the bit I heard made me think she might be having an affair. It sounded so secretive. I have a hunch it has something to do with why she's selling up and moving onto *Aurora*."

"What exactly did you hear?"

She relayed what she'd remembered of the conversation to Frank.

"Thanks Amy. You've done the right thing coming to me. We're continuing to investigate Dean's death and any information is helpful at this stage."

"I hope you find the truth soon. Goodbye Frank."

Amy ended the call and started the engine. It was done and now it was up to Frank.

*

Later that evening, after Maddie and Tracy had gone to bed, Amy was sitting with Terry having just watched an episode of a series they'd been following on Netflix.

"I came across some stuff at Ella's today that looked suspicious," Amy said.

"What sort of stuff?" he asked.

"I was wrong about the Bitcoin. Instead of making money it seems they may have lost a fortune by buying close to the peak and they don't appear to have cashed it in."

"Did Ella tell you?"

Amy's guilt made her look away. "No, I saw it in a file."

"Amy, please! Getting involved like this is not good for your health, especially after the stress of your diagnosis, followed by Dean's death and now your redundancy. And then there is the family relationship thing that you should be working hard to protect as big sister. You're not a detective."

"Well, I want justice for Dean—he deserves it. It's because I'm his big sister that I did what I did today." She took a deep breath. "And do you know what else I found out? Sara wasn't provided for in his will."

Terry looked up, his interest now piqued. "What? She's not?"

"No, Ella is the sole beneficiary. Don't you find that odd?"

"That is unexpected. I wonder what possessed Dean to do that?"

"That's what I thought. It had to be Ella. He must've been more under her control than I'd guessed." Amy added, "And she will benefit from his death with an insurance payout to the tune of 1.5 million dollars."

Terry's eyes widened. "You're kidding me."

"No, I'm deadly serious." She paused, realising how appropriate that particular turn of phrase was. "I passed the information onto Frank. He said they're still investigating it. I promise to leave it with him now."

Terry said gently, "Amy, I am upset that you poked your nose in where you shouldn't, especially after we'd discussed it. I thought you were going to help Ella out of goodness and not with an ulterior motive. Despite that, I know how strongly you feel about getting justice for Dean. I just hope you will now put it behind you, because we need you to focus on your own health and on slowing down the progress of this disease."

"I know, I will. I did work out again today—I'm trying but it's hard. You know it's not my natural default." Amy stood up and took his hand, pulling him to his feet. "C'mon, let's get to bed."

It'd been a long and enlightening day.

17

Frank was at home with the movement of the sea under his feet. The early autumn day was perfect with a clear sky and water that sparkled under the sun. *Deodar III* made steady progress on her way out to Great Barrier Island with her two passengers on board. Standing at the stern with the wind blowing in his face, Frank breathed in the salty air and realised how much he missed being out on the water. The distinctive smell of the ocean was to his nose as a good melody was to his ears. Being out here motivated him afresh to get the case wound up soon so he could return to his position behind the wheel. He missed the excitement of the sea and the changing daily caseload.

Ahead of them loomed Great Barrier Island, also known as Aotea, a volcanic island that was the jewel in the crown of the Hauraki Gulf. At nearly 45 km in length and 285 square kilometres, it made up the eastern border to the Gulf. Running between Coromandel to the south and Little Barrier Island to the west, it sheltered the inner Gulf from the relentless swells of the Pacific Ocean. Just 88 kilometres from Auckland, with a coastline full of beaches, harbours and bays, its interior covered in native bush, Aotea was the perfect island getaway and one of Frank's all-time favourite places. A sense of anticipation grew in him as they neared the island.

Deodar III was being skippered by Colin Bell, one of the younger Coastal Masters in the force. As he stood holding the wheel and manoeuvring her through the chop, he wore a wide grin under the bold handlebar moustache that only someone in the

Maritime Unit could get away with. Frank had been pleased to see Stephen Blackett was crewing for Colin today.

He turned to Anahera before asking over the noise of the engines, "Have you been out to Barrier before?"

"Never—although it's been on my bucket list," she answered, the wind blowing her hair across her face. "How many people live out here?"

"There're around one thousand or so residents who live largely off-grid, being mainly self-sufficient and relying on renewable solar power and the collection of fresh water."

"Sounds like bliss. It's just moved up my bucket list."

"Its remoteness attracts hermits and recluses, people who want to escape the busyness of life and those who want peace and solitude or to simply be at one with nature. That's what makes it the perfect place to hide."

"What's there to do out here?"

"Lots—that is if you're a hiker and into the outdoors. Such a pity this trip is purely business as I'd like to have shown you around. There are some great walking tracks threading across the interior." He pointed to a prominent peak. "The highest peak is Mt Hobson. A climb to the top is worthwhile as the views are 360-degrees and sensational. The Pacific Ocean on the east side rolls in over pristine white sandy beaches with clear aqua-coloured water. It's nothing short of paradise."

Her face broke into a broad smile. "You're beginning to sound like a travel brochure."

He grinned. "I've always loved this place. My parents owned a modest 28-foot yacht that we'd sail out here for holidays. They were some of the best times."

"Sounds idyllic."

"It was." He pointed to the harbour that was getting closer with its backdrop of sharp peaks. "That's Whangaparapara Harbour, our destination. We should be there in ten minutes."

"I can see what I've been missing," Anahera said, gazing at the majestic scenery with awe.

Entering through the headlands, Colin slowed to five knots and they made their way up the length of the harbour to the wharf, flanked by a hilly coastline covered in native bush. They passed the old whaling station on their port side. Two yachts were anchored adjacent to the wharf and beyond them were mangroves and mudflats.

As they neared the wharf, Frank spotted Dave Watson waiting for them. Stephen threw him the mooring lines and he secured the vessel. Frank and Anahera disembarked.

"Hi Dave, how are you?" He shook the other man's hand. "Meet my colleague Anahera Raupara. We're working the case together."

Dave was middle-aged and shorter than Anahera, with a generous girth. Dressed casually, he had a relaxed air about him. His face was weathered and seemed to be permanently creased in a broad smile. He offered Anahera his hand. "Pleased to meet you."

"Same here." Anahera shook his hand then tucked her windblown strands of hair behind her ears.

Frank turned back to *Deodar III*. "Thanks fellas. We'll meet you back here at 1300 hours."

"We'll be here Frank." Colin waved. "Glad to be your taxi service."

Stephen had looped the mooring lines from the boat around the piles and was already releasing them. He waved and *Deodar III* slowly pulled away.

"Frank, I understand you're looking for some information regarding the movements of people that were out here on the yacht you mentioned on the phone."

"That's right. It's a Beneteau Oceanis 43 footer with a dark blue hull. We believe two people were on board and she was anchored here for a couple of nights around three weeks ago. The man was tall. His most distinctive feature would have been his beard." Frank pulled out the photo of the bearded version of Dean and showed Dave. "He was lost overboard, turned up drowned. The other occupant is the suspect who was his wife, a stunning blonde woman—tall, slender, long hair. Anyone who saw her would likely remember her. Here, I have her Facebook profile." He tapped the screen of his mobile, then held it up for Dave to see.

Anahera continued, "We have reason to believe the wife, er... widow, has been having contact with someone based out here at Barrier. We're hoping to find any information that might tell us whether they entertained anyone while they were here."

"Or any other relevant information. For instance someone may have witnessed them fighting," Frank finished. "So far what we have is circumstantial and we need a bit more to get the search warrant and bring the widow in for questioning. You mentioned a local who might help?"

"There's an old-timer who lives up there." Dave pointed up the hill behind the wharf. "Jock Jones is his name, but everybody calls him Jonesy. He's a bit of a loner by all accounts. Hardly ever leaves his bach unless to go fishing in his aluminium run-about. Like many of the locals he's fairly self-sufficient. Never makes any trouble and keeps to himself. He spends hours with his eye behind the lens of a telescope, watching all the goings-on around the harbour—especially on the boats that anchor here, and there are a lot of them. He's an odd chap, but I'd trust him to tell the truth."

"Let's hope he can remember."

Anahera asked, "Would you mind if I take a look at that photo?"

Dave passed it to her.

"I've been focusing on the clean-shaven photo on the evidence board. He looks so different with all this facial hair." She looked pensive.

"There's no road up to Jonesy's place—only a steep walking track so we'll have to walk from here. He's expecting us and he'll know you've arrived."

The track, wide enough for a vehicle, wound its way steeply up the hill. They passed two old baches nestled in the bush and a neglected caravan that was partially secluded behind a thick curtain of trees and fernery. The track narrowed into an overgrown path that zigzagged even more steeply up to the crest of the hill then followed the ridge to a clearing that revealed a small house. Its wood cladding was badly in need of a paint job and some rotten weatherboards were visible. Dave led them along a concrete path and up three steps before knocking on the rickety door.

A scruffy man in his fifties with greasy hair, a face covered in stubble and hair that sprang from his neck, emerged. His faded green tee shirt and jeans were stained and ripped.

"Jonesy, meet Detectives Frank Smythe and Anahera Raupara."

Jonesy's hand was calloused and rough. "Pleased to meet you." His accent was strong backcountry.

Breathless, Frank said, "Good to meet you Jonesy. It's quite a climb up the hill to your house."

"Yer get used to it." Jonesy looked at Anahera but didn't move to shake her hand. "Anahera was it? Detective you say?"

Anahera replied in a smooth tone, "Yes, that's right. Detective Anahera Raupara."

Still breathing hard from the exertion, Dave asked, "Can we come in? As I explained over the phone, these are colleagues from Auckland who'd like to ask you some questions about a yacht that was anchored in the harbour a couple of weeks ago."

"Come in, come in." Jonesy waved them in.

The interior of the house was as much in need of a spruce up as the exterior. Ancient wallpaper was lifting and peeling. A 1950's style Formica table and four chrome-framed seats stood beside a small kitchen comprising an old fridge, a wooden bench and an enamel sink. An old-fashioned Chesterfield couch with a spring showing through the grubby brown fabric and a lounge chair were the only other furniture in the room. A telescope, the one item in the room belonging to the current century, was placed strategically in front of the window that framed the extensive view over the harbour and to Mount Hobson beyond.

"Wow, great view!" Anahera exclaimed.

"Mind if I take a look?" Frank asked, indicating the telescope.

"Go ahead," Jonesy replied.

The telescope was trained on one of the yachts at anchor below and Frank could clearly see the two occupants reading books in the cockpit.

"What is it yer wanna know?" Jonesy asked.

"Mind if we sit down?" Dave sounded determined to extend island hospitality despite their host.

"Be m' guests." Jonesy took his own seat in the lounge chair.

The three police officers all perched on the sofa. Frank, shifting about uncomfortably, had got the exposed spring and he took pains to avoid being pinched.

He cleared his throat. "Jonesy, around three weeks ago a Beneteau Oceanis 43 foot yacht with a dark blue hull named *Aurora* was anchored in the bay."

Frank held up his phone with the photo of *Aurora* taken at the marina. Jonesy stared at it without commenting.

"We believe there were two people on board. I can show you some photos." Frank pulled out the photo of Dean and passed it to Jonesy. Using his phone, he flicked to the Facebook photo of Ella and held it up for Jonesy to see. "Do you by chance remember the yacht and recognise this man and woman?"

Jonesy took his time before answering. "Yeah, I remember 'em. Why do yer wanna to know?" He handed the photo back to Frank.

"The man was knocked overboard and drowned after they left Whangaparapara. It would help us with our inquiries if you could tell us what you remember," Frank said.

Anahera opened her notebook and took out a pen.

"Yeah, I remember her alright, the woman was a right stunner," Jonesy leered. "She wore a teeny bikini—yellow I think it was. Yeah, that was it—looked good with 'er tan."

Frank exchanged a look with Anahera, who was trying to hide her disapproval.

"What else do you remember?" Frank asked.

"I seem to recall they were in the harbour for two nights, possibly three." He hesitated. "No, I'm pretty sure it was only two nights. She did lots of swimming and sunbathing. They came ashore a few times; he rowed the dinghy. I remember that 'cos they had an outboard, but he seemed to like to row."

"Anything else?"

"There were three of them for a while."

Frank sat up straighter on the couch. "What do you mean three of them?"

"Just what I said, they had a visitor, another man. I thought she must like threesomes." His weathered face twisted into a sleazy grin revealing the gaps where teeth were missing. "Lucky buggers."

"Can you describe this third man?" Frank asked.

"Well, I don't tend to take so much notice of men you understand." He smirked at Anahera before continuing, "He didn't have two heads, if that's what yur asking." Another toothless grin. "Nah, as far as I remember, he were just another bloke. Come ta think on it, they both might've been growing a few whiskers like most of the blokes round here. Nothin' special. But who could forget her?"

Frank exchanged another look with Anahera. "How long was this third man on board?"

"I didn't see him on the first night or the next morning. I'd thought there was only the two of them on board. Maybe they picked him up from the shore, or maybe he was down in the cabin for that first night—he might have been crook below decks. I can't say for sure." He paused to pick up a toothpick from the arm of his chair and proceeded to pick at his remaining teeth, before adding, "I first saw him that next afternoon and am pretty sure all three stayed on board overnight. The wind strengthened that evening and came round to more west'ly. Not a good anchorage in a west'ly so I wasn't surprised when they upped anchor and left."

"Did you see all three of them leave together then?" Frank asked.

"Nah, nah. The three rowed ashore that morning and the girl and one of the men rowed back before pulling up the anchor and leaving." He sniggered. "I remember they had to fight the current and a strong wind to get back to the boat 'cos they'd anchored quite a ways from the wharf. They were taking on a bit of water and I reckon she was mad with him for being such an idiot."

"Anything else?" Frank asked.

"No, I think that's about it." Jonesy looked pleased with himself.

"You've been a big help, thanks."

Anahera closed her notebook and put her pen back in her pocket.

"Yer not gonna ask me to go to the big city for a trial, are ya? I don't like leaving here, there's too many people in Auckland for my liking."

"If we need you, we could always have you testify on a zoom link," Frank said.

"Zoom link? What the hell is that? Some fandangled technology I 'spose."

"It's videoconferencing."

Jonesy looked bemused.

"We can sort something out if it comes to a trial. I'm assuming you'd be happy to give the evidence you've given us today?" Frank asked.

"Yeah, course I can do that." Jonesy's chest seemed to swell with importance.

Frank and Anahera stood up, followed by Jonesy and Dave. "I be seeing yer then," Jonesy said, walking them to the door.

After navigating their way back down the hill, they walked the short distance to the Whangaparapara Lodge to see if the proprietor remembered the couple and take the opportunity to get some lunch.

Situated further up the road from the wharf, the Lodge was in a prime location on a rise that afforded views of the harbour. A

Norfolk pine stood tall in pride of place on the lawn in front of the lodge and across the road bordering the mangroves were some gnarly old pohutukawa trees. A path led up to steps and onto a silvery wooden deck with a weathered outdoor table.

"I'll get this," Frank said, leaving Anahera and Dave to take their seats. It wasn't difficult to relay their orders at the bar—fish and chips all round and a glass of lager each to wash it down. He explained who he was and asked the proprietor if they could have a few minutes of his time when he got the chance.

Back outside, Frank asked Anahera, "So what do you make of what Jonesy had to say?"

"To be honest, I thought he was a creep and I wouldn't be happy with him watching me through that telescope. Have you ever had a problem with him Dave?" Anahera asked.

"No—he's an odd one. He keeps to himself and is harmless enough. So long as he only watches and doesn't touch. I've never had a complaint about him."

"That aside, it's interesting that he remembers three people on board." She looked at Frank. "Obviously a friend or acquaintance of both Dean and Ella."

"Does that rule out the lover motive?"

"No, not at all." Anahera looked pensive. "What if the mystery visitor was Tony Newton? Remember the loner I told you about who'd gone A.W.O.L. and then had used his debit card out here on Barrier?"

"I suppose it's possible." Frank frowned.

"It's as good a guess as any at this stage. They knew him, his bank statements showed he'd paid Dean's dental practice and so I assume he was his dentist."

"But how likely is it that this...er..." Frank stuttered.

"Tony Newton," Anahera filled in.

"Tony Newton is a friend?" Frank paused. "How likely is it that a loner would socialise and stay overnight with his dentist?"

"I don't know," Anahera answered. "Tony Newton kept a beard. Maybe Ella has a thing for the rugged type."

"Are you suggesting Ella might be having an affair with this Tony Newton?" Frank asked.

"Maybe—although it would be surprising given everything I know about the guy. A loner, a conspiracy theorist, not known to be a sailor." Anahera played with her phone. "His mother did think he might be seeing someone."

"If she's planning to live on the boat, and if he's not a sailor, then that does sound strange." Frank paused, considering what they'd learned. "Maybe they knew Tony was out here on holiday and invited him to visit them on *Aurora*. They could've picked him up from the wharf here and had him to stay overnight, which could make sense if they were having a few drinks. It could all be innocent and unrelated to Dean's death."

"We know that there was no third person on board when Coastguard boarded her after Dean went missing so they must have dropped him off at the wharf before they set sail just as Jonesy said." Anahera's voice betrayed her excitement. "Isn't it strange that Ella never mentioned it when questioned about that day? Surely, she would've said they'd entertained a visitor and dropped him off."

"Unless she was hiding an affair. It could also account for the phone calls to Ella that pinged off Barrier," Frank said.

They sat in silence for a while before Anahera said, "It may not have been Tony at all, simply a coincidence that he was out here. We don't know if he was on Barrier the whole time he was missing nor even if he was here at the same time *Aurora* was here."

"You know what I think of coincidences," Frank said with a wry smile.

Dave had been watching and listening intently as the conversation had flowed between them. He said, "There's lots of accommodation on the island, especially at this time of year when schools are back. This lodge is popular, plus there are many more places around the island including baches to rent through the likes of Air BnB."

"We'll need to check out where he might be staying and how he travelled out here. I'll check in with the Land Search and Rescue guys who were wrapping up the paperwork where I left off," Anahera said.

Frank leaned forward, planted his elbows on the table and rested his chin on his hands. "It's possible that all three of them left Auckland for a holiday. When they arrived in Whangaparapara, Tony was seasick and down below, which could be why Jonesy hadn't seen him. That could make sense given he's not used to the motion of the sea. Then he surfaced, when Jonesy saw him. Then they would've had to leave him on the island for some reason. Maybe because he couldn't face more seasickness."

"Didn't Ella say they'd been at Port Fitzroy before coming down here? Surely you wouldn't be down in the cabin sick for all of that time."

"We need to interview Tony Newton," Frank said.

The proprietor arrived carrying three plates of fish and chips garnished with salad greens; one plate was balanced on his forearm and one in each hand. "I'll just bring out the lagers and we can have that chat if you'd like."

"Looks yum," Anahera said, selecting some utensils from a jar and popping a chip into her mouth.

The proprietor came back with the beers and took a seat at the table. "What was it you were after?"

Frank introduced Anahera and took out the photo and placed it in front of him before getting Ella's photo up on the screen of his phone. "Do you remember seeing this couple?"

"I can't be sure, sorry. We have a lot of folks through here."

"They had a Beneteau Oceanis 43 footer with a blue hull. They were anchored in the harbour for two nights around three weeks ago."

"No sorry, I don't remember them."

"Do you recall if you've had a Tony Newton staying at the lodge?" Anahera asked.

"No, I'm fairly confident I'm right in saying no one by that name."

"Not to worry, it was worth a try." Anahera smiled, her dimple showing. "This is great fish and chips, thanks."

"Our pleasure. I hope you find what you're looking for," he said, getting up and going back inside.

"I have a register of all the accommodation on the island. I can send it to you when I get back to Claris later today," Dave said. "Many of them are holiday baches owned by Aucklanders. Most don't have telephones, so it's a bit of a mission to find out which are occupied and by whom."

While they finished their meals Dave filled them in on the type of work he handled out on Great Barrier. Back at the wharf, *Deodar III* was waiting for them and they farewelled Dave who made an offer to follow up if they needed anything more.

Later that day, Anahera added Tony Newton's name with a question mark to the whiteboard in their office.

Frank said, "I think we should apply for that warrant. I reckon we have enough to persuade a judge to grant it. What do you think?"

"It's time. I doubt we'll make any more progress until we question Ella and search her place." Anahera sat back down.

"I don't expect she'll confess and make it easy for us."

"We'll see."

Frank lodged the request for the warrant and believed the net was finally closing. Following a short meeting with Brad to update him on their progress, he called it a day. As he reflected on the strange yet fortuitous meeting with Jonesy, he was hopeful that they were on the cusp of solving the case and finally shedding light on the circumstances surrounding Dean's death.

18

Anahera and Frank parked down the street from Ella's house, waiting for the search team to arrive. From their position they could see the *For Sale* sign standing boldly on the berm.

"I called Sandie who took over my caseload at Land Search and Rescue. They're no further along with locating Tony Newton," Anahera said. "The case has continued to be on the back burner ever since he surfaced on Barrier using his debit card. He still hasn't come home. They believe he remains off grid somewhere out at the island. She was going to follow it up and get back to me, but there's still no word."

"We need to rule him out of our inquiries if he's not involved." Frank picked up his mobile phone. "I'll give Dave Watson a call and ask for his help in chasing up accommodation places, starting with those in the vicinity of Whangaparapara. I'll suggest he looks for Tony Newton in the first instance and then anyone who may have gone aboard *Aurora* on the dates in question."

"Good idea."

Frank made the call and Dave said he'd get onto it immediately.

He ended the call just as two squad cars pulled up behind them. The rain was light as they walked quickly to Ella's door. Anahera's face was grim as she rang the doorbell. The four uniformed constables, three men and a woman from the other two cars, came up the path behind them and huddled under the portico to stay dry. Ella opened the door, immaculate as ever in tight jeans, a black sweater and hair pulled back into a high ponytail. Her eyes widened with surprise when she saw the contingent of police.

"Yes?" she asked, a deep frown creasing her forehead.

"I have a warrant to search your house and yacht," Frank said, flashing the warrant paper in front of her.

"What's this about?" Ella asked sharply, her eyes narrowing and jaw jutting out.

"We are investigating Dean's death and would like to ask you some questions." Frank shuffled his feet. "We would like you to accompany us to the station to help us with our inquiries."

"I suppose so." Ella frowned before standing back to allow them to enter. "You'd better take your shoes off then."

"Ella, this is my colleague Detective Anahera Raupara. She will be interviewing you with me today," Frank said.

"I suggest you get your coat and shoes and prepare to come down to Auckland Central Police Station. Frank and I will take you down there as soon as we've finished here." The authoritative tone in Anahera's voice sounded like a schoolteacher addressing her pupil. "When you are ready, I suggest you wait in the kitchen."

"Do you have a hairbrush or anything of Dean's that we could get a sample of DNA from?" Frank asked.

Ella looked at him with contempt, replying, "I've thrown all of Dean's things out in preparation for the move. Nothing left, sorry."

Frank followed the constables as they went from room to room, peering into cupboards and leafing through papers. Looking through the walk-in wardrobe and chest of drawers he found she had indeed removed any trace of Dean. A masculine-looking manicure set was on a shelf in the ensuite vanity and Frank asked for it to be put in an evidence bag. In the study he instructed them to pack up the computer and bring it down to the station where he'd get one of the techies to go through it. Two packing boxes were stacked in the corner and after a quick check he discovered they contained the archives of files that Amy had mentioned so he asked that they too be brought back to the station.

Ella appeared to be sulking on a barstool in the kitchen when Frank entered.

"Could you please give me the keys to *Aurora*?" Frank asked.

Without a word, she retrieved them from a drawer in the kitchen and passed them to him.

"And your mobile phone?" he asked.

"When will I get it back?"

"This shouldn't take long. All going well, you should have it later today." He looked at her and added in a softer voice that he hoped would take some of the tension out of the situation, "Ella, I realise how much of a shock this must be and how inconvenient it is. If you have nothing to hide, then we'll soon be able to complete our investigation and put a line under the whole thing, but right now there are too many unanswered questions. Please bear with us."

"What questions Frank?" she asked.

"We'll explain everything back at the station."

She retrieved the phone from her handbag and reluctantly handed it over, glaring icily at him. He placed it in an evidence bag.

Ella paced the kitchen. After a while, she asked, "How much longer?"

"It'll take as long as it takes," Anahera answered. Then added less aggressively, "We shouldn't be too much longer."

Once satisfied that they had what they needed, he ordered Jimmy, one of the constables, to go to Westhaven and search *Aurora*, and to take the old oar without the price sticker from the cockpit locker and deliver it to Forensics. He also asked him to arrange for Forensics to go over the boat and to get a techie to go through the GPS data to see if they could recover the tracking information for the trip back from Barrier. To prevent the possibility of a mix up, Frank went over the information twice, outlining where she was berthed and what to look for.

He and Anahera accompanied Ella to their car where Frank opened the back door and held it for her to get in, ensuring she didn't knock her head in the process. A neighbour watched from their window, and another was in their front garden despite the light rain. The four constables carried the contents uplifted in the search out to their vehicles and drove off. All in all, it had been a seamless operation.

*

Back at Central, Anahera took Ella into the interview room while Frank contacted Forensics to advise them to expect the oar for matching with the one they'd already processed. For now, the manicure set could wait. Then he made a quick call to Brad to let him know they were about to conduct the interview.

Anahera and Ella were seated in the small windowless interview room when he joined them.

"Am I under arrest?" Ella sounded defiant.

"No, you're just here to answer some questions," Anahera answered levelly. "You have the right to remain silent, you do not have to make a statement, anything you say may be recorded and given as evidence in court. You have the right to speak to a lawyer without delay and in private before deciding whether to answer any of our questions. The police have a list of lawyers you may speak to for free. Do you understand?"

"Yes." Ella glared at Anahera. "I don't want to say anything without my lawyer present."

Anahera looked at Frank, who answered, "That's fine Ella. You can make a call to your lawyer." He went out and brought in a phone which he plugged into a wall jack and passed to her.

"Can you get me the number for Suzie Laselles from Laselles Fenwick?"

Anahera raised her eyebrows at Frank who then looked up the number.

Ella made her phone call and was instructed not to say anything without her lawyer present, so they left her to stew in silence. Half an hour later they were back in the interview room where Suzie Laselles introduced herself as Ella's lawyer. The sides of her head were short shaven with a longer shock of blonded hair on top that flopped over to the left side. She wore a black pants suit with a white shirt buttoned up to the neck. Her manner reflected her reputation of being a fox terrier in the courtroom where she'd made her name defending career criminals. How she came to be Ella's lawyer of choice was an interesting question.

"I need some time alone with my client." Suzie wasted no time on preliminaries.

"We'll wait outside in the corridor." Anahera sounded equally brusque.

Anahera and Frank stood outside in the corridor for ten minutes planning their approach to the interview in hushed tones before Suzie invited them back into the room.

"Let's get started." Anahera looked at Ella. "Ella, we are video recording this interview. For the record, please state your full name, date of birth and address."

Ella looked at Suzie who nodded in the affirmative and she complied in a submissive voice.

"Ella, we are interested in the events surrounding the man-overboard incident that led to Dean's death. I know you've already told us your story, but we need to go over it again. So please bear with us." Frank spoke with a conciliatory voice.

He looked at Anahera, who took over. "Ella, for the record can you please tell us what happened on the day Dean drowned?"

Ella looked at Suzie who said, "Just tell them the truth, you have nothing to hide."

Ella answered, "We were on holiday and had anchored in Whangaparapara Harbour for two nights. On the second night the wind got up and was blowing up the harbour making it an uncomfortable night at anchor, so we didn't get a lot of sleep because the boat was rocking around in the chop and the wind was noisy in the rigging. We only had three days of holiday left and so we decided to head for home. We left the harbour and were sailing for Westhaven. But then Dean wanted to go down to Coromandel because he didn't want the holiday to end and so we changed direction. We were running downwind under full sail when a swell forced *Aurora* to jibe and the boom hit him on the back of the head knocking him overboard." Ella stopped, tears brimming in her eyes, before lowering her head to cover her face with her hands.

"What did you do then?" Anahera asked.

Suzie placed her hand on Ella's back and said, "Ella, you don't have to answer if you don't want to."

"It's okay." Ella raised her head, wiped her eyes with the back of her hand and took a deep breath. "I rounded up into the wind, then I took the sheets out of the cleats and let the sails flap. I had to reach down and turn the motor on to get control of the boat. All this time I had my eyes off him and by the time I looked again, he'd gone from view. Behind the swells. I searched for a while, I'm not sure how long, before I went down into the cabin to call in the mayday."

"Where was Dean when he was hit?" Frank asked, taking over the questioning.

"Standing on the starboard cockpit seat."

"And why was he standing there? What was he doing?"

"I don't know."

"Where were you?"

"Sitting on the port cockpit seat."

"Did you actually see him get hit?"

"No, but I heard the impact and saw him go over." Her gaze was steady.

"Did you see him in the water?"

"Only initially, before I got busy with the sails."

"You had said he was hit on the back of the head."

Ella looked like she'd been cornered but recovered quickly. "I must have seen it hit him—I've obviously forgotten. It was all so traumatic."

"And you were sure he was hit on the head?"

"Yes."

"I seem to recall Dean was about my height, is that right?"

"Yes." Ella said it slowly, as if unsure.

"When I stood on the cockpit seat the boom was nowhere near my head level. How do you explain that?"

"I... I don't know," she stuttered.

"Did you adjust the topping lift?"

Ella frowned. "No, why?"

"It's all part of the scene. Why would he have left the wheel if you were sailing on the point of the jibe?" Frank asked.

"I don't know."

"Did you in any way cause Dean to fall overboard?" Frank eyeballed her.

Ella held his gaze. "No."

With a look from Frank, Anahera took over the questioning. "Did you argue that morning?"

Suzie interjected, "You're badgering my client and she doesn't need to answer these questions. This is nothing more than a fishing expedition."

Ella looked from Suzie to Frank, saying, "I've nothing to hide. We had a disagreement over whether to go home, but I wouldn't call it an argument as such."

"Where were you when you changed direction?"

"I'm not sure."

"How long had you been sailing before changing direction?"

"I don't know. Maybe an hour, maybe more."

"When you put the sails up after leaving the harbour, what was your heading relative to the wind?"

"We were on a starboard tack."

"Did you have the sails reefed?"

She hesitated. "Yes, we had two reefs in. We took them out when we turned off the wind."

Suzie quickly intervened and saying, "That's enough. Either charge Ella or this interview is over."

Frank responded calmly. "We just have a few more questions. We'd appreciate your cooperation."

Anahera stepped back into the fray and turning to Ella, she said, "Ella, this shouldn't take much longer." She paused for effect, looking at her notes. "There is a new oar on board. When did you lose the old oar?"

Ella looked surprised. "We lost it prior to our holiday and had to buy a replacement. Why?"

Anahera ignored her question and asked, "When did you buy the new one?"

"I'm not sure."

"Was it before or after your holiday?"

Ella's eyes darted from Anahera to Frank and back to Anahera. She answered in a quiet resigned voice, "After."

"So, when did you lose the oar?"

"Like I said, before the holiday."

"So, you went away to Great Barrier on holiday for a week with only one oar to row the dinghy with. Is that what you're telling us?"

"Yes. We have an outboard motor for the dinghy."

"Isn't that unusual? To not have a pair of oars on board?" Anahera held Ella's gaze.

Ella didn't comment.

"Just so you know, an oar was found that matches your one and we currently have Forensics analysing it."

Ella maintained a poker face. "If you're trying to insinuate that I killed Dean, you're wrong. I loved him and would never hurt him. You've got this all wrong."

"Forensics found a hair in a crack in the blade, which is away for DNA testing."

Ella stared with lips slightly parted.

"Did you have a third person on board at any time when you were out at Whangaparapara?" Anahera asked.

A fleeting look of surprise passed over Ella's face and she looked at Suzie.

"I would like to speak to my client alone," Suzie said firmly.

Anahera formally suspended the interview and turned off the recorder. She and Frank picked up their things and left the room without a word, closing the door behind them.

Outside Anahera asked, "What do you think?"

"Her story about the jibe is consistent with her earlier account, but that's not surprising. She's had a lot of time to think about it," Frank answered, looking thoughtful. "Her answers about the missing oar are weak. And you caught her off guard with your last question. It certainly makes me think we're on the right track."

"I think we have her worried. She knows we're onto her."

"We're going to need more if we're going to charge her. We can't keep her in for too long without an arrest."

"We need to establish her motive." Anahera looked like a hunter going for the kill. "I'll pursue the third person when we get back. Once we exhaust that avenue I'll switch to the finances."

"You're doing a good job in there. Given you've not been involved with her before, I think you should keep the lead." He grinned. "I'll play the good cop and get the coffees."

She smiled. "We make a good team."

"I'll go check on the lads. Give me a call when we're back in."

Frank went back to their office and sank into his chair. He was more convinced than ever that Ella was guilty and was determined to get justice for Dean. He pulled out his mobile and found Jimmy in his contacts.

"Jimmy, Frank here. How's it going with *Aurora*? Did you find the oar?"

"All good Frank. I have the oar. Just to be certain, it was the one without the price sticker you wanted, correct?"

"Yes, that right. Can you take it into the Forensics lab for me?"

"Will do. I've searched the boat, but I can't see anything of interest on board. Forensics have one of their team here and I'm waiting for the techie to arrive to get the GPS information."

"Good. I had a look at the chart plotter myself when she first came in from the trip and noted the tracking was turned off. I'm hoping he can still recover it—that sort of thing is beyond my skillset," Frank said.

"I know what you mean. I'll let you know if they find anything."

"Thanks." Frank ended the call.

At that moment Anahera poked her head in to tell him they were back on. They re-entered the interview room and took their seats.

After advising that they were again recording, Anahera asked, "Ella, did you have a third person on board your yacht when you were out at Great Barrier?"

Ella stayed mute.

Suzie said, "I have advised my client not to answer that."

Anahera looked at Frank. They were definitely onto something.

"Do you know a Tony Newton?" Anahera asked, pressing the line of questioning further.

"Who?" Ella asked, sounding vague.

"Tony Newton."

A look of panic flittered across Ella's face before she turned to look at Suzie, who said, "You don't need to answer that."

"It's okay." She looked back at Anahera. "There was a Tony Newton who was a patient of Dean's."

"Did you happen to see him out at Great Barrier?" Anahera persisted.

Again, Ella looked at Suzie.

Suzie said, "I advise my client not to answer that question."

"Who called you from Great Barrier after you returned home following Dean's drowning?"

The colour drained from Ella's face. Suzie intervened once more saying, "I advise my client not to answer that question."

Frank checked his watch. "How about we take a break and get you some refreshments. Would you like some sandwiches and a drink?" He gave Ella his best good cop smile.

Frank left the room to arrange for someone to take care of their requests while Anahera ended the recording before joining Frank for lunch in their office.

"The extra person is a touchy point," Anahera commented to Frank between mouthfuls of salad.

"You're right. We don't yet know who or why they are relevant. We're assuming Tony Newton, but we may be wrong. We need to find him." He tucked into another sandwich.

Anahera paused to take another mouthful. "I think I'll start on the finances after lunch and see where we get to there."

They finished their lunch and Anahera went along to the staff kitchen to make them coffees. While she was away Frank's phone rang.

"Frank," he answered.

"Jimmy here. You'll be pleased to know the technician retrieved data from the GPS. He's analysing it and will send you a report. Unfortunately, Forensics didn't find any other evidence on board that might help with the conviction, but they now have the other oar. I'll let you know if it's a match as soon as I hear back from them."

"Good work Jimmy. Text me when you hear. And thanks." Frank ended the call as Anahera returned with the coffees and he relayed the news to her.

Anahera checked the time on the wall clock. "Let's get back into the bull ring."

As they were picking up their notebooks, Brad appeared in the doorway. "How's it going?"

"Good. I'll put my reputation on the fact she's as guilty as sin. A cool customer though," Anahera answered.

"Do you think she'll break?"

"Not showing the signs at this point. Wouldn't be drawn in on the third person—she refused to answer those questions under the advice of her lawyer. We're still trying to establish motive." Anahera stood up and gathered her things.

"Keep the pressure on. I'm hoping we'll have an arrest by the end of the day." Brad turned to walk away.

"We'll do our best," Anahera called after him. She looked at Frank and asked, "Ready?"

"Let's do this."

Frank steeled himself as they made their way back to the interview room.

19

Dave Watson had been enjoying a typically quiet day at the station in Claris when he'd received the call from Frank Smythe. Frank had explained the urgency of the request and said they needed to locate the person who had visited *Aurora* when she was anchored in Whangaparapara Harbour. The first priority, based on a hunch it was Tony Newton because he was known to the owners of *Aurora*, was to track him down and determine if he might have information regarding the events that led to the death of the victim.

Dave turned to his computer and brought up the list of accommodation providers on Barrier, focussing on the handful in the vicinity of Whangaparapara. The list provided the numbers for the owners or their agents, so he decided to start by calling them to ask if they were letting their places out to a Tony Newton.

He left his desk to make himself a coffee before making his calls. To be involved in a homicide inquiry was a rare thing on the island and he relished the idea of tracking this man down. It would be a pleasant change from the usual range of petty crime he dealt with daily. Keeping the lid on the marijuana plantations kept him busy, as did the minor traffic offenses and community policing. Just last evening he had received a complaint from a woman in Tryphena whose neighbour had built a fence that blocked her view without her consent. While hardly a police matter, the neighbours had engaged in a fight which led him to intervene and de-escalate the situation before one of them did something to hurt the other or damage property.

The jug boiled and he made the coffee, stirring in a heaped spoonful of sugar, and took a Gingernut from a jar on the benchtop. Back at his desk he dunked the Gingernut into the steaming coffee and sucked on the soft sugary treat. Whoever invented Gingernuts should've been awarded a medal.

The first call on the list was answered by a woman with a broad Kiwi accent, who informed him her property was currently vacant and no, she hadn't let it to a Tony Newton. He finished the Gingernut and tried the second number on the list, but it rang unanswered and went to voice mail. The Whangaparapara Lodge where they'd had lunch confirmed there had been no Tony Newton on their register. He finished his coffee before trying the next number, and again got no answer. The following number was answered by a man who also had never heard of Tony Newton. And on it went until Dave had exhausted the list for the accommodation within easy access of the Whangaparapara wharf. Of course, he could be staying anywhere on the island, nonetheless Dave decided to keep the focus on Whangaparapara.

His next task was to call the island's rental car companies, although he didn't expect a man who wished to remain off grid would be driving around the island like a tourist. He placed a call to each of the operators on the island who confirmed they hadn't hired a car to a Tony Newton.

A visit to the locations where there had been no response would be his next best option and he shut down the computer. Putting his police issue jacket on over his casual blue check shirt and navy trousers, he locked up and went around the back to his car.

The drive over to Whangaparapara was beautiful. The early morning rain had cleared and sunshine sparkled on the water. Some days he really had to pinch himself that he was lucky enough to be living in paradise with the best policing job in the country. The island had one road over passes with grand views that went from Tryphena in the south to Fitzroy in the northwest with branches to Whangaparapara and Blind Bay. Claris was in the middle of the island near popular surf beaches and where the island's aerodrome welcomed punters seeking sun, surf, bush treks and tranquillity away from the crowds.

The road took him past the track to the hot springs and wound its way down to the harbour. The first of the properties he planned to visit was potentially the most likely as it was well isolated, situated on 1.5 acres of dense native bush above the harbour and three kilometres from the wharf. Dave slowed to a crawl and turned into the narrow gravel track, bumping from one pothole to another as he wound his way up the steep hill to a clearing in the bush. A tidy wooden bungalow, its walls stained dark brown in contrast to its white window joinery, sat proudly in the middle of the clearing. Large solar panels were visible on its iron roof and a LPG cylinder was attached to the exterior wall.

Dave parked the car and walked up the path that led to a beautifully stained wooden door. Adjacent to the door was a small deck with a table and chairs for two. He rapped sharply on the door and heard movements inside. A tallish thin man with a scruffy beard and moustache opened the door, looking surprised at the intrusion.

"I'm Dave Watson, Great Barrier Police." He flashed his badge at the man.

The man looked startled.

"I'm looking for Tony Newton," he said. "Would that be you?"

"Um... yes that's me." The man looked past Dave and then down at his feet, before looking up and asking, "What is it you want?"

"Could I please see some identification? A passport or driver's license would do."

The man looked surprised.

Dave added quickly, "Just procedure, you know how it is."

The man disappeared inside, coming back waving a New Zealand passport. Dave took it and flipped it open. The black and white photo was a poor likeness with Tony Newton staring at the camera looking like a criminal, but then whose passport photo doesn't look like that?

He handed the passport back. "Could we sit down?" Dave asked, used to island hospitality and not the way of these visitor types.

They sat facing each other at the round wooden table on the veranda.

"We are interested in the events surrounding a tragic drowning that occurred off a yacht three weeks ago. The yacht is a 43-foot Beneteau called *Aurora*. We have a witness who says a man matching your description visited *Aurora* the day before the drowning incident and we are after any information that will help our inquiries." Dave paused, watching for a reaction but saw none. "Do you know Ella and Dean Hampton?"

Fear flickered across the man's face, before he composed himself and answered levelly, "Yes, Dean Hampton is my dentist. Did he drown?"

Dave paused. He didn't think he'd mentioned the victim was a man. "Yes, Dean Hampton unfortunately drowned."

"I'm so sorry to hear that. He was a good dentist."

"Did you by chance visit *Aurora* when she was in Whangaparapara Harbour?"

The man hesitated. "Yes, they were kind enough to invite me on board."

"Tell me about that visit." Dave took out his notebook.

"It would have been about three weeks ago. They picked me up from the wharf and we had dinner and quite a few drinks on board. They invited me to stay the night to save walking all the way back here after dark. It wasn't much of a night with the wind and noise. They dropped me off next morning and sailed for home."

Dave finished making a note. "How long have you been out here?"

"A little over a month."

"Why did you come to Barrier?"

"I don't trust the government, the whole Covid thing was a farce. They've been using it to control the population. I figured I'd go off grid for a while—where better to achieve that than out here?"

"When did you arrange to meet up with the Hamptons?"

"When I had my last dentist appointment we talked about Great Barrier. They were coming out for a holiday and since I was planning this trip we agreed to meet up."

Dave consulted his notes. "Did you make three calls to Ella since she's been home?"

Tony Newton looked out over the veranda and took a moment, before answering in a quiet voice, "Yes."

"What was the nature of those calls?"

"Do I have to answer that?" Tony asked.

"No, not if you don't want to." Dave waited, but there was nothing forthcoming. To push the point further, he asked, "Were you having an affair with Ella?"

"I'd prefer not to answer that." Tony looked defeated.

"One last question. Did you witness any fighting or bickering between Ella and Dean that last time you saw them aboard *Aurora*?"

"No, definitely not."

"Did you see anything unusual? Anything at all?"

"No."

Dave put his notebook away. "Thanks for your time Mr Newton. You've been helpful."

With no cell tower in the locality, Dave had to drive to the outskirts of Claris before he stopped and placed a call to Frank.

"Frank? Dave Watson here."

"Dave, how did you get on?"

"I did a little detective work and found your Tony Newton. I've just come from him now. He confirmed he knows the Hamptons. He did visit them on *Aurora* and stayed the night before they upped anchor and sailed home."

"That's great news, thanks. Was he able to shed some light on their moods? Did he witness any issues with them?"

"No, but the funny thing was he didn't want to talk about Ella. He made the calls to her, and I'd hazard a guess that he was having an affair with her. He was somewhat uncomfortable when I asked the question. When I put it to him, he refused to answer."

"Interesting. That may be another part of the motive. We still have her in for questioning and we're hoping to arrest her today."

"Let me know if I can be of further assistance."

"There is one thing. Could you keep an eye on Tony Newton and let us know if he's leaving the island?"

"I'll contact the ferry operator and the airport."

"Thanks Dave, you've been a great help already."

Dave ended the call and drove the rest of the way back to the station happy to have been involved in some real police work.

*

Anahera and Frank entered the interview room and Anahera sat down while Frank cleared the lunch rubbish. She turned on the recording and stated the time, then flipped through her notepad.

"Ella, please can you tell us the state of your finances at the time you went on your holiday to Barrier?" Anahera asked.

"We were in debt."

"Is it true that you had a first mortgage as well as a second mortgage on your home and a revolving credit account that was in overdraft?"

"Yes."

"Is it true that you lost significant funds on Bitcoin?"

"Yes."

"Whose idea was it to invest in Bitcoin?"

Ella hesitated, looking down at her hands. "Mine."

"Where did the money come from for the Bitcoin investment?"

"We took a second mortgage out on the house and used the revolving credit account with the bank."

"How is this relevant to the case?" Suzie asked curtly.

"We believe it's related to the motive," Anahera answered equally curtly.

"Why did you invest money you didn't have in Bitcoin?"

Ella suddenly looked crestfallen. "I'd read about how people were making a killing from it and it seemed like easy money. Bitcoin was on the rise and people thought it would keep going up. I convinced Dean to put everything into it and..." She wiped a tear. "When it started to fall it just kept going."

"Is that what you and Dean argued about?" Frank asked softly.

"Yes." She sniffed and searched her bag for a tissue. "We started arguing a lot."

"Ella, how much money are you expecting to collect from Dean's insurance policy?" Anahera asked.

"One and a half million."

"Did you increase the policy recently?"

"Yes." She folded her arms. "We thought if he were to die, then at least I wouldn't be destitute as he was the major earner." She dabbed her eyes with a tissue.

"So, it was a joint decision?" Anahera persisted.

"Yes."

"Did you kill Dean to collect his life insurance?" Frank asked, his tone formal.

Ella's eyes narrowed and she spat the words out. "I did not kill Dean. How many times do I have to tell you?"

Suzie looked daggers at Frank. "That's enough. Unless you're charging my client, I'm calling an end to this interview."

"We'll get to that shortly." Frank looked at Anahera, signalling for her to take over the questioning.

"Please bear with me—I have a few more questions. Ella, why did Dean not provide for Sara in his will?" Anahera asked in a measured voice.

"Because he wanted to make sure I would be okay."

"Was he not concerned as to whether his only child would be provided for?"

"She has her whole future ahead of her and she will be a graduate with the ability to live comfortably under her own steam."

"Don't you think it a little unusual for a father not to consider his only *blood* child in his will?" Anahera had stressed the word *blood*.

"How other people run their families is up to them." Ella was looking fatigued.

Frank's mobile beeped with an incoming text. He looked at the screen and said, "We'll take a short break—something has come up."

As he was leaving the room, he turned back to face Ella and asked, "Is the beard trimmer on *Aurora* Dean's?"

She looked confused. "Yes, why do you ask?"

"Just checking."

Anahera paused the recording and followed him out of the room.

In the corridor he said, "The oar is a match, with ninety percent certainty. Assuming the DNA test proves the hair is Dean's, then it will remove any doubt it belonged to *Aurora*, but there will still be some doubt as to whether it was the actual murder weapon. What do you think? We have the motive—it was the money. It had to be."

"The third person is still a puzzle. Can we charge her without solving that piece?" she asked.

"It could be important, or it could be a red herring. Let's see if we can chat to Brad and our prosecutor. We can't detain her indefinitely without a charge, and I don't think we're going to get any further with this line of questioning. I'm reluctant to let her go, even though I don't see her as a flight risk."

"I'll call Brad now and ask if he can arrange a meeting with the prosecutor as soon as possible."

Anahera made the call and explained their thinking to Brad. He agreed their logic was sound and he undertook to set up an immediate meeting with the prosecutor.

*

Frank and Anahera entered Brad's office where he was talking to Pam Downer, a prosecutor with the Police Prosecution Service.

She stood up and shook hands with them before the four of them sat down around the coffee table in the corner of the office. Frank had worked with Pam in the past and knew her to be an efficient and very capable operator, her counsel always measured and wise. She was a well-groomed woman in her late thirties and dressed in the corporate style that signalled *don't-mess-with-me*.

Frank provided a background on the case and Pam listened intently, taking notes on her i-Pad and asking the occasional question for clarification.

"How long have you had her in for questioning?" Pam asked.

"Three hours. The problem we have is that all the evidence is circumstantial. She denies having played any part in the drowning."

"How sure are you that she did?"

"I'd put my career on it," Frank said.

"So would I," Anahera added. "She's guilty alright, but do we have enough to charge her?"

"Let's go over the motive again." Pam paused, checking her notes. "You say she and Dean were in serious debt from a speculative gamble on Bitcoin and she stood to benefit from the life insurance payout. Some months prior they had increased his cover."

"That's correct, it was enough to nearly clear the debt."

"I'm a little confused about this..." She checked her notes again. "This Tony Newton. What part do you think he played?"

This time, Anahera answered, "We're not sure. What we know is that he was known to them, they entertained him at Barrier, and he has since phoned Ella Hampton three times from an unregistered phone. We suspect he was having an affair with Ella, but neither will answer those questions."

"Do you think he was involved in some way as an accomplice?"

"I can't see how he could be, as he was on Barrier when it happened. Unless of course he helped plan it." Anahera looked at Frank.

"We have no proof of that at this stage."

"And you're waiting on ESR for the DNA test on the hair?"

"Yes, we should have it by the end of the week. We expect it will be Dean's. Forensics are ninety percent certain the oar came from *Aurora*. We think it may have been used as a weapon to knock him overboard."

"Even if it's his hair, it doesn't absolutely prove it is the murder weapon." Pam looked thoughtful as she rubbed her chin with her forefinger. "Would Ella have the strength to do that?"

"If she had the opportunity when he was standing on the transom, for example," Frank said thoughtfully. "I doubt she would be able to drag Dean's body over the side on her own. She wouldn't have the strength to get a dead weight like that over the lifelines or the stern. Then there's her story about the jibe—it just doesn't add up. And she lied to her family member about when the oar was replaced. The family member was the sister-in-law and I'm confident she will agree to testify if it comes to that."

"Do you think it was premeditated?"

"Almost certainly," Frank answered. "The fact they'd upped the life insurance cover speaks to that."

"So, you want to charge her with murder and not manslaughter." Pam paused. "It's borderline whether a judge will toss it out without the murder weapon. The hair would help make the case and could lead to a confession. Do you think she's a flight risk?"

"I don't think so. Until she sells her house, she doesn't have the money. Even if she set sail on her own, she wouldn't get far aboard *Aurora* without us being able to pick her up. And we could place a stop at the airports." Frank looked at Anahera for confirmation.

"I agree," Anahera said. "But placing her under arrest might just force a confession by making her feel scared and vulnerable."

"That would be by far the best outcome," agreed Pam. "Okay, you have my support. You can go ahead and book her."

"Good work, team. You've done it," Brad said, grinning broadly. "Let's hope a night in a cell will break her. I want to hear the minute you book her so I can arrange the media conference. This will make good press."

"Let's not celebrate quite yet." Pam's expression was grim as she looked at each of them in turn. "We still must prove each element of the offense for the charge to stick and these types of cases are extremely tricky to prove. You'd better hope that you get that confession. As a murder charge, and if it gets as far as a trial, it will require a near unanimous decision by a jury of peers and that is never a foregone conclusion. Never forget your suspect remains innocent in the eyes of the law until you can prove beyond reasonable doubt that she is guilty. We will need to rely on expert opinions to substantiate your assumptions. I've come up against Suzie Laselles before and she's no easy opponent. There's a lot of work yet to be done."

Frank and Anahera thanked Pam and left Brad's office.

"Why is it that I'm left feeling like we've lost the trial already and we haven't even arrested the culprit yet?" Anahera asked.

Frank sighed. "I know what you mean, I feel the same."

"Do you mind if I take a short walk in the fresh air to clear my head before we charge her?" Anahera ran her hand absentmindedly through her hair.

"Ten minutes won't make any difference."

"Great. I'll see you back here in ten."

Frank had just sat down at his desk when his phone buzzed.

"Frank Smythe."

"Frank, it's Jimmy here. We've recovered the data from the GPS aboard *Aurora*. I've sent you the report."

"Great. Anything unusual?"

"Well, I'm not sure what exactly you were looking for. It appears *Aurora* tracked out of Whangaparapara, took a southwest heading then zigzagged about as if searching. Best if you check it for yourself."

"Thanks Jimmy. You may have provided the missing piece of evidence we need to slam this one home."

Frank punched the end call icon and turned to his inbox. Moments later a new email pinged. He was reading the file when Anahera returned.

Frank relayed the information from Jimmy. "I just need half an hour to check the GPS information. I have a good feeling about this."

Anahera grinned. "This is such good news. But Frank, let's make the arrest. I don't see any reason why we should delay that—after all, we've been given the approval to go ahead. That gives you more time to analyse the data."

"You're right. I just know this is going to be the cream on top." He grinned at her, basking in the moment, fully believing they'd made their case. "If I can show that with the wind and tide vectors there was no way *Aurora* could have been running downwind and therefore the jibe wasn't possible as Ella described it, then we have the evidence to show she lied about how Dean fell overboard. And with only the two of them on board, she's looking more and more guilty."

Although confident that Ella was guilty, Frank re-entered the interview room with some trepidation. Suzie and Ella looked up at the intrusion and a momentary trace of fear clouded Ella's face when she spied Frank's grim expression.

Anahera looked directly at Ella. "Ella Hampton, I am charging you with the murder of Dean Hampton. I remind you that you have the right to remain silent, you do not have to make a statement, anything you say may be recorded and given as evidence in court. Do you understand?"

"You can't arrest me; I didn't kill Dean! You must believe me, I love him. I'm innocent," Ella protested, her eyes darting about wildly.

"You're making a grave mistake," Suzie said sharply. "My client has not done anything wrong. Your evidence is merely circumstantial. This will not stand up in court."

"Ella, please come with me and we'll get the formalities over with," Anahera said, her manner brisk and business-like.

Frank watched them leave the room, knowing that justice for Dean wouldn't be served until the jury sealed her fate. Ella's protests of innocence were audible all the way down the corridor as she was taken away to be processed, Suzie at her heels like the terrier she was. He could only imagine the humiliation that a woman like her would endure being fingerprinted and locked up as a common criminal, which he believed her to be.

It had been a long and exhausting day, so Frank took Anahera's advice and left the chart plotting data from *Aurora* until the next morning. Instead, they arranged to meet at Smugglers' Bar for a well-deserved drink once Frank had advised Brad of the arrest.

20

Frank was in the office early the next morning, his mood cheerful. Yesterday's rain had cleared and a large slow moving high covered the country, promising good weather right through to the weekend. The progress they'd made on the Hampton case was pleasing and he'd enjoyed the old camaraderie working with Anahera again, but he was eager to resume his post behind the wheel of *Deodar III*.

While his computer was booting, he pulled out the chart of the Hauraki Gulf with his pencilled estimation of the course *Aurora* may have travelled and laid it out on the desk. He retrieved the parallel ruler and other chart plotting paraphernalia from his bag. Jimmy's email contained a file attachment with the chart plotter data from *Aurora*. It took him a few minutes to orientate himself with the data on the screen.

"You're here early. Did Margie kick you out?" Anahera swept into the room and put a coffee-to-go in front of him. "I saw your car in the carpark and thought you might be needing this."

He grinned. "Thanks, you're a life saver."

"Is there any news of Ella?"

"No. She'll still be in a remand cell cooling her heels."

Anahera stood looking at the chart spread out on the desk. "Is that your workings?"

"That was before I received the data from Jimmy. I sketched the course *Aurora* would've had to sail accounting for the wind and tidal flows if the jibe occurred in the way Ella described. I'm about to re-plot it with the data from the GPS."

"You're an old-fashioned guy Frank Smythe." Anahera chuckled. "That's what computers are for."

He smiled and took a sip of his coffee. "If you don't understand how to do these things manually, how will you get on if the power is out? Or worse if you're at sea and the chart plotter fails?"

"I get your point," she said, sipping her coffee.

"But you're right, I still like seeing it on paper. I guess that's why I still like to carry a notebook; some habits are hard to break."

Frank consulted the computer and drew the actual course taken on the chart in pencil, lightly marking the pings that the chart plotter had recorded. He then checked the wind strength and direction from MetService records for those exact times and showed it with small arrows alongside the course. Satisfied, he sat back and studied it.

"What do you make of it?" Anahera craned her head over the chart.

"This is the course they actually followed." Frank used the point of the compass to indicate the newest lines he'd drawn. "And here's where she obviously started to search backwards and forwards. Now this was the direction of the wind. At no time were they on a downwind course that would've caused a jibe. And there's no sign that they changed direction and headed for Coromandel. Ella's story doesn't add up."

"That's sounds like fairly solid evidence."

"It is. An expert on the stand should have no problems in pointing out the flaws in her story."

"Do you think she was even sailing?"

"Hard to say, but *Aurora* would've had the wind hard on the nose if she was."

Anahera looked blankly at him.

Frank explained, "Hard on the nose means sailing close to the wind direction and you need to haul the sails in tight to get forward motion. That would mean the boom would have been held close to the centre line of the boat and not swinging through a big arc. This is the first hard evidence we have that isn't circumstantial and that proves she lied about the events surrounding Dean's death."

"Great work partner. Brad's going to want to hear about it."

"Don't praise me, it's the techie who did the hard yards and recovered the data where I couldn't." Frank swung his chair back to face his workstation. "I'll give Brad a call now."

Brad was delighted with the news as it meant the decision to go ahead with charging Ella had been a good move.

Next Frank looked up Amy Fagin's number and gave her a call.

"Amy? Frank Smythe here."

"Frank, I was wondering how you were getting on, so it's good timing. How's the investigation going?" She sounded relaxed.

"We've made some good progress. I thought I should let you know that we have charged Ella with Dean's murder."

Amy gasped. "What? You have?"

"Yes. We brought Ella in for questioning and charged her yesterday afternoon."

"Oh my goodness! I don't know what to say."

The line went quiet. Frank waited while the news sank in.

"So, Dean will get justice." Her quavering voice was little more than a whisper.

"Yes, he should now get justice. But you need to know that if this gets to court the jury will have to decide whether the charge sticks, so there's still a long way to go."

"Did Ella not confess?"

"No, she is continuing to deny she did anything to cause his death. There is some fairly damning evidence against her. I'm hoping you will sign a witness statement regarding your comments about the jibe and especially the conversation you had with Ella about the oar. Also, we may need you as a witness if it goes to trial. Would that be okay?"

"Of course. Anything to help get the truth out."

"Thanks Amy. This wouldn't have happened if it weren't for you coming forward. It was a brave thing to do, and I really appreciate it."

"I'm glad I did."

"How's your health?"

"Good, thanks. I'm getting fitter and have modified my diet and I'm feeling better for it."

"That's good. Take care Amy. Is it okay if I come around this afternoon and get that statement?"

"Sure. As you know my time is very flexible these days, so tell me when suits."

"Two pm?"

"Fine, I'll see you then."

The call had reminded him of the near miss and how he'd allowed his own judgement to be clouded by his acquaintance with Dean. Ella very nearly got away with it and would've if it hadn't been for Amy alerting him to those initial inconsistencies. He vowed never again to let anything get in the way of his objectivity when it came to police work.

*

Over the next two days Anahera and Frank continued to work the case, collecting witness statements and getting the information together in preparation for trial. Brad had informed them that their secondments would finish at the end of the week, at which time Frank would go back to the Maritime Unit while Anahera would go back to working the Land Search and Rescue cases.

Frank's mobile phone rang.

"Frank Smythe."

"Frank, Cyril Williams, Forensics."

"Cyril, what news do you have for me?"

"Not good, I'm afraid." He paused. "The results of the DNA testing of that hair sample just came back from ESR. It's not a match for the clippings, so it's probably not from your victim."

Frank drew in a deep breath through his teeth. "That's not what I wanted to hear."

"How certain are you that the clippings came from your victim?"

"The beard trimmer was on his boat and the widow has confirmed it is his. Should I bring you another sample to check we have Dean's DNA with the clippings? I have a manicure set in evidence that may turn something up. The body was cremated, and the widow has already disposed of his things."

"My, that was quick! It would be better to get something more clearcut than the manicure set."

"How about one of your team goes down to the boat and looks for a hair in the cabin? I doubt it's been thoroughly cleaned."

"We can do that."

They made a time for Frank to meet a forensic technician at the marina that afternoon and Frank ended the call.

"I gather the hair was a disappointment," Anahera said.

"It doesn't match the clippings from the beard trimmer. We'll go down and try to find another reference sample for Dean."

"It doesn't change the fact that the oar is almost certainly the missing oar," Anahera pointed out. "But was it the murder weapon? How else did the hair get there?"

"Forensics said it must have taken significant force for the hair to be lodged in the crack. It's unlikely that it got stuck there by chance—and they'll testify to that."

"If not Dean's, whose hair is it?" Anahera sat back in her chair with her arms folded behind her head.

"That is the question!"

"It's puzzling alright. Where are we at with the witness statements?" she asked.

"We've pretty much ticked them all off the list. The obvious one that we're missing is from Tony Newton." Frank sat up a little taller. "How about we make another trip out to Barrier and get a witness statement from him? There's something we're missing in this whole thing and I'm sure it's got something to do with him. The fact that Ella opted for silence in response to our questions about him makes me suspicious. And from Dave's report, he was a bit cautious when asked about her. He may well have been in cahoots with her and is an accessory to murder."

"I think you're right, it's time we paid him a visit."

They arranged to be taxied out to Whangaparapara aboard *Deodar III* first thing the following morning.

The remainder of the afternoon was spent with a forensic technician combing *Aurora*, looking for something that could be used as a DNA reference sample for Dean. After much searching, they found a number of blonde hairs beside the mattress they assumed to be his as they were too short to be from Ella. They would need to take a DNA sample from Ella to eliminate that possibility.

*

Another perfect early autumn day dawned on Auckland and the Hauraki Gulf. Frank met Anahera at the Maritime Unit office and they boarded *Deodar III*. Colin was again skipper, ably assisted by Stephen.

Once they left the dock, Colin offered the wheel to Frank who readily accepted. It felt good to feel the vibrations through the wheel once again and to manoeuvre her over the small swells that were coming on to *Deodar*'s port bow. He felt alive.

"When are you back with the Unit?" Colin asked over the engine noise. "We're having to stretch out our shifts because we're so short staffed. Covid has been doing its rounds and we don't have enough cover."

"I'm told Monday."

"That's great news."

"I can't wait to get back—I miss it." Frank tapped the wheel affectionately and grinned. "I miss her!"

"How about us?" Colin smirked in mock offense.

"No, just the boat," laughed Frank.

Midway across they saw a small pod of orca, consisting of three adults and a calf. These majestic apex predators cruised through the water effortlessly, their sleek black and white bodies glistening with water as they surfaced for breath. Frank slowed right down and pointed them out to Anahera who was in raptures. This was her first encounter and she pulled out her phone and snapped some photos. They watched them as they slowly went by, appearing to be curious about the intrusion of the boat in their realm.

As the island got closer the detail in the vegetation became clearer until they finally got to the entrance to Whangaparapara Harbour.

Once again Dave was waiting for them on the wharf. They didn't expect to be long, so the *Deodar III* crew agreed to wait for them. As soon as Frank and Anahera disembarked, Dave took them to his vehicle and drove them up the road to a driveway where he turned in and navigated the deeply rutted track. It led to a small house that was at the top of the hill and nestled amongst the bush. Once parked they walked the short distance up the path to the front door.

Frank knocked sharply. Silence. They looked at each other. Frank knocked again, louder this time. After a long pause they heard footsteps making their way to the door. It swung open, slowly, and a familiar face emerged.

His hair was darker, he had a scruffy beard, but there was no mistaking his old friend Dean Hampton.

21

Frank stood rooted to the spot, not believing his eyes. Standing before him was the last person he'd expected to open the door. Something was very very wrong. His heart raced and words failed him.

Dean's eyes locked onto Frank with recognition registering on his face before his brow furrowed in a deep frown. "Frank, what are you doing here?" Dean looked from Frank to Dave and his jaw dropped as he took in the reality of his situation.

Trying to pull himself back into his professional persona, Frank said in a faltering voice, "Dean, we... er... thought you were dead."

"Dean?" Anahera asked.

Dean looked from Frank to Anahera to Dave and back to Frank, saying nothing, yet his eyes were wide, his breath coming in gasps.

"This is Dean Hampton," Frank said, wishing it were different.

"But you showed me your passport... Tony Newton's passport." Dave looked dumbfounded.

Anger replaced his initial shock as Frank realised Dean was mixed up in something big, something worse than bad. "Dean, what on earth is going on? What have you done?" Frank's face was grim, his voice harsh and the words rapid.

Looking panicked, Dean said, "I have nothing to say until I see my lawyer."

"You've got some explaining to do, that's for sure. Are you aware of the trauma you've put your family through, letting them believe you're dead?" Frank shook his head. "Sara. Amy. Why Dean? Why would you do it?"

Dean shuffled his feet and looked down, saying in a quiet defeated voice, "I want my lawyer."

"How did you come by Tony Newton's passport?" Frank asked.

Dean said nothing.

"What did you do to Tony Newton?" Frank persisted.

Dean continued to stare at his feet, mute.

"Take him inside for a minute, would you Dave? Get him out of my sight. I want to speak with Anahera." Frank took in a deep breath to calm his anger.

Dave propelled Dean inside and shut the door behind them. Anahera and Frank wandered a few metres back down the path for privacy.

"That's a turn up for the books," Anahera said.

"You're not wrong there. I'm assuming Dean and Ella had planned this all along and Tony Newton's body was the cadaver that washed up on the Port Jackson beach."

"But we don't have enough to charge him with accessory to murder unless we get a confession."

"Let's bring him in for questioning and hope he breaks." Frank ran his hand over his balding head. "I'm quite certain the Dean of old would never have done something like this—he must be feeling remorseful. We can book him on the identity theft charge and use that to take him into custody. We should be able to find the passport somewhere in the cottage; besides we'll have Dave's testimony to say he used a false identity when questioned."

"Brad will want to know what's going on. I'll give him a quick call once we're back in reception and let him know we're bringing him in," Anahera said. "Meanwhile I suggest you book him."

With a heavy heart Frank walked back to the stained front door and entered the cottage. His eyes took a moment to adjust to the gloomy interior. Dean was sitting at a heavy wooden table opposite Dave. The room was divided into three functional zones by a couch that was positioned between the dining and lounge areas and an island bench with sink separating the kitchen from the lounge. A hallway led to what appeared to be the private living quarters.

He walked across to the table and stood looking at Dean for a long moment. Dean looked away, not meeting Frank's eye.

"Dean Hampton, I am arresting you for the identity theft and identity fraud relating to Tony Newton. You have the right to remain silent, you do not have to make a statement, anything you say may be recorded and given as evidence in court. You have the right to speak to a lawyer without delay and in private before deciding whether to answer any of our questions. The police have a list of lawyers you may speak to for free. Do you understand?"

"Yes." Dean's voice was timid, like that of a child caught stealing a lolly. "I want to see my lawyer."

"Can I assume they're in Auckland?"

"Yes."

"Well then, as soon as we get you back to Auckland you can make that call. We will take you into Auckland Central Police Station for questioning. We have the *Deodar III* police launch standing by."

Dean still could not look his old friend in the eye.

"I would like to take the opportunity to do a quick search of the property. You can either grant us that right now or we can come back with a warrant later. Do you consent to us conducting a search now?"

Without looking up, Dean said, "I suppose so."

Frank took the cue and went through the doorway to the small hall. The cottage had two bedrooms and a bathroom. One bedroom had views of the native bush behind and was obviously unused; a quick search showed it had nothing of interest inside. The other bedroom had a view of the harbour as well as bush. This was obviously the room Dean had been using. A wardrobe contained a few hanging clothes and other clothes were neatly folded on a set of shelves. Beside the bed was a set of drawers and on top was a small mobile phone, which Frank put in an evidence bag. The top drawer contained a wallet with a large wad of cash but no personal identification of any sort; no bank cards, no driver's licence, nothing that would tie Dean Hampton or Tony Newton to it. Just the cash. Underneath the wallet was a New Zealand passport. The photo inside was of a bearded man and the details were Tony Newton's. Tony was surprisingly close to being Dean's doppelganger and Frank let out a low whistle.

"Found anything?" Anahera asked, her footsteps sounding in the room.

"Tony Newton's passport is here. He could be Dean's twin." He held it out for Anahera to see.

Anahera nodded in agreement. "I hadn't joined the dots. The Hamptons must have been responsible for the robbery at Tony Newton's place that we were investigating."

"I can't find any other identification for either Dean or Tony Newton. It seems Dean has tried to erase his old identity."

"Perhaps. We've enough to make the identity theft charge stick and that'll do for starters."

"Have you got an evidence bag on you? How about you pop the passport and wallet into one while I check out the bathroom."

"Sure."

Frank went next door to the bathroom. He checked through the vanity but couldn't find anything more that could be used as evidence.

Back in the living area Frank slipped handcuffs on his friend, more for effect than any risk of losing him. Then Dave drove them down to the Whangaparapara wharf where *Deodar III* was waiting. On board they cuffed their prisoner to the boat to prevent any attempt at bailing overboard.

Dean remained quiet for the entire trip, affecting the mood on board. The sea failed to weave its magic over Frank who sat forlornly watching the surface rise and fall with the small swells rolling in from the north. Memories of the good times spent sailing the classics felt like myths. At the funeral he'd grieved for his old buddy, but it was all a lie. Could you ever really know a person, ever really know what they're capable of? It was easier to think the Dean he knew still existed somewhere inside this man who was wearing the handcuffs, perhaps under layers of manipulation that'd changed him and made him into a man capable of murder. Then again, Dean could have been the mastermind behind it. Frank wasn't ready to contemplate that thought. Could a man really change that much? Regardless of whether Dean was victim to a conniving and manipulative wife or a cold-blooded killer, he was a grown man who could think for himself, and Frank was bitterly disappointed in him. How he'd ended up as Frank's prisoner was beyond comprehension. The thought was depressing.

If only Frank had wised up to this whole saga earlier. He'd missed clues that should have alerted him to Ella, but he'd lost objectivity through having been friends with Dean. Could he have saved Amy and the family some of the grief they'd had to endure?

The guilt would be with him for a long time, he could only hope it'd turn him into a better cop.

They disembarked at Maritime HQ and Dean rode in the back of Frank's car to Central where he was taken to an interview room. They left him there to mull things over while he and Anahera met with Brad.

"So, this is an interesting turn of events," Brad began. "The husband comes back to life. It's damned inconvenient after my press release!"

"We've booked him with identity theft and have yet to find out if he was involved in any way with the drowning of the man-overboard, who we now assume to be Tony Newton."

"I thought the John Doe identity was confirmed by dental records." Brad looked puzzled.

"It was. I suspect the dental records were tampered with."

"I recall you knew Dean Hampton from years back. Did you recognise him?"

"Yes. He's not changed much apart from his hair colour and facial hair. I would've known him anywhere."

"This must be hard on you." Brad's voice had taken on a friendly note. "Would you two like a coffee before you go into the interview?"

"That'd be very much appreciated," Anahera chipped in. "White and strong for us both."

Brad got up and put his head through the doorway to ask his assistant to get them three coffees. Back at his desk, he asked them for a full update and Frank obliged, beginning with Dave's initial meeting and how he was led to believe the man was Tony Newton with the showing of the passport, and finishing with telling him how he'd recognised Dean instantly the moment he'd opened the door. Anahera added that the stolen passport was now in evidence and by all accounts it looked like Dean had gotten rid of any identification that would tie him to being Dean Hampton.

As they were finishing their coffees, Brad said, "Frank, you'd better leave the questioning to Anahera given your relationship with the prisoner."

"Yes, I thought that would be the case. I'd like to be present, perhaps having a familiar face in the room might just help him open up. What do you think?"

"It could work, I'll leave that to your judgement. Are you quite sure you have not had contact with Dean Hampton in recent years?"

"I'm certain."

"Then that's okay with me. It's no different to small town policing where you know everyone. Does Ella know yet?"

"No, she's in a remand cell and we thought it best to leave her for the time being while we see what we can get out of Dean." Anahera took a last mouthful and emptied her mug. "If we can get a full confession from him that implicates her in the murder of Tony Newton then she might just confess all."

"I suggest you drop the current charges against her as soon as possible and charge her with the murder of Tony Newton, preferably before the end of day. We don't want her lawyer finding any loopholes on technicalities."

"Will do. We'll see what's forthcoming from Dean first." Anahera stood up.

"Keep me posted." Brad looked down at the papers on his desk, signalling the meeting was over.

Anahera and Frank took their seats in the interview room where Dean was sitting at the table, his shoulders hunched and his head hung low, nothing like the self-assured and gregarious man he once was.

"I want to speak to my lawyer, Simon Burke of Burke Simmonds Family Law." He paused and looked at Frank. "They've been my lawyers for years and Simon helped me through my messy divorce. I trust him."

This explanation was unnecessary, as though Dean was chatting to an old friend, causing Frank to bristle. Without a word he left the room, returning with a landline phone and the number for the law firm. He plugged it in and passed Dean the number. While they waited for the lawyer to arrive, Frank brought Dean a cup of coffee from the staff kitchen.

Simon Burke arrived and was shown into the interview room. Smartly dressed in a black shirt and chic tie under a blue suit with pointed black shoes, he had a calm gentleman's manner about him that complemented his usual work in the field of family law.

Once the introductions were concluded, he asked for time alone with his client. Anahera and Frank left the room.

"The hair in the blade of the oar could be Tony Newton's. I'll ask Sandie at Land Search and Rescue if she could take a forensics techie over to his house and get a sample to match the DNA." Anahera dug her hands into her pockets. "Without a confession we'll need the hair in the oar to be Tony Newton's to tie it all together."

"It's about time we had a bit of luck with that hair. If we can match it to Tony then we might just have the murder weapon. At the very least it will link him to *Aurora* and show he was on board."

"A match will certainly provide weight to the circumstantial evidence. Without it we may struggle to get a conviction." Anahera shook her head.

"And see Ella Hampton walk free? No way. We need that confession from Dean."

Anahera placed the call to Sandie and made the request. They continued to confer quietly in the corridor for ten minutes before Simon Burke announced they were ready for them to begin the interview.

Anahera formally announced the interview would be video recorded and began by asking him to state his name, date of birth and address. Dean responded in a low voice that betrayed a slight quaver.

"How long have you known Tony Newton?"

Dean sat mute.

"My client wishes to exercise his right not to answer any questions relating to the passport found in the location at which he was staying." Simon's demeanour was businesslike.

"Dean, did you conspire with your wife Ella to stage your murder so as to get your life insurance payout?"

Dean continued to exercise his right to silence.

"I advise my client not to answer."

Anahera tried again. "Dean, was it Ella's idea to stage your death?"

Again, they were met by a wall of silence.

"My client does not need to answer that question."

"Dean, we have Ella in custody. We will find the truth in this matter and if you answer our questions, it will likely help your case." Anahera paused as if considering what might induce him to break his silence. "Are you aware of the seriousness of your situation? A charge of false identity could buy you prison time as well as a hefty fine."

"I have nothing to say to you." Dean spoke in a monotone.

Anahera looked at Frank and he nodded. She formally suspended the interview before leaving the room.

Once outside, she said, "This is getting nowhere. What do you think?"

"I agree. I suspect he's trying to protect Ella."

"Perhaps we should let him stew for a while. Then we could start with the evidence we have against Ella. If he's trying to protect her then he may well break his silence if he thinks we're already onto her."

"I think I'll give Amy a call and let her know her brother is alive. After all the grief she's been through, it's the least I can do for her."

"Fair enough. Do you think we should bring Ella in for questioning while Dean stews? Like Brad said, we need to change the charge as soon as possible to that of Tony Newton, poor sod. If we tell her that we have Dean in custody it might entice her to open up some more."

"It's worth a shot."

Frank went back to the office to call Amy while Anahera arranged for Ella to be brought up to another interview room. Frank punched Amy's number into his mobile phone.

"Amy, it's Frank Smythe."

"Hello Frank."

"Amy, I have some news for you." Frank hesitated, not sure how best to say it. "We've found Dean—he's alive Amy."

An audible gasp was followed by a pause. "What did you say?"

"Dean is alive. We have him down at Central." Frank waited for the news to sink in.

"But I don't understand. How can that be? His body was found. We cremated him." A long pause ensued before she added quietly, "Are you really sure Frank?"

"Yes, I've been with him myself."

"Where did you find him?"

"Out at Great Barrier. He's been living off grid out there ever since the... incident."

Another long pause, before Amy said in a voice that was barely audible, "I thought Ella killed him."

"So did I," Frank replied in a soft voice.

The line was silent for a bit. "If it wasn't Dean, who was it that we cremated?"

"It was someone else, we have yet to confirm his identity. I just wanted you to know your brother isn't dead."

"Can I come and pick him up?"

"No, we have him in custody."

"Why?"

Frank paused again, considering how much to tell her. "He stole someone's identity and is implicated in the murder of this other person."

"No! He can't have, he wouldn't have." Her denial was impassioned.

"I'm sorry Amy."

"Has he confessed to it?"

"Not as yet. He's not saying much at all."

"Frank, I want to see him. Please let me talk to him. Whatever he's done, it's not him. Please believe me. Ella would've manipulated him. He's so under her..." She paused, before continuing, "Under her spell."

"I'll give it some thought. But I need to get going now. Please understand I've called you out of courtesy and I would appreciate you keeping this to yourself for the time being. It's early days for our investigation."

"I understand. This is such a bolt out of the blue, I don't know what to say. I appreciate you taking the time to update me."

"I'm sorry I don't have better news for you. Bye Amy." He ended the call.

Frank joined Anahera who was leading Ella into an interview room down the corridor from the one where Dean sat with his lawyer. He shut the door behind them. Ella no longer looked like a woman straight out of a fashion magazine. Instead, her hair was dishevelled, her make-up smudged. She wore the same clothes as the previous day. Her face was set in an unbecoming pout.

"Ella, we are dropping the charge of the murder of Dean Hampton. Do you understand?"

Ella's eyes went wide in disbelief. "You are?"

Anahera almost looked smug. "Ella Hampton, I am charging you with the murder of Tony Newton. You have the right to remain silent, you do not have to make a statement, anything you say may be recorded and given as evidence in court. You have the right to speak to a lawyer without delay and in private before deciding whether to answer any of our questions. The police have a list of lawyers you may speak to for free. Do you understand?"

Ella's shoulders collapsed and she shrank back into her chair. "Yes."

"You should also know that we have Dean in custody," Frank added.

Ella looked at him, her mouth open and eyes wide. "What?"

"Dean is helping us with our inquiries." Frank stared at her. "Would you like to give us your version of the events that led to Tony Newton's death?"

"I'm not admitting to anything, and I won't say another word without my lawyer present."

"Have it your way." Frank stood up. "Anahera, I'll arrange for her to be taken back to the cell."

Frank walked out as his phone buzzed with the front desk advising that Amy Fagin was waiting to see him. Once he'd instructed the sergeant to return Ella to her cell, Frank let Anahera know before going to meet Amy. He found her pacing the reception area, looking out of place among the assortment of gang members and young teens who were occupying the space.

When Amy saw Frank, she rushed over to him. "Frank, please let me see Dean. This is so out of character for him, I need to talk to him."

"Amy, it's not that simple. Dean isn't cooperating right now, so it's likely to be some time before he's out of the interview room."

"I can get him to cooperate, I know I can." The set of her jaw showed a steely determination as she eyed him intensely, her vibrating arm revealing her stress.

"Normally the answer would be a definite no. But given the help you've already supplied and your determination to find the truth, I wonder if maybe you could help us. I get the feeling Dean is not cooperating in order to protect Ella. If he tells the truth, it will go better for him. And maybe you can convince him of that. Leave it with me and I'll discuss it with my partner." Frank left her near the front desk and went in search of Anahera.

She was waiting in their office and held out a coffee for him as he entered. "Thought we could do with a caffeine injection before we climb back into the ring."

"Thanks. Amy Fagin turned up at the front desk asking for me. She wants to see Dean." He sipped on the hot coffee.

"I assume you told her to go home?"

"Actually no. I've got an idea. It's a bit unorthodox but hear me out. She has been close to her brother in the past and could have a positive influence over him. She has little regard for Ella and has been chasing the truth ever since the incident was called in. What would you think if we allow her to visit him on the condition that she advises him to tell the truth?" Frank took another sip and savoured the strong coffee taste.

"We would need to be careful it couldn't be construed as manipulating the suspect."

"I can't see how it would create a problem. There really is no downside. We would obviously monitor the conversation and step in if there's any sign of an issue."

Anahera looked thoughtful. "It may work. No question we need Dean to start talking. Let's clear it with Brad just to make sure."

Frank called Brad and after careful deliberation he sanctioned the visit. Having finished her coffee, Anahera went into the interview room to explain to Dean that Amy was in the station wanting to see him and to ask if he'd accept a visit from her. At first Dean had been unsure, possibly out of guilt or shame, but after discussing it with his lawyer he'd agreed to see her. Frank went down to fetch Amy.

*

Amy continued to pace the reception area at the police station. Here was not a place she'd spent any time in the past and she felt at odds with the two gang members who wore their brotherhood tattooed on their faces, the homeless man carrying his belongings in shopping bags and a group of youths wanting to get an impounded car released.

She was relieved to see Frank come hurrying through the door from the interior.

"Can I see him?" she asked.

"Yes, but only on the condition you encourage him to tell the truth. Do you understand?" His manner was brusque and not the friendly approach she'd come to like.

"Yes. Oh Frank, thank you." She could've hugged him.

"You'll only have ten minutes with him and his lawyer." In a gentler voice he said, "This way Amy."

Frank led her to the lifts and down a corridor. Stopping outside the interview room door, he said, "We'll be listening next door. Good luck in there."

Frank opened the door and closed it behind her. The room was small with a large mirror along one side that she assumed to be one way glass. Dean was sitting at a table next to Simon Burke, whom Amy recognised from the tumultuous days that surrounded Dean's acrimonious divorce.

Simon stood up and shook Amy's hand, but all the while she was aware of Dean sitting at the table. He made no move towards her. His eyes were red, his face partially hidden by an unkempt moustache and beard. She'd never seen him look so wretched, not even during those black days negotiating child custody.

Her emotions were super-charged, making it a struggle to hold it together. Now was the time to be strong and she wiped her tears away with the back of her hand, only to be replaced by more tears.

"We thought you were dead." It was barely more than a whisper. "We held your funeral, you were cremated, we scattered your ashes. Where were you?"

"I'm sorry Amy."

"Sorry?" She was vaguely aware she'd raised her voice, once more the big sister scolding her younger sibling. "Why Dean? Why did you do this to us, to Sara and to Mum? To me? How could you?"

"I'm so very sorry Amy, I never meant to hurt anyone. One thing led to another, things got out of hand and before we knew it, we were in too deep." Dean looked miserable.

"Careful Dean. No need to disclose too much," Simon said quietly. "Remember they're listening."

The implications of Dean sitting here dawned on Amy and she asked in hushed tones, "Who was the body we cremated?"

Dean looked down at his hands. "I can't get into that."

"Look Dean, I don't have long." She breathed in deeply through her nose and slowly exhaled out her mouth. "You have to tell the cops the truth. Please, do it for Sara."

"Amy, I know you mean well—it's just that you don't understand. I can't." He caught her eye and quickly looked away.

"Dean you can, and you must, or you'll get in more trouble than you're already in. Don't you see you're being implicated in a murder Dean? A murder! I'm sure a judge will factor your willingness to cooperate into your sentence. Telling the truth is the only way forward for you. We must believe that honesty pays or what else do we have?" Her hand trembled violently so she sat on it to hide it from him. Through tears she said, "Let Ella deal with her own consequences. You have other responsibilities— Sara needs you, and so does Mum."

He didn't look up.

"Please Dean!" she pleaded, desperate for him to see sense.

This time Dean looked at his sister for a long time. "Amy, will you ever find it in you to forgive me? For everything? I had time to think on Barrier and I realised how poorly I've treated you in the last few years. I thought I'd never have the chance to see you again. And after all you did for Sara and me—you were my rock for so long."

"Then trust me now and tell the truth, even if it means confessing your part in this. Please, please Dean." Tears sprang into her eyes as she reached forward with her good hand and gave his hand a gentle squeeze, but she quickly retracted it when she came in contact with the handcuffs.

Dean put his head in his hands and his shoulders heaved.

"If you don't mind Amy, I'd like some time alone with my client," Simon said in a fatherly voice.

"Of course." Amy went around the table to where Dean was sitting and hugged him. "I was so devastated to lose you, we all were, and now I can hardly believe we've got you back. I'll be there for you, no matter what lies ahead. I love you Dean."

"Amy, please believe me when I say I'm sorry," Dean said, still slumped in his chair.

Amy walked to the door and was holding the handle looking back at her brother, still not quite believing it was him, when Frank opened it and ushered her out. They walked in silence to the front door where he left her to make her way to her car.

Sitting behind the wheel she stared out the window at the concrete wall of the carpark building, seeing nothing through tears that flowed freely. Her emotions were in turmoil. Relief gave way to annoyance that gave way to anger that gave way to loyalty and most of all love. He was such a fool to get involved in whatever it was that they'd done. And even more of a fool to protect Ella. It had to have been Ella's fault, Ella's idea, Ella's plan. Ella had always controlled him while he'd always been a sucker for her charms. Amy was doubtful that Ella would protect him if it meant burning her own chance at a reduced sentence.

22

Frank left Amy at the door out to the street. She'd done a good job pleading with Dean to tell the truth. Now he could only hope that the fool would take it on board and start talking. It wasn't looking good for Dean, but it would be a whole lot worse if he didn't confess—a judge may well be more lenient if he did.

Anahera was waiting for him in the corridor and they entered the interview room together. Dean was pacing and looking distraught, his hands still cuffed in front of him. Simon sat upright at the table watching his client.

"Sit down please Dean," Frank said sharply, barely containing his anger and disappointment.

Dean sat beside Simon and Anahera formally restarted the interview.

"Dean, I am going to ask you some questions relating to your disappearance and the events aboard your yacht *Aurora*. Please be mindful that we have already interviewed Ella." She paused for effect.

"My client has decided to help you with your inquiry." Simon's voice was quiet but firm.

Anahera looked at Dean, saying, "Thank you Dean, it will go better for you this way. Let's start with how long you have known Tony Newton."

"Tony has been a patient of mine for around five years." He spoke in a subdued tone while looking down at his hands that were cuffed and on the table.

"How about you tell us what happened to Tony Newton?"

Dean sighed a long breath and dropped his shoulders. "Tony drowned when Ella clubbed him with the oar and pushed him off *Aurora*."

Anahera looked at Frank. There it was. The confession they needed.

Frank sighed, his feelings a mixture of relief that they'd cracked the case, quiet elation that he'd been right about Ella, and a deep sadness to see how far Dean had fallen.

"How did he come to be aboard *Aurora* making that passage with Ella?" she asked.

"We'd met him at Whangaparapara Harbour on Great Barrier. We knew he was staying there because he'd been in for a dental check-up six weeks before and we'd talked about his upcoming holiday. He'd rented an Air BnB cottage and wanted to go off grid for a while. He was paranoid about the government being in a conspiracy with big pharma. We happened to be planning a holiday out there ourselves and that was when Ella came up with the idea."

"What happened?"

He paused and took a deep breath. "We invited him on board for drinks and dinner. It got late and we'd had quite a few drinks, so he stayed the night rather than going back to the cottage where he was staying."

"Go on."

"Ella and I staged a mock argument. I said I wanted to stay on the island while Ella wanted to go home. She asked Tony to help her crew *Aurora* back to the marina, which he was happy to do because he was obviously sweet on her. The plan was for them to head out into the middle of the Gulf and Ella was going to knock him overboard and claim I fell overboard when hit on the head by the boom in a jibe manoeuvre." Tears formed and ran down his cheeks. "I'm sorry. I'm so sorry!"

"How did she manage to get him overboard?"

"I don't know exactly, I wasn't there. The plan was for her to get him to go into the stern locker on the transom to look for a fishing lure—it's where we keep the fishing tackle. While he was occupied, she was going to hit him on the head with an oar and knock him overboard." He placed his head in his hands and wept. "She was... going to... leave him to the sh-sharks."

"Whose idea was it that you take on his identity?"

He looked up, his eyes red. "Ella's. She thought if I could impersonate him then she would come out and pick me up with *Aurora* and we'd head up to the islands and disappear. She'd noticed how alike we were—we could've been brothers." He pulled a handkerchief out of his pocket and blew noisily. "When everything went pear-shaped, she suggested that I pretend to be him so that we could collect the life insurance. He was a loner— we assumed it would be some time before he'd be missed."

"Help me understand this. Ella came up with a plan to kill Tony Newton, who looked remarkedly like your double, in order for you both to collect a life insurance payment. And then she was going to come for you and together you were going to sail away to anonymity. Is that correct?"

He hung his head. "More or less."

"Which part do I have wrong?"

"It sounds a little too trite when you say it like that."

"Trite? It's premeditated murder, simple." Anahera's voice betrayed her anger.

Frank sensed she was struggling and formally suspended the interview. "Please excuse us for a minute," he said, getting up and ushering Anahera into the hallway.

"What just happened in there?" His voice was controlled despite the turmoil of feelings that were going on inside his head.

"I was in danger of losing it, that's what happened. Trite he says, it's a murder for goodness sake." She drew in a deep breath. "I need some time out to process what we've just heard."

"Hey, you're doing well in there. How about we take a short break before going back in? He's talking and we have our confession. Just hang in there and eke the details out of him." He put his hand on her shoulder. "Can I get you a coffee?"

"More coffee?" She laughed. "Well perhaps another one won't hurt."

They arranged for drinks to be offered to Dean and Simon before making their own coffees which they took back to their office. For a while they sat in silence, each lost in thought.

Frank was struggling to believe the incredible story Dean was telling. How could Dean have stooped so low? Why had he not put an end to this madness before it resulted in murder? He was clearly culpable, although he was making Ella out to be the mastermind. Or was she? Was Dean more cunning than Frank would've given him credit for? Ella was certainly guilty of murder, no question. Yet was it her idea?

"How can we determine who the real mastermind behind this elaborate plan was. Him or her?" Frank was as much thinking out loud as asking a question.

"I was thinking the same. She's guilty of murder and he's an accomplice to the murder. But which one planned it?" Anahera got up and stared at the whiteboard, looking for anything they'd missed.

"I'd have put money on Ella, but I'm not so confident anymore."

"Maybe we need to pit them against each other. If each of them thinks the other has 'fessed up, then it may become obvious which one was the instigator." She placed her mug on the corner of her desk and rearranged the photos of her kids. "Okay, I'm ready. Shall we go face him?"

"Ready if you are."

"Let's do it." Anahera led him down the hall and back into the interview room.

Dean, who was slumped in his chair with his head resting on his forearms, looked up as they entered. His eyes were bloodshot and he looked exhausted. Simon was busy with his phone and put it down when they entered. Anahera formally restarted the interview and with the recording rolling once more, she began.

"Did you exchange Tony Newton's dental records with your own?"

Dean looked at her then looked down at his hands. "Yes, Ella changed them over. It was easy given we had both at the clinic."

"How did you get Tony's passport?"

"Ella broke into his house a couple of months ago and took it. We knew he wouldn't be home because he was with me having a filling done."

"Do you admit to colluding with Ella to break in and steal Tony's passport?"

"Yes." Dean raised his head and looked directly at Frank. "Frank, you know me. I'm not a bad person. I didn't think Ella would go through with it. It's like a game that got out of hand. At first, they were just ideas—I never really wanted anyone to get hurt. You have to believe me."

Frank held his gaze for a long moment, before speaking in measured tones. "Murder isn't a game. And a life isn't yours to take, and now you'll have to live with the consequences. You've changed Dean. The man I called my friend wouldn't have done this. If you're lucky, the fact you're helping us with our inquiries will be looked on favourably at sentencing time. But you've been a fool."

Dean hung his head.

"Let's talk motive," Anahera said. "Ella has helped us to understand your motive. Now this is where you get to tell me your version of events. What drove you and Ella to take this course of action?"

"We invested a large amount of our money in Bitcoin, some of which we mortgaged the house to get. It was supposed to be a short-term speculative investment to make a fast return, but it peaked and began to fall—and never stopped falling. We stood to lose everything. The payments on the mortgage were crippling. Our revolving credit facility was heading south rapidly. It was a desperate situation."

"Whose idea was it to speculate on Bitcoin?"

Dean looked up. "Ella came up with the idea, although I admit I didn't take much convincing."

"And whose idea was it to increase the life insurance?"

"Again, it was Ella's and I went along with it. I realise now I shouldn't have." His voice was flat.

"And whose idea was it to stage your death and collect the life insurance?"

He didn't answer, instead, he hung his head. They waited. Then in what was little more than a whisper, he said, "Ella's."

Anahera formally ended the interview. With a quick look at Frank who nodded, she said, "Dean Hampton, you are charged with being an accessory after the fact to the murder of Tony Newton. You are also charged with being an accessory to the theft of Tony Newton's passport. I remind you that you have the right to remain silent, you do not have to make a statement, anything you say may be recorded and given as evidence in court. Do you understand?"

"Yes." Dean looked up at Frank. "I'm so sorry for everything. Please Frank, believe me. I'm so very sorry. I wish I could change things—it should never have happened."

Frank couldn't resist his urge to respond in anger. "You're damn right it shouldn't have happened. Didn't you stop to think Tony Newton was someone's son? That he had as much right to live as you do?" Realising he'd overstepped, he added in a calmer voice, "What you and Ella have done is inexcusable and you're going to have to face the consequences and take your chances with the judge at sentencing. Dean, I've counted you as a friend and I can't help but be disappointed that you'd be party to such a callous crime."

"You will be taken away for processing and will stay in a remand cell overnight," Anahera said curtly.

Frank left the room to make the arrangements. His mood was deeply melancholic and he suddenly felt very tired. Although they'd cracked the case, he took no satisfaction in the outcome. To believe that Dean Hampton, dentist, father, fun-loving friend, was the same man as the one wearing handcuffs was hard to contemplate.

*

The next morning Ella was brought into the interview room where Frank and Anahera were waiting. Despite her dishevelled state, she walked upright, her jaw jutting out ever so slightly and her eyes blazing. Her hands had been cuffed in front of her, not for safety or flight reasons, but because Anahera had thought it might induce her to face the enormity of her plight.

"I won't say anything without my lawyer present." She stared at them defiantly.

The call was made to Suzie Laselles and they left Ella to simmer on her own while they waited for the lawyer to arrive. It didn't take long before Suzie was shown into the interview room where Anahera and Frank joined them.

Anahera formally began the interview.

"Ella, Dean has testified to the fact that you murdered Tony Newton and we'd like to hear your account," Frank started.

Ella's face clouded and she looked panicked before she composed herself, turning her face into a blank mask.

"We know about the fishing lure and the oar. How about you tell us exactly what happened aboard the *Aurora* that day?" he asked.

"I have nothing to say." She spat the words out.

"Ella, we have Forensics working to match the hair found wedged in the oar with Tony Newton's DNA. The evidence against you is compelling. We want to give you the opportunity to give your version of events." Frank held her in a steady gaze.

Ella became wide eyed, her mouth slightly open as if she realised the net was closing about her.

"Tell us the truth Ella," Frank persisted.

"I'm innocent. You can't send me back to that cell! I don't belong there!" Her eyes were wild and her protest had a desperate edge to it.

"Stop badgering my client," Suzie said sharply.

"Ella, this will go better for you if you cooperate. Please tell us what happened to Tony Newton aboard *Aurora*." Anahera entered the fray.

"Alright, I did it. Satisfied? I did it!" Her eyes blazed. "I hit Tony Newton with the oar and knocked him overboard. I saw him floating in the water, bleeding but still alive, so I ran over him—I was afraid he'd be recognised."

Suzie interjected, "Ella, I must caution you to..."

Ella ignored her. "He was a nobody, a weirdo, and no one was going to miss him. Don't you see, it was such a clever plan. I even changed the dental records. I convinced Dean to grow his beard and to up his life insurance. It was the only way out of our financial troubles. I planned it all, but I did it for Dean, for us. Dean loves me, he'll do anything for me. We would've lost everything." Ella stopped abruptly and put her hand to her mouth as if physically stopping any more words from escaping her lips. She looked at the faces intently watching her.

Suzie looked as shocked as Frank felt.

"One more thing Ella. Why did you want to view the body?" Frank asked quietly.

"Because I wanted to make sure I was the one to identify him and not anyone else." Her voice now subdued, Ella looked dazed.

"And why change the will?"

"The money from Dean's assets had to come back to us." The fight had left her, she hung her head.

Frank charged Ella with breaking and entering and the theft of Tony Newton's passport.

Anahera formally ended the interview before standing up and leaving the room with Frank close behind her. While Ella was taken back to her cell, they went up to Brad's office to give him a full update. It was over. They'd achieved the right outcome, and yet there was no cause for celebration.

23

Amy arrived at the café where she'd arranged to meet Frank and took a seat at a table by the window so she could watch the passers-by. It'd been two days since Frank had called her and told her that Dean had confessed to being part of the murder.

Ever since then she'd been on a rollercoaster of emotions. It was like a bad dream. To believe her beloved brother could possibly have been involved in something so despicable was a struggle. It didn't add up. Dean had been a good man, kind and caring. He'd poured his heart and soul into Sara, especially when his first marriage was coming to an end. She could not reconcile that person with this man who'd allowed, even helped orchestrate a murder.

There were times over the last two days when she was filled with rage. How Dean could have been so stupid to go along with Ella's plan when he should have stood up to her and stopped it before it was too late was a mystery to Amy. She hated his weakness. Hated what he'd done to her family, to Sara, her mum, to her girls and to herself. Hated the stress he was causing them. Her anger had surfaced, flowing out of her to target Terry and the girls, sniping at petty things until she managed to reign it back in.

If only she had known what was going on, had better understood the hold Ella had over Dean, she might have been able to save a man's life as well as saving them all the heartache. In the early hours when lying awake in the dark she had been overcome with feelings of guilt that she hadn't been more proactive in keeping Dean close. Her acceptance of the distance that he and Ella had put between them was unforgivable and she'd spent many hours berating herself and thinking how she could have intervened. Her focus on her own health and on her immediate family had caused her to miss the signs that things were amiss with Dean.

And then there had been the times when she'd hit rock bottom, feeling total desperation for her brother's plight. How he'd cope in prison was a scary thought. If she'd captured the tears that she'd cried over these last two days she could have filled a lake. At these times her Parkinson's symptoms would increase and she'd find herself falling into a dark abyss of pain and fear. No matter how hard Terry and the girls tried to humour her, she couldn't be cheered. The picture of Dean sitting at the table in the interview room, his hands in cuffs, would not leave her and she'd grieved for her younger sibling.

There were moments when she had resigned herself to the truth, accepted what had happened and become determined to make the best of it. Dean had made some huge mistakes and now he'd have to face the consequences. There had to be consequences, she understood that, and she'd stand by him and be there when he was released. They all would. He would pay for the terrible things he'd been party to and one day he'd be able to move on with his life. At least he was alive. There was a good chance he'd get to see his daughter finish her studies, have a career, perhaps get married and have children of her own. His grandchildren. After all he'd done, she still loved him.

She had wanted justice for her brother and had pleaded with Frank to seek the truth. Never did she imagine what that justice would mean. Truth had always been a central tenet of her life, and she wouldn't change that now. It had to be the best path for Dean.

Frank came hurrying across the pedestrian crossing close to the café. Once again he was wearing the blue overalls which she'd come to recognise as the official uniform of the Maritime Police Unit. When he entered the café and spotted Amy his face broke into his good-humoured grin as he wound his way through the tables to where she was seated.

"Sorry I'm late," Frank said, putting his hand out to shake Amy's.

"You're not, I was early," she said, smiling.

"Have you ordered yet? Can I get you a drink and something to eat?"

"No, I haven't ordered and yes thanks, a green tea would be lovely." Frank turned to go and place their order.

Amy watched him as he waited for service. This was a good man, not unlike her Terry, and she was extremely grateful for the way he'd dealt with first Dean's disappearance and then the investigation.

Frank returned and took a seat opposite Amy.

"How're you doing?" Genuine concern showed on his face.

"I'm coping, thanks. Still coming to terms with what has happened, but I suspect that's going to take some time." She paused. "How about you?"

"Much the same. I've been involved in many cases—you don't get to my age without having a lot of runs on the board—and this one was by far the hardest. It's the first time I've had to lock up an old mate. And I always liked Dean. It's so hard to comprehend how on earth he got himself into this mess."

"I know what you mean." She picked up a sachet of sugar and played with it. "Frank, please tell me how they pulled it off. I need to know."

Frank filled Amy in on the whole elaborate plot, starting with Ella noticing Tony was a double for Dean, the theft of the passport, the switching of the dental records, the facial hair, the dinner on Barrier and finished with how Ella had carried out the murder.

They were interrupted by the waitress who brought them their drinks.

"And the motive was their financial situation?"

"Yes. The life insurance would more or less have pulled them out of the debt they'd accrued with the speculative Bitcoin investment."

"How did Tony Newton's family take it?"

"He only had his mum. It'd apparently been a long time since she had seen him and I hear she was devastated. No parent ever expects to hear of their child's death, especially when it's through circumstances such as these." Frank shook his head.

Amy put her hand to her mouth. "I'm so sorry."

"It wasn't your fault Amy. You have no reason to feel any guilt at all. In fact, I wanted to thank you in person for the part you played. You've done the right and honourable thing—firstly alerting us to your suspicions which prompted the investigation and then helping to encourage Dean to tell the truth. I doubt we'd have solved this without you."

"What happens now?" She sipped her tea.

"Like I told you on the phone, Ella confessed to the murder during the interview process. We'll now have to wait and see how she pleads in court, but the evidence against her is damning. She'll get a sentence of life imprisonment with a non-parole period of at least ten years. That's the minimum under the law."

"And Dean?"

"The sentence for being an accessory to murder is imprisonment for a term not exceeding seven years. Assuming he pleads guilty, and with his willingness to help us with our inquiries and this being his first offence, the judge may well give him a favourable term.”

“We’ll be waiting for him when he gets out and will help him adjust to life after this nightmare.” Amy gazed out the window. “It won’t be easy for him to readjust to life on the outside.”

“It won’t be straightforward after being incarcerated. At least he seemed to me to be remorseful. That gives me hope the old Dean will come back.”

“It’s a bit late for Tony,” she said sharply, before looking embarrassed. “Sorry, I don’t know where that came from.”

“No need to apologise.” He sipped his coffee.

“One of the things that still baffles me is how upset Ella was in the early days after Dean allegedly drowned. She had me fooled.” Amy frowned.

“She’s a good actress, I’ll give her that. Although I suspect the emotions you saw were real. She says she did it all for Dean, that she wanted to have a nice life with him. It’s likely she was upset when the reality of what she’d done sank in—I can’t say for sure. I suspect she was also living in fear that she’d be caught.”

“And what about the will?” Her hand shook as she went to pick up her cup, so she sat on it and used her other hand.

“Ella convinced Dean to change it in order to keep the income from the sale of their assets.”

They were silent for a while.

“How’s your health?” he asked.

“I’m doing okay. I’m still trying to optimise my drug regime. It’s different for everyone and it takes time to get it right, balancing the symptoms with the side-effects of the drugs. I know stress exacerbates it and so all I want is for this whole mess to be behind us. Until that happens, I just need to get through each day, for everyone’s sake.”

"Hang in there Amy. You seem to me to be one strong lady and your family depend on you. You'll get through this, just keep fighting one day at a time."

"Thanks Frank. I have no other choice."

They finished their drinks and said their goodbyes. With a clearer understanding, she walked out of the café determined that for the sake of her family she would face whatever else life threw at her. If they could come through this, and they would, then they could deal with anything, Parkinson's disease and all.

About the author

Robyn Cotton grew up in South Taranaki and studied at Massey University, before embarking on her career in the dairy industry then as a management consultant and director. Late in her career she discovered creative writing and launched *A Skylark Flies* and *Mary & Me*, both based on personal experiences. *The Jibe* is her first mystery story.

She now enjoys life on the Hibiscus Coast where she can indulge her love of sailing while exploring the beautiful Hauraki Gulf. This passion became the inspiration behind *The Jibe*.

Robyn is a Christian living with Parkinson's disease and likes nothing more than spending quality time with family and friends. Her other interests include photography, travel, various sports and exploring Aotearoa New Zealand's natural environment.

A Skylark Flies
By Robyn Cotton

Rose, a young Kiwi, is on a working holiday in the United Kingdom to discover her roots. When in Scotland, she is subjected to a brutal assault by a local man, Tommy.

Their lives will never be the same again. While Rose fights to recover from her emotional trauma, Tommy, a victim of a lifetime of abuse, struggles with guilt. The choices they make will ultimately determine whether they live life as victims or rise above it.

Inspired by true events, *A Skylark Flies* is a poignant story of forgiveness. It gives the reader a window into the souls of two very different characters whose stories converge at critical points.

The assailant has power over the victim, induced by fear—and the victim has power to release him from his guilt and shame.

Mary & Me

Two women with Parkinson's disease two hundred years apart
By Robyn Cotton

Mary lives with Parkinson's disease in the early nineteenth century. Rose has it in the twenty-first century. Separated by two hundred years their experiences are vastly different, reflecting the change in attitudes and understanding.

Rose's story is inspired by the author's own experience of living with Parkinson's. It is deeply personal and honest and will take you on an emotional rollercoaster, from the shock of diagnosis to hope and resilience.

This journey illustrates the importance of responding positively to a life with a debilitating disease.

Mary & Me provides a novel approach to unpacking Parkinson's and the mix of emotions that may accompany it.

9 780473 708863